MW01127823

*T*ill *W*e *M*eet *A*gain

ALLEN SWEETSIR

Copyright © 2022 Allen Sweetsir
All rights reserved
First Edition

PAGE PUBLISHING
Conneaut Lake, PA

First originally published by Page Publishing 2022

ISBN 978-1-6624-6960-2 (pbk)
ISBN 978-1-6624-6961-9 (digital)

Printed in the United States of America

*C*hapter 1

Berlin 1936. Sidney Klein was an American exchange student at the Berlin Polytechnic Institute, a premier military preparatory school where Germany's future military officers were taught academics and military traditions prior to attending officers training. Sidney had attended the school since the sixth grade. He had been granted admission to the school based on his academic grades, his fluency in German, and the fact that his father, Lieutenant Colonel Jacob Klein, was the US military attaché to Germany. Sidney was considered to be one of the brightest students in his class with a class standing of 98.9. Sidney had become best friends with Klaus Bergman, the son of *Obersturmbannführer* (Lieutenant Colonel) Reinhard Bergman, a staff officer assigned to the SS (*Schutzstaffel* or Protection Squad) headquartered in Berlin. Klaus was running a very close second in class standing at 98.7.

The two boys enjoyed each other's company immensely. Klaus was impressed with Sidney's language abilities. In addition to German, Sidney spoke fluent Russian and Polish. Klaus thought that Sidney's analytical mind would make him an ideal candidate for an intelligence officer. Sidney was amazed at Klaus's total recall of famous battles and the formations and tactics employed. They would spend hours after class discussing military history and dissecting campaigns and successes and failures of the military leaders involved. Both boys were considered by their instructors to be wise beyond their years, and they predicted that the boys would go far in their pursuit of a military career.

Although Sidney got along well enough with the other students, there was an underlying tension in their relationship. Klaus had already been counseled by his father and several instructors not to become too close to Sidney. They were all fervent believers of the new National Socialism and the preaching of Der Führer Adolf Hitler and reminded Klaus that although Sidney was a nice enough boy, Klaus must remember that he was, after all, a Jew. Klaus had seen all the required propaganda films depicting European Jewry as backstabbing vermin and the cause of all of Germany's woes after the Great War. Klaus just couldn't place Sidney in that category and so continued to be friends with him. When it came to the propaganda films, Sidney was offered to be excused from the viewing but decided that the content might be handy in assessing a possible future enemy to the United States.

As their last year at the school was coming to an end, Klaus and Sidney were making plans to attend the XI (Eleventh) Olympic Games to be held in Berlin during August 1–16. Klaus knew that he would be attending the *Fahnenjunker Schule* (Officers Candidate School) in September, so he was looking forward to going to the Olympics in August. Sidney said his father had another year left on his assignment to the embassy, and Sidney wouldn't be starting high school until September. He just didn't know where he would attend school yet. He was also looking forward to the Olympics. They started planning which events they wanted to attend and when they needed to be at the different venues. With their plans made, they prepared for their eighth grade graduation ceremony.

On the last day of school, Sidney was informed that he had maintained his number 1 class standing rank and would be the class valedictorian. Klaus congratulated Sidney and kidded him about being a Jew selected as the valedictorian for a German military school. He told Sidney, "If Herr Goebbels was to find out about this, he would probably have the entire school staff arrested!" Sidney knew that Klaus was just kidding him, but he considered the possibility real. He discussed this with Klaus, who realized the possibilities and asked Sidney what he planned to do. Sidney told Klaus that he would go to the school headmaster and suggest that they make Klaus the valedictorian to avoid any negative publicity. Klaus sarcastically thanked Sidney for the "honor," for now he must write a speech, which he hated to do. Sidney graciously offered Klaus his speech, which he had already prepared, and went to see the headmaster. The headmaster was both surprised and grateful for Sidney's forethought. He promised that Sidney's diploma would reflect that he graduated first in his class and would write a letter of recommendation detailing Sidney's academic and leadership qualities.

After the graduation ceremonies, Klaus's and Sidney's families met for the first time. Both sides were cordial and polite, but both boys could sense an undercurrent of tension. Sidney and Klaus began speaking of their plans for the summer vacation and of attending the Olympic Games in August. Klaus's father informed him that the plans he had made for the summer would have to be canceled as Klaus would be attending the Hitler Youth Camp near Tegernsee for summer training prior to attending the Fahnenjunker Schul in September. This was obviously news to Klaus, and his disappointment was quite obvious. Before Sidney could assure his friend that he would provide him with reports on the Olympic events they had intended to see together, Sidney's father dropped his own bombshell. Lieutenant Colonel Klein had been selected to attend the Command and General Staff College at Fort Leavenworth, Kansas, starting in September. They would be leaving Germany in one month, around the fifteenth of July. Sidney and Klaus would have less than a month before they would be heading their separate ways.

When they figured Sidney's family packing and Klaus's preparations for camp, they would be lucky to have two weeks to socialize over the summer. Not exactly what they had planned on. They managed to squeeze in a camping trip on the last weekend they would spend together. They spoke of their plans for the future. Sidney planned to begin his preparations for admission to West Point. Klaus could not believe all the work that was involved in attending the US Army's premier officers training academy. He could understand and accept the requirement for high academic standards, but the application and acceptance process just escaped him. That Sidney would need to be recommended by a politician in order to attend just made no sense to him. Sidney possessed all the necessary qualities to become an exceptional officer, and that should suffice. For Klaus, the academic requirements were also mandatory. After that, he submitted his application, and if his grades were good enough and he had attended the right schools and he passed the genealogy test, he would attend officer school.

Klaus explained to Sidney the purpose of the Hitler Youth Camp and what it entailed. It was basically a summer camp in which officer prospects were involved in physical training and basic military skills, such as drill and ceremony, land navigation, inspections, National Socialist programs, racial purity, and small arms training. This was conducted over a period of eight weeks. Klaus would then attend the Officers Candidate School. Because Klaus had applied for the Waffen-SS, the elite forces not associated with the regular army *Wehrmacht*, Klaus would attend school at the Waffen-SS school at Bad Tölz in Bavaria. There, he would be taught everything necessary to become a Waffen-SS officer.

On the last night of their camping trip, the two friends discussed their futures and their opinions of the coming world events. Klaus was in favor of many of the changes coming to Germany's economy and resurgence in industry. Although Sidney was his best friend, he didn't discuss changes in the German military that he had overheard when his father was talking to other officers. Many of the changes in the German military would be considered to be in violation of the Treaty of Versailles, which severely restricted parts of Germany's military. Sidney expressed his concerns with Japanese expansion into China and its increasingly aggressive behavior in search of natural resources to feed its growing industrial capacity. He was also concerned with Germany's treatment of Jews, Gypsies, and the handicapped. Klaus agreed with Sidney on this topic but warned him to be extremely careful to whom he voiced his opinions on this subject. The Gestapo *Geheim Staatspolizei* (State Secret Police) had informants everywhere.

Klaus and Sidney made a vow that they would stay in touch. It was then that Klaus produced a small bottle of *slivovitz* (Polish plum brandy) that he had smuggled from home. Klaus raised the bottle to Sidney and promised, "Till we meet again." He took a goodly pull at the bottle and handed it to Sidney, who repeated the toast and finished the bottle.

In the morning, the boys packed up their gear and hiked back to the bus line and boarded their respective busses back to their homes. In the morning, Klaus would leave for the Hitler Youth Camp, and Sidney would help his parents start packing for their move back to the United States. Although he and Klaus had promised they would stay in touch, Sidney had a strange feeling that their promise would not hold for long.

Chapter 2

Fort Leavenworth, Kansas, in July of 1936 was, in a word, miserable. Hot, dusty, and brown. There was no comparison between Fort Leavenworth and Berlin. This time of year in Berlin, everything was green and lush. The people were strolling through the parks, sunning themselves, and swimming in the lakes. Families were enjoying picnic lunches in the parks or partaking of coffee and cake or ice cream at street-side cafés. In the evenings, the biergartens were serving schooners of Berliner *Weizen bier* (wheat beer) accompanied by soft large pretzels. Young couples toured the Kurfürstendamm, the Champs-Élysées of Berlin. With its nightclubs and restaurants, it was the most popular spot in Berlin.

Fort Leavenworth, in comparison, had the Army Command and General Staff College and the Army Disciplinary Barracks. Not much of a comparison to Berlin. The high school in which Sidney was enrolled was not much of a challenge for Sidney, but that just meant that he could place more time into subjects that would be advantageous toward his application to the United States Military Academy at West Point. The only advantage to this school compared to the school in Berlin was, this was a coeducational school, and there were some very pretty girls here. Sidney had already met one whom he was very attracted to, a raven-haired, blue-eyed beauty named Rachel. They hit it off right away, and there was a definite attraction for both of them. Rachel was intrigued with Sidney's travels in Europe and wished to travel herself. At first blush, one would think that they were a totally incompatible couple. Sidney was very strait-laced and conservative, studious and grounded in science, and principled. Rachel, on the other hand, was artistic, liberal, and always reaching for the stars. She dreamed of becoming a star one day. In school, she had the voice of an angel, well suited for classical music, a field that her parents hoped and encouraged her to pursue. Rachel dreamed of being a star too. But her dreams were much different than her parents'. She saw herself as a famous nightclub singer and future recording star. In the blink of an eye, she could switch from opera singer to jazz artist, and Sidney just loved to hear her sing.

The school band had a jazz combo that would gather after school to play, and sometimes Rachel and Sidney would stop by and listen. One afternoon Sidney talked to Steve, the leader of the group, and told him about Rachel's singing voice. Steve said he had heard Rachel singing in the choir but didn't think her voice was suited for jazz music. Sidney convinced him to give Rachel a chance. Steve asked Rachel if she would like to sing a song with the band, to which Rachel readily agreed. The band played "Pennies from Heaven," which had just been recorded by Billie Holiday. At the conclusion of the song, Steve just looked at Rachel and told her, "I have just one word. *Wow!*" Everyone was stunned by the rendition sung by Rachel. Some said that if they closed their eyes, they could imagine Billie Holiday was in the room. There was no doubt that Rachel had real talent and was destined to go places in the music field. Steve asked her if she would consider performing with the band and outlined the band's rehearsal and current booking schedule. Rachel wanted desperately to join the band but knew that if it began to interfere with her grades, her parents would put an end to her plans. Sidney promised her that he would help her with her studies. After all, by helping Rachel with her schoolwork, that gave him opportunities to spend more time with her. Rachel said that if Sidney would help her with her schoolwork, she would join the band. For Sidney, it was a definite win-win situation. He got to hear Rachel sing and spend more time with her doing homework.

Sidney got to be a regular fixture at the Silberman household while helping Rachel with her schoolwork. Luckily, Mr. and Mrs.

Silberman not only approved of Sidney but they had also become friends with Sidney's parents. Mr. Silberman, who was a lawyer, taught military justice classes at the Command and General Staff College, and Mrs. Silberman worked with Sidney's mother on the welcoming committee at the Jewish Temple in town. Both families often met socially and were becoming good friends. When they got together, they often discussed the evolving political scene in Europe.

Lieutenant Colonel Klein, having just spent three years as the US military attaché to Germany, was a wealth of knowledge when it came to the developments in German politics. He and Mr. Silberman would spend hours discussing what each thought Adolf Hitler's next move would be. Both agreed that Hitler's plans for expanding the Reich were not over. The only point they disagreed on was the fate of the Jews in Germany. Mr. Silberman didn't feel that the Jews would be mistreated by the Nazis. They had, after all, fought for their German homeland during the Great War and had shown that they were valuable citizens. Lieutenant Colonel Klein felt otherwise. He suggested that Mr. Silberman read Hitler's book *Mein Kampf* (*My Struggle*) in order to understand Hitler's deep-seated hatred of the Jews and communists. Hitler blamed all of Germany's woes on the Jews. He believed that the German Army was not defeated but that rich and powerful Jewish factions had forced Kaiser Wilhelm to sue for peace and abdicate his throne, throwing Germany into the state of financial ruin that he, Adolf Hitler, had rescued it from. Mr. Silberman still found it difficult to believe that the German people would allow the discrimination or mistreatment of its own citizens. Lieutenant Colonel Klein tried to convince him of the things he had personally observed. Jewish shops were marked with a yellow Star of David so that citizens would know it was a Jewish-owned establishment. If that wasn't enough to discourage non-Jewish patrons from entering, there was usually a contingent of brown-shirted SA (*Sturmabteilung* or Storm Troopers) outside the shop to discourage anyone from entering. Mr. Silberman thought that these were isolated incidences and couldn't be happening all over the country. Lieutenant Colonel Klein consigned himself to the fact that unless some people saw something with their own eyes, it didn't occur. He decided to change the subject to a more neutral one, their weekly bridge game that they all looked forward to playing.

Sidney arrived home from school to find a letter in his room from Klaus Bergman. He eagerly tore open the envelope to read what his friend had written. Klaus was away at the Hitler Youth Camp near Tegernsee for summer training. Classes consisted of plenty of physical fitness, hiking, camping, field craft, singing of inspirational marching songs, and rifle marksmanship. There were also lectures on racial purity, the duties of every good Aryan to support the Reich, and solemn vows to honor and obey Adolf Hitler. The reading of *Mein Kampf* was also a mandatory subject. Klaus said he especially enjoyed the hiking, camping, field craft, and marksmanship. He was not overly enamored with the classes on racial purity and the anti-Semitic lectures. Having Sidney as a friend, he had a hard time comparing the Jews depicted in the films and lectures to Sidney. He dutifully attended the classes but did not take them to heart. Klaus asked how Sidney's summer was going and if he were to write to him, to send the letter to his home address as he would be done there in two weeks.

Sidney sat down and responded to Klaus's letter right then. He described the bland Kansas landscape and the classes he was taking, none of which were a real challenge. The only bright side to being here was Rachel. Sidney went into great detail describing her looks, her voice, her demeanor, basically everything about her. Sidney was surprised to find that he had filled up two pages just about Rachel. He finished off the letter with best wishes to Klaus and his parents and hoped to hear from him again soon. He sealed the envelope and, grabbing his bicycle, pedaled to the post office on main post to mail his letter. The postal clerk gave Sidney a funny look before announcing it would be ten cents to mail his letter to Germany. Sidney paid the clerk and left. The postal clerk placed a ten-cent stamp on the envelope and then stamped it. He looked at the envelope address one more time. It read, "Klaus Bergman, Am Rothenberg 34a, Berlin, Germany." The postal clerk tossed the letter into the mailbag for New York.

That evening, when Sidney's father returned home, he told him of the letter from Klaus. They talked about how Klaus was doing and if he gave any indication of how things were going in Germany these days. Sidney said that the letter concerned itself with Klaus's attendance at the Hitler Youth Camp and his favorite and least favorite subjects. After dinner, Sidney announced that he would be going to help Rachel with her French homework for about an hour or so. When Sidney left, his mother sat down with her husband and asked if he thought they were seeing too much of each other, if he thought that Sidney should see other girls or other friends. The thought that ran through Jacob Klein's head was, *What other girl can possibly compare with Rachel? She is beautiful and talented and genuinely enjoys being with Sidney. What more can a fellow want?* He replied to his wife's question that they seemed to suit each other very well and that there was nothing wrong with that. Miriam Klein was not too sure how she felt about the two teenagers' apparent attachment to each other and thought that a separation might do them good. Not a permanent separation, just a period long enough for them to see things beyond each other. This was a subject that Miriam would ponder over the coming weeks.

Sidney and Rachel were working on her French homework. She had improved quite a bit since Sidney began tutoring her. Even though he was in the same year as Rachel, he had been placed in an advanced course, mainly because of his fluency in three other foreign languages. Sidney just had a knack, an ear for foreign languages. This was a talent that Rachel admired about Sidney. She had never learned a foreign language until now and was doing her very best to master it. With Sidney's help, she was doing very well. Her teacher was impressed not only with her growing vocabulary but also with her pronunciation. When Rachel asked Sidney how he managed to do the French pronunciation so well—she thought the French spoke through their noses—Sidney said he had borrowed records from the school library.

They had just finished their studies for the evening, and Rachel asked Sidney if he would care to go for a walk. They walked down the street and through the park before starting back to Rachel's house.

They were watching the moon rising over the flat Kansas landscape when they shared their first kiss. If you asked either one later who initiated the kiss, neither one could say. One minute, they were watching the moon; the next, they were kissing. No matter how it happened, it would not be their last. Sidney brought Rachel to her door and kissed her good night.

"See you in school tomorrow," Sidney said.

Rachel smiled and said, "Can't wait."

The rest of their freshman year seemed to fly by. That Sidney and Rachel were constant companions seemed to be as natural as night following day. As the year ended, the jazz band that Rachel had been singing in had been hired to perform at the graduation dance for the senior class. This could pose a problem for Rachel because her mother had volunteered to help on the decoration committee at school. This meant there was a good chance that her mother would be at the dance that night and that her father might be in attendance also. Rachel talked to Sidney about the coming catastrophe, and Sidney said, "It is going to have to come out sooner or later. May as well be now. You can't tell the band you can't appear. Their entire program is now based around a singer." Rachel agreed and decided that the worst that could happen was that the band would have to find a new singer for the next school year.

The night of the dance, there was a certain air of anticipation. The master of ceremonies introduced the band and invited the members of the senior class to go onto the dance floor and dance the first dance. As the lights came up on stage, Sidney was standing next to Mr. and Mrs. Silberman. He turned to them and said, "I hope you enjoy her performance. She's worked very hard on it." At first, they didn't understand until they heard Rachel's voice. The audience was astounded. No one would've thought a sixteen-year-old girl could sing like that. Rachel's parents just stared in surprise. Their hopes of an opera singer appeared doomed.

Chapter 3

June 1938. Another school year ended, and Sidney was looking forward to spending more time with Rachel. There was an end-of-year party scheduled for 8:00 p.m. at the lake, and their close circle of friends were all planning to attend.

At dinner that night, Sidney's father had news for him. Sidney's Uncle Saul wanted Sidney to come to New York City and help him in his deli over the summer. Sidney was less than pleased and pointed out to his father that it was a waste of time. He didn't intend to pursue a career as a counterman in a deli. He would become a career army officer like his father. Jacob said that it would be good for him to go to New York as he was concerned that Sidney and Rachel might be seeing too much of each other. Besides, he had heard from Rachel's father that Rachel would be accompanying her Aunt Sylvia to Germany in order to assist her in closing her uncle's business in Germany in order to relocate to Holland. Sidney was shocked to learn of this. Germany was becoming more dangerous for Jews every day.

At the party that night, they discussed their much-changed plans for the summer. Rachel was unaware of her pending trip to Germany but was now looking forward to it. Sidney expressed his concerns over Rachel's travel to Germany. She expressed her excitement at the opportunity to see the world. With both leaving the next day, this would be their last time together for several months. With a passionate kiss and a whispered "Till we meet again," they left to face their futures.

* * *

Klaus had just finished his second year at Bad Tölz and was looking forward to a two-week leave back to Berlin. The first two years were comprised mostly of indoctrination into the Waffen-SS, what was expected of an SS officer, organization of SS units, extreme discipline, hard physical training, marching, drill and ceremony, but the most disconcerting was the family lineage investigation—an investigation going back 150 years to ensure that there was only pure Aryan blood in the candidate's family. Failure to pass the investigation resulted in immediate dismissal from the school. Four of his classmates had been so dismissed. One, as a result of the shame he felt, committed suicide by hanging himself in his barracks room. The other three were formed before the corps of cadets and were stripped of their badges of rank and uniform tunics. As they were marched out of the *kaserne* (military post), the assembled cadets performed an about-face to turn their backs on the three as a final act of shame.

Klaus arrived home to find a much-changed climate. The treatment of the Jews had become even harsher and more open. It was not just the brown-shirted SA who harassed the Jews; even the common citizens had become more prone to acts of violence. The police did nothing to stop these acts as the Jews had no rights under German law. They were no longer citizens of the Third Reich. It was as if Herr Hitler's virulent speeches and Dr. Goebbels's propaganda films had infected the entire populace with a virus. People who had been friends and neighbors and done business together for decades were now total strangers. Jewish shops, marked with the Star of David, were off-limits to non-Jews. Klaus was expected to feel the same way, but somehow, it didn't feel right.

Klaus's parents were proud of his accomplishments at officer's school. His father was expecting a new assignment and promotion to *standartenführer* (colonel). All he could say about the assignment was that it was to a "special" unit with great responsibilities. He had been selected for this assignment by Reichsführer Himmler personally. A great honor indeed!

That evening, Klaus met with some old childhood friends at a local *gasthaus* (pub). They talked of work and other friends but were more interested in Klaus and his life in the military. Although conscription had been instituted in 1935, it was very lenient as to when men would be inducted into the service. They were interested in his experiences so far. Klaus painted his experiences with a very broad brush, not wanting to get into some aspects of SS training. There was much talk of the great things Hitler was doing for Germany—more and more jobs were being created, and the standard of living was improving. Everyone was in awe at Hitler's audacious demands for *Lebensraum* (living space), which were being granted without resistance from the world. The return of the Rhineland and the mostly peaceful annexation of Austria were amazing feats of statesmanship. No one seemed to see the storm clouds on the horizon.

*C*hapter 4

New York City in the summer of 1938 was quite different from Leavenworth, Kansas. The sights, sounds, and smells were so much different. Walking down the streets, you could imagine yourself in different countries by the aromas of cooking meals—Italian sauces, German bratwurst, Polish sauerkraut, and Irish cabbage. It was quite interesting. Working at Uncle Saul's delicatessen was quite an experience. Saul was not only a salesman / sandwich maker but also a showman, entertaining the customers with his banter describing the various meats and specialties, giving a taste of the brisket, a slice of salami, a piece of corned beef so tender it would make you *meshuggena* (Yiddish for *crazy*). Uncle Saul knew every customer by name, their usual order, and the side dishes they liked. He flirted with the old ladies and talked baseball with the men who came in.

Sidney learned the business from the ground up, literally. He started with sweeping and mopping the floors and taking out the trash. He progressed to running errands and then making deliveries to nearby businesses and construction workers. He would inventory and store supplies and would eventually help his Aunt Miriam in the kitchen. Although he was kept quite busy, he couldn't stop thinking and worrying about Rachel.

* * *

Crossing the Atlantic on the SS *Normandie*, Rachel was looking forward to visiting Germany. Her Aunt Sylvia, who was more like an older sister, had filled her head with all the things they would experience, especially the nightlife. Sylvia knew several friends in the nightclub business who would get them into several of the better-known clubs. Although Rachel was underage, with the right makeup and low lighting, she could pass for someone in their twenties.

It seemed rather strange when they were arranging their passage. The travel agent looked at their passports and asked if they weren't going in the wrong direction. When Sylvia asked why, the agent pointed to the names in their passports and asked, "You're Jewish, aren't you? Right now, there aren't any Jews trying to get to Germany. They're all trying to get out." Sylvia explained they had business in Germany. The agent shrugged and issued the tickets without further comment.

The trip across the Atlantic would take a little over four days, in which time they had nothing to do but relax and enjoy the accommodations aboard the *Normandie*. There were passengers from several nations on board, the majority being American. There were also French, British, and Italians, as well as a large contingent of German and German Americans. The passengers had sort of segregated themselves by nationality or political leaning.

The British and French were in one group; the Germans and Italians in another. The Americans and German Americans were scattered between the two main groups, depending on how they felt about European politics. Dinner conversations were diverse. Depending on the group, topics ranged from the danger Hitler posed to world peace in the Anglo-Franco group to the deportation of unwanted peoples from Germany, to include the Gypsies, communists, and of course, Jews. For Sylvia and Rachel, these were very uncomfortable topics. Topics such as these were not discussed in their circles. Several of their fellow travelers advised them that the Germany they might have known or heard of was no more, and if they were wise, they would remain on board the ship and return on the next sailing. Others said that being an American might offer them a little more protection as Germany had no quarrel with America.

Their arrival in Bremen was definitely an eye-opener. As they disembarked, they noticed a fenced and barbwire compound containing around two hundred people—men, women, and children—with a minimal amount of baggage. The containment area was patrolled by armed soldiers in black uniforms with large German shepherd dogs. One of the British passengers whispered to Sylvia, "SS, they are guarding the Jews being deported."

They approached the gate marked Zoll/Douane/Customs and presented their passports. The customs officer smiled at them and looked at their passports, then his demeanor changed immediately. He looked at them and said, "Juden?" (Jewish?)

Sylvia replied, "American."

The customs officer merely grunted and stamped an entry visa and then a large red *J* in their passport. Tossing the passports back, he waved them on. That was their welcome to Germany.

The train ride from Bremen to Berlin, for the most part, was uneventful. The German countryside and cities were quaint and peaceful. As they passed through the cities along the way to Berlin, they noticed that several shops had yellow Stars of David painted on the storefront windows. They asked the British passenger from the *Normandie* what the purpose was. He glanced around to make sure no one was listening before telling them the shops that were owned by Jews were marked that way so "Germans" knew not to shop there. Since 1935, the Jews had lost their German citizenship and were considered "subjects of the state." They were subject to all laws and taxes but were provided no rights or representation. Sylvia thanked the man but still found it difficult to believe that such laws could be implemented in a modern, just society.

The remainder of the trip was mostly spent in quiet contemplation. Sylvia wondered if maybe she had made a mistake bringing her young niece on this journey. Upon their arrival in Berlin, they were met at the *Hauptbahnhof* (main train station) by Aunt Sylvia's uncle, Abraham Silberman, who had a huge smile and flowers for both ladies. He welcomed them to Berlin and helped them load their bags into his car, a 1937 DKW. Aunt Sylvia knew that Uncle Abraham was a successful jeweler and could easily afford an automobile, but she also knew him to be extremely frugal. She asked him about the car, to which he replied that he bought the car so he would not have to rely on public transportation "in case of emergency."

The ride to Uncle Abraham's apartment took only fifteen minutes, but in that short time, Sylvia and Rachel got an upfront and personal view of "normal" life in Nazi Germany. As they had seen along the way, stores and shops were painted with yellow stars to indicate Jewish establishments, with the addition of groups of brown-shirted SA members harassing customers and basically creating a disturbance for the owners. Uncle Abraham explained that the SA was there to ensure no "Aryans" patronized the Jewish shops and to discourage Jews from entering the stores either. Uncle Abraham stated that it had been very bad for business, with many shops having to close their doors because of the inability to buy products to sell and out of a need to protect their families. Many of the owners were leaving the city and the country, hoping to go to Holland and France, and some even to England and America. Many of Uncle Abraham's customers who had consigned pieces of jewelry for sale had recovered the items or offered them for sale at ridiculously low prices in order to generate cash. This had prompted Uncle Abraham to read the writing on the wall and close his store and move to Holland.

For the next week, the girls were kept busy inventorying and packaging jewelry. Sylvia would oftentimes leave the store to deliver jewelry back to customers. One day a gentleman entered the store. He was well dressed and arrived in a large Mercedes automobile. He and Uncle Abraham greeted each other as old friends. Albrecht Rheinhaus and Uncle Abraham had been colleagues for years. He was here to make Uncle Abraham an offer. He was willing to purchase the remainder of Uncle Abraham's merchandise. Uncle Abraham was pleased to be able to liquidate everything, except what he would take to Holland, in one sale. He quoted Herr Rheinhaus a price of 30,000 reichsmarks. Herr Rheinhaus smiled and offered 3,000 reichsmarks. Uncle Abraham couldn't believe his ears! He argued that the price was totally unreasonable. He was already taking a significant loss at the price he quoted. Herr Rheinhaus told Uncle Abraham that 3,000 reichsmarks was still better than nothing. If he were too blind to see what was happening and waited for the Reich to seize all his assets, he would be a fool not to accept his offer. He asked Herr Rheinhaus to reconsider his offer. Herr Rheinhaus said if he reconsidered, it would be a lesser amount. With regret, Uncle Abraham accepted the offer. Herr Rheinhaus nodded and said he would return tomorrow with the money and a bill of sale for Uncle Abraham to sign. Uncle Abraham felt betrayed by his old colleague whom he also thought of as a friend. He realized that this was the new normal for Nazi Germany and the best indication to leave as soon as possible.

The next morning, Herr Rheinhaus arrived with the cash and bill of sale. They concluded their business, but before Herr Rheinhaus left, he offered Uncle Abraham a bit of advice, "If I were you, I wouldn't put your money in the bank. There are rumors of Hitler nationalizing the banks and confiscating any accounts belonging to Jews."

Uncle Abraham thanked him for his advice. He already had close to 100,000 reichsmarks from jewelry already sold and had no intention of placing any of it into a bank. At the current exchange rate, even with black market traders, he expected to receive at least 60,000 Dutch guilders, which should be enough money to support himself for three years or more in Holland. By then, he expected to reestablish his business.

With the business all but completely liquidated, Uncle Abraham told the girls that they had worked enough and deserved some relaxation. *Finally,* thought Rachel, *a chance to see the famed Berlin nightlife.* Aunt Sylvia had two close college friends who lived nearby. She would contact them and arrange for a night on the town.

Luckily, Aunt Sylvia's college friends were extremely liberal and were not at all in favor of Hitler's anti-Semite ideas and programs. They arranged to meet at Fritz's on the Kurfürstendamm at 8:00 p.m. Rachel was very excited about the evening, but Aunt Sylvia was having reservations considering all she had seen in the past two months, but she didn't want to dampen the spirit for Rachel's sake. Aunt Sylvia and Rachel meet Hildegard and Renate at Fritz's as planned. They were told that Rachel was only seventeen and therefore underage, but when they met her, they would've sworn she was in her twenties. Renate said that Fritz's was known for not being too strict on age when it came to pretty, single women, so they were allowed in and shown to a table not far from the stage.

Renate had already learned from Aunt Sylvia that Rachel was quite a singer, so she had spoken with her friend, the bandleader, about allowing Rachel to sing a song with them. He agreed and went to the table to arrange a song. It was then that it came out that Rachel didn't speak German, only English, French, and Polish. They went round and round trying to decide on a song when Rachel asked if he knew of the show *Porgy and Bess* and the song "Summertime." Of course, he knew the show and the song; he just hoped there weren't any intelligent Gestapo in the audience tonight. He reminded Rachel that the composers, the Gershwin brothers, were Jews—a fact not appreciated by the Nazis no matter how talented they were.

Rachel took the stage. The houselights dimmed. She sang the song and brought down the house. Rachel returned to her table and was roundly applauded by the three ladies. Soon, a waiter appeared with a bottle of champagne and glasses, with the compliments of the gentlemen from a table. The waiter indicated a table occupied by four young German Army officers. Hildegard and Renate smiled and waved, Rachel just nodded, and Aunt Sylvia's blood ran cold.

One of the young officers approached the table, clicked his heels together in the approved Prussian style, and introduced him-self as *Oberleutnant* (First Lieutenant) Heinrich Gross. He smiled at Rachel and asked her name. Aunt Sylvia answered that her name was Romy Sullivan, an American who didn't speak German. He turned to Aunt Sylvia and asked who she was. "I am her aunt, Cynthia, also an American, here to visit my college classmates."

"I see," he replied. "Well, I just wanted to compliment your niece on her singing and hope you enjoy the champagne." He gave a short bow to the ladies and returned to his table. For the first time, Rachel took a breath.

Aunt Sylvia decided, and Rachel agreed, that they had enough excitement for one evening. As they walked home, Aunt Sylvia thought that as it was approaching August and Uncle Abraham was ready to make his move to Holland, it might be a good time to arrange their return to the United States. The trip back should take about ten days, and they both wanted some time to unwind before Rachel returned to school and Aunt Sylvia back to work. They knew the next passage back to New York from Bremen would be on the ninth of August, so they planned on leaving Berlin on the seventh of August.

As they approached the store and apartment, they noticed a small crowd gathered out front and an ambulance. They ran to the storefront to see Uncle Abraham carried out and placed on a stretcher. He was swathed in bloody bandages and appeared to be unconscious. A neighbor said that he had been beaten and robbed. Aunt Sylvia asked if the police had captured anyone. The neighbor shook his head and said the police wouldn't respond to a crime involving a Jew unless the Jew was accused of the crime. They were told which hospital Uncle Abraham was being taken. They went into the apartment. Uncle Abraham's strongbox was broken open, the money and jewelry gone. More importantly, their passports were also missing. There was nothing they could do about the missing passports at the moment. They had to see about Uncle Abraham. Aunt Sylvia found the keys to Uncle Abraham's car, and they set off for the hospital.

At the emergency room, the nurse told them the doctor was still examining Uncle Abraham and for them to take a seat. After about an hour, the doctor approached and gave them Uncle Abraham's condition. His injuries were severe. In addition to a concussion, he had a broken jaw, three broken ribs, a fractured left wrist, and bruising to his kidneys. It would be several weeks before he could be released, and even then, he would require at-home care for at least a month. When asked if they could see him, the doctor told them they could go in for a few minutes but that he was still unconscious, and if he were to awaken, they would have to sedate him because of the pain he would experience from his injuries. They entered Uncle Abraham's room and were shocked to see him. His face was one huge bruise. They both knew that even if they had their passports, they couldn't leave Uncle Abraham in his present medical condition.

After about thirty minutes, they returned to Uncle Abraham's apartment to clean up and revise their travel plans. The first priority was to obtain replacement passports. The second priority was to get Rachel home before the start of school. Luckily, they still had their tickets for the *Normandie*. It then dawned on them that money was going to be an immediate problem. They hoped that Uncle Abraham had a secret stash somewhere "in case of emergency," and this was a dire emergency. Tomorrow, after they checked on Uncle Abraham, they would make their way to the American Embassy at Pariser Platz to inquire about replacing their passports.

The next morning, Uncle Abraham's condition had not changed. He was still unconscious and being fed intravenously. Being unable to do anything for Uncle Abraham for the moment, they proceeded to the embassy. They exited the bus at the top of Pariser Platz to see a crowd of people lined up at the entrance to the American Embassy. The line of people stretched from the entrance, down the street, and around the corner toward the *Brandenburger Tor* (Brandenburg Gate). They walked down the street toward the entrance of the compound. At the gate, a sign was labeled *Visumantragsteller* (Visa Applicants). This was where the huge line was headed. A sign to the left was labeled US Citizens. At the head of both lines stood an embassy employee and a nattily dressed US Marine in blue dress uniform and wearing a sidearm. They approached, and the embassy employee asked the purpose of their business. Aunt Sylvia related their tale of woe concerning the theft of their passports.

"Do you have any type of identification?"

Aunt Sylvia thought then said she had their cruise line tickets with their names, which showed they had passports to enter Germany, and she had a Kansas State driver's license. Rachel had a Leavenworth High School identification card.

The embassy official said that it wasn't much. "Do you have anyone who could vouch for your identity here in Germany?" The only person was Uncle Abraham, and he was unconscious. The embassy official said that the little identification they had would allow them to be issued an American identity card and submit the forms for a passport replacement.

They entered the embassy, completed the mountain of forms, had their pictures taken for their identity cards and passport applications, and were told they would be notified to pick up their passports in sixty to ninety days.

Chapter 5

All things considered, Sidney had enjoyed his summer with Uncle Saul and Aunt Miriam but was also ready to get back home. He was rather disappointed that he had not received one letter from Rachel. He was thinking that she probably was having such a good time in Berlin that she couldn't find time to write to him. He and Uncle Saul were going to Grand Central Station to purchase his return tickets to Kansas. Afterward, he would call home and tell his folks when he would be arriving in Kansas City. It was about an hour-and-twenty-minute drive from the train station back to the Fort Leavenworth Military Post. Hopefully, his father would be able to get time off from the Command and General Staff School to pick him up at the train station. He knew how much his mother hated driving into Kansas City.

That afternoon, he called her and relayed his travel plans. Almost as an afterthought, she mentioned that he had received two telegrams from Rachel. One arrived three days ago and the other today. When asked what was in the telegrams, she stated that she had not read them. She figured they were addressed to Sidney and were personal in nature. He told his mother that he had not heard from Rachel all summer and asked if she would please read them. She opened the first telegram and read:

Reichspostamt (Government Post Office)
7552 Berlin, Deutschland
27 Juli 1938
My dear Sidney,

Plans are set for trip home (STOP) Leaving Bremen 7 August (STOP) Should be home in about 14 days (STOP)

Rachel

That was great news! His mother opened the second telegram and read:

Reichspostamt
7552 Berlin, Deutschland
31 Juli 1938.

Sidney, Drastic change of plans (STOP) Sylvia's Uncle Abraham XXXXXX and XXXXXX (STOP) Our passports have been XXXXXX (STOP) New passports to take 60–90 days (STOP) Don't know when we'll be home (STOP)

Rachel

Sidney and his mother were both perplexed by this second telegram and what the Xs meant. Sidney's father came home at that moment, read the telegram, and said that the telegram had been redacted. He said that Germany was redacting any references to crime. This meant that Rachel and Sylvia's passports had been stolen. Sidney's heart sank down to his shoes. The thought of Rachel stuck in Nazi Germany at this time just made his blood run cold. His father told him that his replacement at the German Embassy was an old academy classmate and would contact him to see if there was anything he could do to help or get more information. He told Sidney to trust him and would see him at the Kansas City train station in three days.

* * *

Klaus was glad to be back at school in Bad Tölz. His other classmates were straggling in groups of twos and threes. As uniforms were squared away, bunks made to exacting standards, and footlockers rearranged, there were the usual discussions of home and how their leave was spent.

One guy noticed the new training schedule had been posted. He noticed something very unusual. The training schedule was normally posted for seven days at a time with a new schedule posted every Sunday afternoon for the following week. This schedule was posted for the next thirty days, entitled "Ubung mit Panzer im Angriff und Verteidigung" ("Training with Armor in the Attack and Defense"). So they were finally going to see some tanks. The training was scheduled to take place at the Grafenwöhr Training Center. One cadet asked if anyone had heard of this Grafenwöhr. *Oberjunker* (Cadet Staff Sergeant) Dieter Hannauer, the group historian and bookworm, stated that Grafenwöhr had been a military training center since around 1900. It was about three hundred kilometers from Bad Tölz and would take about five–six hours by truck. Klaus announced that they had best pack their equipment now to allow them a few more minutes of sleep in the morning. He was sure that *Scharführer* (Staff Sergeant) Winter would be gently awakening them extra early in the morning to prepare for a road trip.

As promised, Scharführer Winter awakened the cadets in his usual way by launching a large metal trash can down the middle of the barracks and banging on the lid while haranguing the cadets with vulgar references regarding sexual congress between themselves and various barn animals and, worse, Jews. After two years of his repertoire, the insults no longer had the sting of the first year. In fact, they barely heard the words anymore; they concentrated more on the instructions that were mixed in his tirade.

Breakfast was at 0530, weapons issued at 0600, and field equipment loaded on trailers by 0645. Cadets would assemble before the barracks by 0715. They would embark the trucks by 0730. Estimated arrival time in Grafenwöhr would be approximately 1500. It was going to be a long, bone-numbing ride on the wooden slat seats of the three-ton Opel Blitz trucks. The convoy of five three-ton trucks and three *Kübelwagens* (German Jeep) departed the Bad Tölz Kaserne at precisely 0800. It was a pleasant morning for a drive. The pleasant part would, of course, diminish after a couple of hours on wooden seats and August sun beating down on the cadets in the back of the open trucks.

At 1200, they received a slight reprieve when they pulled into a rest area for a midday meal of field rations and tepid water. At least they were afforded the opportunity to stretch their legs and relieve themselves. One cadet had already experienced trying to urinate from the side of a moving truck. The wind whipping around the side of the truck made the trajectory of his stream, at best, unpredictable and did not endear him to his comrades who had managed to fall asleep. The cadets and their cadre reembarked in their vehicles, and the journey resumed. It would be approximately two more hours until they reached their destination.

The convoy was about one kilometer from Grafenwöhr when the sound of rifle and machine gun fire, punctuated by the rapid thumping of heavier guns, could be heard. The convoy stopped at the main gate to present their orders and receive instructions as to which training range they were being assigned. They proceeded another two kilometers when they were halted by Military Police blocking the road. About the time people were wondering what was going on, three tanks came crashing out of the underbrush, bounded over the road, and disappeared into the underbrush on the other side of the road. As this was the first time most of the cadets had seen a tank, they were quite impressed. Klaus informed his comrades that they were Panzer II light tanks, armed with a 20-millimeter automatic cannon and a 7.92-millimeter MG-34 machine gun. The other cadets were impressed by his knowledge of modern tanks. This was not the first time Klaus had seen a Panzer II up close.

After talking on their radio, the MPs moved their motorcycles and waved the convoy on. After three more kilometers, they arrived at their training site. A complex of four-man tents around two larger tents was to be their home for the next twenty-eight days. All around them, they could hear the growl of tanks maneuvering, coupled with rifle, machine gun, and automatic cannon fire. They asked Scharführer Winter if this noise kept up all night. He told them that the tanks and infantry usually ceased maneuvers around 1900. That way, the heavy artillery and antiaircraft guns could fire without fear of hitting anyone. They, he said, fire until dawn.

They were formed up in class formation and assigned tents. They had until 1700 to square their gear away before evening meal, and then they were dismissed. They were lined up for evening meal and marched into the dining tent. They would have until 1800 for dinner and then would reform before the command tent where the *Untersturmführer* (Second Lieutenant) would give them a briefing on the coming training exercises, after which they would be released until lights out at 2100. At that moment, the sound of what everyone thought was an approaching freight train flew overhead, followed in five seconds by a huge detonation. The artillery was at work.

At 0530 the next morning, the cadets were awakened to the sound of…silence! The entire night, except for a forty-five-minute "meal break," the artillery had fired one round a minute for five minutes, followed by a fifteen-minute pause, and then repeated the cycle. The first few fifteen-minute pauses had lulled the cadets into thinking they could fall asleep, only to have the next firing cycle start. It had been a very long night with very little sleep. They tried to catch a few winks of sleep before their day started at 0600. At the moment, they were not great fans of the "King of the Battlefield"—the field artillery.

After breakfast, the cadets were marched to the first training area, a large tent intended for classroom instruction and lectures. The next two days would consist of lectures and sand table exercises dealing with the deployment of panzer grenadier units in support of armored forces. These were absolutely fascinating topics after a night with no sleep. Most of the cadets spent the lectures standing so they wouldn't fall asleep. To fall asleep would result in severe repercussions that Scharführer Winter was expert at handing out. Klaus figured that was why they spent two days studying the same topics. The cadre figured the cadets were only absorbing about half the information per day. During the midday break, most of the cadets passed on lunch and collapsed into sleep for forty-five minutes. The others wolfed down their lunch and then slept. After the third day of this routine, the cadets noticed that they were starting to ignore the roar of the artillery and were actually sleeping through the night.

The following week was the beginning of practical field exercises. They were introduced to their secondary mode of transportation (primary being their feet), the *Sonderkraftfahrzeug 7* or *Sd. Kfz. 7* (Special Purpose Vehicle Model 7)—an eight-ton half-track truck built by KrausMaffei. This vehicle would allow the panzer grenadiers to travel at the same speed and over the same terrain as the tanks until contact with the enemy, at which point they would disembark and provide infantry support for the tanks. The Sd. Kfz. 7 was a massive piece of machinery that carried a ten-man squad with storage for all their gear. During the field exercises, they also learned that they would not spend much time in their Model 7 but would make great use of their primary mode of transportation.

They spent days chasing Panzer II tanks up and down the ranges, assaulting gun positions, clearing trench works, and choking on dust and gasoline fumes. They quickly learned that the life of a panzer grenadier was not one for the weak. They each took turns leading their squad during the assault. Because they were using live ammunition, two cadre members accompanied each squad as safety observers. Each squad consisted of the squad leader, armed with an MP-38 9-millimeter submachine gun, a three-man MG-34 machine gun crew, two fire team leaders armed with MP-38s, and four riflemen armed with the Mauser 98K 7.92-millimeter rifle. The drill consisted of the squad leader having the machine gun team lay down suppressing fire on the enemy gun position while the two fire teams would conduct a pincer movement to come up on either side of the gun position. The machine gun team would cease fire, while the two fire team leaders would engage the position, and one rifleman would toss a hand grenade through the gunport.

Klaus was leading the left team, and Oberjunker Dieter Hannauer would lead the right team. Klaus's team would deploy the grenade. The exercise was proceeding with textbook efficiency. They reached the gun emplacement, and the machine gun team ceased fire. Klaus and the rifleman with the grenade stepped out from the left side and Dieter from the right. The rifleman armed the grenade and threw it at the gunport. Klaus and the rifleman dove back to cover. Klaus heard the thump as the hand grenade bounced off the front of the gunport. Klaus looked up to see that Dieter was staring down at the grenade at his feet. He screamed for Dieter to move, but it was too late. The grenade exploded, hurling Dieter five feet backward, shredding his legs, abdomen, and chest. *Unterscharführer* (Sergeant) Hartz, the cadre safety observer nearest to Dieter, took one look at him, turned, and vomited. Klaus rushed to Dieter, yelling, "Sanitäter!" (Medic!) Dieter's wounds were horrific. His right leg was practically severed above the knee, several inches of intestine were outside of his abdomen, and he had several shrapnel wounds to his chest, both arms, and face. The most severe wound appeared to be the leg as Klaus was trying to staunch the flow of blood shooting from his leg.

The medic soon arrived. He looked over Dieter's wounds and just shook his head. The femoral artery was severed; he would bleed out in a few minutes, long before they could get him to an operating room. About this time, Dieter regained consciousness and was in a great deal of pain. Klaus asked the medic if there was nothing he could do for him. The medic reached inside his bag and pulled out a syringe of morphine.

"At least it'll be painless."

Scharführer Winter approached and looked at the medic, who just shook his head. It only took about five minutes, and Dieter was gone. The medic covered him with a blanket and called for a stretcher. The medic, Klaus, and two other cadets loaded Dieter's body into an ambulance.

Scharführer Winter called for Klaus to walk with him. "*Standartenjunker* [Cadet Technical Sergeant] Bergman, what happened out there?"

Klaus looked at him and said, "He froze. Just froze." Klaus remembered the surprised look on Dieter's face as the hand grenade rolled up to his feet. It was all in slow motion—the smoke from the fuse burning down, his scream for Dieter to move, the flash of the explosion, and Dieter flying through the air. "He just froze."

Training was canceled for the remainder of the day. Klaus, as cadet squad leader, was assigned the task of inventorying Dieter's belongings and separating personal property from "Reich" property. He was spared the task of writing a letter to Dieter's parents but thought that he should. It was a responsibility and duty of command, and as he would be an officer soon, it would be good training. Scharführer Winter said to present him with a draft letter, which he would take to the untersturmführer for approval. He turned to Klaus and said, "Bergman, as a career officer, you will hope you never have to write such letters, but if you have to write one, it will be too many."

The remainder of the training cycle concluded without further mishap.

Chapter 6

Sidney was back at school for a week now. It took all his willpower to concentrate on his studies and not to constantly worry about Rachel. It was already two weeks since he received the telegram and hadn't heard anything since. He guessed that shouldn't surprise him as it had taken over two months to receive the first telegram. Still, he wished he could contact her somehow. Sidney had heard of something called ham radio stations and that they talked to members around the world. He determined that he would check into these clubs and see what they were all about. He would also have to remind his father to contact his former classmate at the US Embassy in Berlin. He thought that he was probably becoming a pain in the neck at the Silberman household. He either called or stopped by every day, hoping for some word from Rachel, and although Rachel's mother promised he would be the first to know if any news arrived, he still checked in daily.

Walking through the hallway at school today, he happened to notice on the bulletin board a flyer advertising the start of the Leavenworth High School Amateur Radio Club. They were seeking students who might be interested in contacting other students around the world. He noted that the club was going to meet that very afternoon at four thirty in the science lab. He would make it a point to be there.

As part of Sidney's curriculum, he was required to study a foreign language. He signed up for German, but after he corrected the teacher's grammar one time, they moved him to French. As there was a great similarity to German, Sidney did well in the class, and he enjoyed it. It also gave him the opportunity to tutor Rachel. As luck would have it, one of his classmates, Paul, was a member of the Amateur Radio Club that Sidney was interested in. At lunch, he met with him and discussed the club and what their purpose was. Their purpose was basically to establish contact with as many amateur radio operators as possible, creating an address book to enable them to pass radio messages around the world, free of charge. Sidney asked who they frequently contacted and if they had contact with anyone in Germany. Paul said that they regularly messaged with operators in Europe, including France, England, Holland, Belgium, and Poland. They had previously messaged Germany and Italy, but it had become more and more difficult as those governments greatly restricted radio traffic from those countries. There were still a few operators, but they strictly limited their transmissions to avoid confiscation of their equipment and jail.

Still, Sidney pressed, "Is it possible?"

Paul answered, "It is, but difficult."

To Sidney this was a ray of hope. Then Paul asked Sidney if he knew Morse code.

Sidney replied, "No, is that a problem?"

Paul said, "Morse code is the radio international language and how amateur radio operators communicate."

Sidney asked Paul how his French was. He answered his French was terrible, and he doubted he'd pass the course. Sidney told Paul, "I think we're going to have a beautiful friendship." Sidney's plan was to tutor Paul in French and Paul would tutor Sidney in Morse code. Paul beamed at Sidney and told him to come to the meeting this afternoon and see if it would be something he would be interested in. Sidney said he would see Paul there.

The rest of the day seemed to drag by as Sidney was anticipating the prospect of finding a means to converse with Rachel. Finally, the final bell for the day rang, and Sidney made his way to the science lab. It was a beehive of activity with students setting up radio equipment, cables being strung, and posters displaying the alphabet, followed by a system of dots and dashes. Sidney knew this to be Morse code, but that was all he knew. How he was supposed to memorize all that, he didn't know. It was then that Paul arrived. Sidney told Paul of his feelings about learning Morse code. He told Sidney that it should be easy for him to master with his knack for foreign languages. He told Sidney to just consider it another foreign language, except he would have to learn letters instead of words.

An instructor approached and asked if they would help string some antenna cables. They both readily agreed. They wanted to know all about this radio business. They were handed over to one of the class seniors who showed them to several coils of cables. He explained that they would run the cables outside to several different types of antennae. He explained that they would use an omnidirectional antenna usually for shorter distances and a long-wire antenna, which were directional, for great distances. Sidney inquired how far their radios could communicate. He was told that depending on weather, atmosphere, and solar radiation, they could broadcast and receive thousands of miles. There was even a report of a military radio site that had broadcast a signal around the world!

Sidney asked, "How about communicating with, say, Germany?"

"Not a problem, as long as the German government didn't shut down the operator in Germany, which they had a tendency to do," replied the senior student.

Many ham operators were allowed to communicate with foreign stations as long as they spread German propaganda and reported all foreign contacts. When Sidney inquired about getting information about a US citizen in Germany, he was told as long as the person was not a Jew, it should be easy. Finding a German operator that would inquire about a Jew would be difficult and possibly dangerous for the person inquired about. It would take time to develop the trust between the two operators before such inquiries could be advanced. This was not what Sidney wanted to hear but was determined to move forward with this amateur radio thing, beginning with learning their "language."

* * *

Just as Colonel Klein was getting ready to leave his office at the Command and General Staff College, Sergeant Walters tapped on his door, stuck his head in, and said, "Sir, a Lieutenant Colonel Mitchell from the US Embassy in Berlin on line two for you."

Colonel Bergman answered the phone, "George, how are you doing? How's the family liking Berlin and embassy duty?"

Lieutenant Colonel Mitchell replied, "Doing great, Jake, or should I say, sir. Congratulations on the eagles." This was in reference to Jacob Klein's promotion to full colonel.

"Thanks, George, you won't be far behind."

The purpose of the call was to provide Colonel Klein with information concerning his inquiry about Rachel and Sylvia. Lieutenant Colonel Mitchell had found that what Jake had suspected was true. Their passports had, indeed, been stolen along with a large sum of cash. Sylvia's Uncle Abraham was in the hospital in critical condition. Expected to recover, but not for several months. He had managed to expedite completion of the passport paperwork by vouching for Rachel and Sylvia's citizenship. This would help on this end by two days. He also spoke to the ambassador's secretary to see if he would provide an endorsement to expedite the request on the State Department end in Washington, DC. So far, he hadn't heard anything back on his request. He was going to pay Rachel and Sylvia a visit to see if there was anything he could do to help their situation but was told by the chargé de'affaires not to go personally. The Nazi SD (*Sicherheits Dienst*) Security Service kept a close watch on embassy personnel, and he probably wouldn't want Rachel and Sylvia to draw any unwanted attention from the SD, especially being Jewish. He dispatched one of the embassy's Marine security detachment with a letter and to wait for any reply. In his letter, he told them that if they were in need of anything to call his private number at the embassy. That was where things stood at the moment.

Colonel Klein thanked Lieutenant Colonel Mitchell for all he had done so far and said he owed him big-time. Lieutenant Colonel Mitchell promised if he had any other news, he would forward it as soon as possible and would keep an eye on Rachel and Sylvia as best he could. Colonel Klein expressed his thanks again and hung up the phone.

Later at home, he relayed everything he knew to Sidney. He told his son that it appeared that Uncle Abraham's assault and robbery might have been committed by someone who knew him, but police officials didn't appear to be interested in either investigating the case or any interest in Rachel or Sylvia. He felt that as long as they kept a low profile, the authorities would probably ignore them. This wasn't the greatest news for Sidney, but at least it appeared that Rachel and her Aunt Sylvia were all right, and someone was trying to watch out for them. He was still determined to pursue the ham radio gambit. He mentioned this to his father, who basically gave him the same advice as to whom he should contact and provide information. His father told him that German ham radio operators were allowed to stay on the air because they were required to report to the German security services any foreign contacts and what was discussed.

Sidney's second meeting of the radio club was spent watching experienced operators sending and receiving messages. He was amazed with the speed that some of the operators worked. He was told that an experienced operator could send and receive up to fifty words per minute. Sidney was paired with Paul on a dummy radio set to start learning Morse code. He started by sending and receiving the alphabet. This was going to take a lot of work, and he wondered if this was the fastest or easiest way to communicate with Rachel. At least it would keep his mind occupied with something other than worrying about Rachel. He asked Paul if he ever contacted anyone in Germany. Paul said he did but that it was always kind of strange. They always went on and on about how wonderful life in Germany was. There was never any talk of problems or unrest, only how Der Führer had made everyone's life so much better. They made life in Germany sound so idyllic. Paul had made the mistake once of asking about stories of persecution of communists, Gypsies, and Jews and of the banning of all other political parties. There followed a long static-filled silence. He never contacted with that operator again.

A week later, Paul's turn to utilize the radio came up again. Sidney sat by his side to watch and become familiar with Paul's "hand." Every radio operator developed a certain rhythm when sending that could be recognized by other operators, like a signature. Paul was scanning through frequencies when he suddenly stopped and started tapping on his typewriter. He typed out the three-character Q code "QNI." (May I join the net?) Paul turned to the radio key and began tapping out a series of dots and dashes. Paul was receiving traffic. He typed in "QRA." (What is your call sign?) He turned back to the typewriter and typed out "ND4W-DE," a German call sign. On the radio key, he returned with his call sign, "AEM1-USA." He went back and forth between the typewriter and the radio key for about twenty minutes, finally signing off with "QSH." (Stay happy and healthy.)

Sidney wanted to know what the entire conversation was about. Paul said everything was very general; he didn't want to press the other operator too hard on any political issues. They would communicate again tomorrow. Sidney wasn't happy with the plan, but as he didn't have the skills to make inquiries himself, he would have to go along with Paul's assessment.

During dinner that evening, Sidney related the radio activities for the day and the information, or lack of information, that had been gleaned. Sidney's father reminded him that he had warned him that German radio operators would be very suspicious of anyone looking for information as the German Intelligence Service monitored all radio transmissions, especially with foreign radio stations. Sidney was determined to learn Morse code faster so he could conduct his own inquiries, security service be damned. There had to be someone out there who wasn't in love with Der Führer and was willing to help him.

Chapter 7

It was the end of October, and Aunt Sylvia and Rachel had still not received any notification from the embassy regarding the status of their passports. Aunt Sylvia vowed that if they received no word by the end of the week, she would make an inquiry at the embassy. Rachel suggested that they call Lieutenant Colonel Mitchell, but Aunt Sylvia was concerned about the possibility of the phones being monitored as Lieutenant Colonel Mitchell had warned they might be. No, the answer was to go to the embassy.

Meanwhile, Uncle Abraham's condition was improving. He had regained consciousness two days after being admitted but was in a great deal of pain, which was to be expected of a man his age and the extent of his injuries. The doctor told them that the damage to his wrist and jaw had required reconstructive surgeries that were impeding his recovery. His age, of course, did not help. The doctor originally anticipated Uncle Abraham's release from the hospital around the first week of October, barring any setbacks. At the end of September, there was a setback. Uncle Abraham's broken ribs caused him to contract pneumonia. He managed to survive, but it delayed his release to the end of October at the earliest.

Aunt Sylvia and Rachel went to visit Uncle Abraham at the hospital, hoping to hear good news concerning his release. Before they got past the ward desk, the nurse on duty stopped them and asked them to wait for Frau Blucher, a hospital administrator. They sat, and shortly, Frau Blucher appeared. She had a sizable folder in her arms, which she laid before Aunt Sylvia, and proceeded to explain that the documents contained in the folder were Uncle Abraham's ongoing medical charges. The charges had reached the point over 1,000 reichsmarks, where hospital policy required payment of at least 50 percent in order to allow further treatment. Aunt Sylvia explained to Frau Blucher that her uncle was in the hospital because he had been robbed. She didn't know if he had any money left. This was a subject that she had not broached with Uncle Abraham as yet. Frau Blucher said that a payment of 500 reichsmarks had to be received by the end of the week, or her uncle would receive no further treatment, would be discharged, and legal proceedings instigated to recover the remaining debt. With that, Frau Blucher presented Aunt Sylvia with a copy of the invoice, turned on her heel, and left.

Aunt Sylvia and Rachel stared at each other in shock. Where were they to come up with such a sum of money by Friday, just four days away? Just that morning, they had been pooling their money to see where they stood. Together they had the impressive sum of 280 reichsmarks and 75 pfennigs. Luckily, there was no rent to pay, and they used very little electricity, which was already paid for next month. The nights hadn't become too cold to require lighting the coal-fired heater in the apartment. They only needed a few briquettes each day for hot water, and there was a goodly supply of them in the basement. Still, the money they had remaining would not last very long, especially if they were to have to take over Uncle Abraham's care at home. Aunt Sylvia didn't want to trouble Uncle Abraham with money problems but could see no other way. If Uncle Abraham didn't have at least 500 reichsmarks by Friday, they would be in serious difficulties and would only get worse. They had to tell Uncle Abraham.

They entered Uncle Abraham's room to see him sitting up and looking very well, better than he had in months. Aunt Sylvia thought it was going to be a shame to ruin the look on his face when she gave him the bad news. Aunt Sylvia tried to put off the subject of money, but Uncle Abraham could tell that something was weighing on her. He told her to get to the point of the matter. Aunt Sylvia showed him the hospital bill and the demand for 500 reichsmarks by Friday. She told him how much money they had left, and they had no idea how much longer it would be before they received their passports, which didn't matter because they couldn't leave until Uncle Abraham had recovered enough to fend for himself. The money situation brought up another problem in how Uncle Abraham was going to make his planned move to Holland. He had the car, yes, but no money for fuel, food, and lodging once he arrived in Holland. The immensity of all this was enough to drive Aunt Sylvia crazy.

Uncle Abraham took the news surprisingly well. He listened to Aunt Sylvia explain their predicament and thought for a few minutes. None of his supposed friends and neighbors had offered any help. As a matter of fact, two of them were actually caught eyeing some of his remaining property through his broken open door. He thought that Herr Rheinhaus might have offered to "loan" them a few reichsmarks to help them out. He was almost positive that it was two of his "associates" who had beaten and robbed him. Uncle Abraham was a shrewd old businessman who knew well not to put all his eggs in one basket. He told Aunt Sylvia to go to his bedroom and push his bed to the right. Under the left leg was a loose floorboard. In the floor was a cigar box containing cash and a few pieces of jewelry. The cash, they were to use as needed; the jewelry, they were to keep for themselves. They tried to argue with him about keeping the jewelry, but he just shushed them and said, "You never know when it might come in handy." He told them to go and take care of paying what needed to be paid.

Aunt Sylvia and Rachel returned to the apartment and did as they were instructed. As Uncle Abraham said, under the floorboard was a cigar box with 5,000 reichsmarks and two beautiful ruby rings. Aunt Sylvia thought to herself that Uncle Abraham certainly was a crafty old fox. They took 2,000 reichsmarks in 100-reichsmark notes from the box and returned the rest, along with the rings, to their hiding place. Tomorrow they would return to pay Frau Blucher and find out how much longer Uncle Abraham would remain in the hospital.

Uncle Abraham was released from the hospital on November 5. Aunt Sylvia and Rachel had gone shopping in the morning and had prepared a coming-home party for him. They went to the hospital at eleven and received final instructions from the doctor concerning continuing care, a prescription for pain, and of course, the final bill. They loaded Uncle Abraham into his car and drove home. He was quite overwhelmed with the flowers, decorations, and meal that the girls had prepared for him.

After the meal, Uncle Abraham motioned Aunt Sylvia to him, removed a small key from his vest pocket, and pointed her to a small cabinet in the wall. He told her to bring what was inside to him. Aunt Sylvia did as she was instructed and returned with a wooden box. Inside was a bottle of Remy Martin VSOP cognac and an Iron Cross medal. Uncle Abraham said that he had brought the bottle back from France at the end of World War I, along with the Iron Cross first class for bravery under fire at the Battle of Château-Thierry in June 1918. The bottle of cognac hadn't been opened in all these years. Uncle Abraham decided it was time to open it. He had Aunt Sylvia bring three brandy glasses from the cabinet, opened the bottle, and poured a healthy dollop of the over twenty-year-old cognac into each glass. Before drinking, he raised his glass and said, "L'chaim." (To life.) And then he poured a small amount of cognac on the floor and said, "In gedenken an die gefallenen." (In remembrance of fallen comrades.) "Bis wir uns wieder treffen." (Till we meet again.) They drank their cognacs in silence.

On Monday, November 7, Aunt Sylvia and Rachel made their trek back to the US Embassy. Once again, they were told that their passports had not yet arrived. When asked what the cause of the delay could be, the embassy staffer couldn't say. Aunt Sylvia asked if they could speak to Lieutenant Colonel Mitchell. They were told that he wasn't available at the moment. Lieutenant Colonel Mitchell was in a high-level briefing and could not be disturbed. If they wanted to wait, they could take a seat, but there was no way to know how long it would be before he would be free. They decided that they had traveled all this way, so they might as well wait for a while.

Three hours later, Lieutenant Colonel Mitchell appeared, looking haggard. Aunt Sylvia and Rachel bombarded him with their usual barrage of questions. Before they got too far into their tirade, Lieutenant Colonel Mitchell held up his hands and told them that he had been in meetings since the ambassador had received word from Paris that a German official in the embassy foreign office had been shot and severely wounded by a German Jew. It was reported that the German government was preparing reprisals. He advised Aunt Sylvia and Rachel to stay home and wait to hear from him. He promised that as soon as he had some news, he would send his Marine messenger. He said he had a bad feeling that things were going to get very ugly in a short time.

Aunt Sylvia and Rachel returned to the apartment to find Uncle Abraham sitting in front of the radio, intently listening to a broadcast. When Aunt Sylvia tried to speak, he just held his hand up. After another minute or two, he said the Jews were really in for it now. Some foolish Jewish boy in Paris had shot an embassy official and confessed to the crime. The Nazis were already announcing that Jewish schoolchildren were barred from attending German schools starting tomorrow. Also, all Jewish cultural events were canceled indefinitely. Jewish newspapers and magazines were banned effective immediately. Himmler had ordered the confiscation of all firearms owned by Jews and made it punishable by twenty years' confinement in a concentration camp for anyone not surrendering their firearms by Wednesday. They just looked at each other for about five minutes, not saying a word.

Rachel spoke first, "What shall we do?"

Uncle Abraham replied by saying that on Saturday, he would call his brother in Amsterdam to tell him he would leave on Monday. In that time, he would gather up all the cash he had and give half to the girls. They could not travel to Holland as they had no passport. Aunt Sylvia refused to take any money, saying that Uncle Abraham would need it when he got to Holland.

"Unsinn!" (Nonsense!) "I helped my brother through law school. He can help me now, and he'll be proud to do it. Besides, I'll feel bad about leaving you two here while I go to safety in Holland."

Aunt Sylvia told him not to be sad. She was certain they would be leaving too in a few more days to a week.

The next day, Uncle Abraham was busy running errands here and there, gathering up packets of cash like a squirrel gathering up nuts for the winter. After each trip, he'd make his way up to his bedroom and put the money into the cigar box under the bed leg. By the end of the day, he was exhausted and slumped into his chair. Rachel went to make him a cup of tea, while Aunt Sylvia removed his shoes and brought him his slippers. Uncle Abraham thanked them both and proceeded to relate the activities of his day. He told them it was as if someone had kicked over an anthill. He normally didn't see this much bustling activity of people going in and out of the shops and stores until the day before Hanukkah. He said that people were more on edge than normal. This shooting in Paris would have far-reaching consequences, and soon. The people were starting to hoard food, medical supplies, candles, and alcohol. In front of the synagogue, there was a growing pile of firearms, mostly shotguns, but also a few hunting rifles and pistols. No one wanted to face twenty years at Dachau or Sachsenhausen.

Wednesday, November 9, started as any other day lately, the usual hustle and bustle as the Jewish community continued to prepare for some tough times. Suddenly, the sound of church bells were ringing in the slow, stately pattern they usually did during a Christian death announcement. Uncle Abraham had been listening to a classical music program when it was interrupted by funeral dirges. An announcer came on and reported that Ernst von Rath, the German diplomat whom had been shot in France, had died of his wounds. The German Reich was in mourning.

Within an hour, members of the SA and Hitler Youth began gathering on the streets. They began by cursing the Jews, physically harassing them, and preventing them from entering non-Jewish shops. A crowd began to gather. The citizens started by cheering on the SA, but soon they, too, harassed their Jewish "neighbors." Uncle Abraham was headed toward the window to see what all the fuss was about when there was the sound of shattering glass and a loud cheer. Someone had thrown a cobblestone, pried up from the street, through the window of the clothing store across the street. As people watched, the SA started tearing out mannequins, dresses, and bolts of cloth and throwing them into the street. The owner struggled with the SA people and called to his neighbors, people who in the past had been customers, to help him. They stood by and watched as the SA beat the man to the ground and continued to kick him until the police arrived and arrested the store owner. This scene played out over and over down the street to each Jewish storefront. The crowds grew larger, and more civilians actively joined in the vandalism and looting.

As night fell, people lit torches to provide better lighting. Eventually, someone threw a torch into one of the businesses. The crowd cheered as the flames grew higher, and more stores were torched. Arrival of the local fire brigade was only to ensure that non-Jewish stores and property were not damaged; the Jewish stores were allowed to burn. From their darkened apartment, Uncle Abraham, Aunt Sylvia, and Rachel watched in horror as this scene from hell played out. Uncle Abraham warned them not to stand too close to the window, lest they be seen from the street. It was then that a great uproar came from further down the street. The entire crowd hurried in that direction. From down the street, they heard someone call out, "The synagogue is burning!" They could not believe what they were hearing. Aunt Sylvia said she would go out and look down the street. Uncle Abraham was against this idea, but Aunt Sylvia said that with her American identification card, she felt that she would be protected.

Aunt Sylvia went down the stairs, peeked out the door, then stepped out onto the sidewalk. It seemed as though she had no sooner stepped outside than she was grabbed and spun around. An SA man pushed her against the wall and demanded to know who she was, what she was doing, and if she was a Jew. When he asked again if she were a Jew, she replied that she was an American. He pushed his flashlight onto her face and said he would determine that. He was so close to her that she could smell his acrid sweat and the alcohol on his breath. He started to grope her when suddenly he was pulled off her by a very large policeman. The SA man told the policeman that this was SA business and to move along. The policeman said that he was responsible for law and order here, and his instructions and that of the SA were to ensure that foreigners were not harassed. The policeman said he had heard the woman say that she was American. He turned to Aunt Sylvia and asked for her identification. She produced the American document from her pocket. The policeman looked at it strangely at first; he studied it a moment before handing it to the SA man. The SA man looked at it and grunted. The policeman handed the document back to Aunt Sylvia, turned to the SA man, and told him he owed Aunt Sylvia an apology. They stared at each other for a long moment before the SA man turned to Aunt Sylvia and said, "Ich entschuldige Mich Fraulein." (I apologize, miss.) He looked at the policeman once more before storming off in the direction of the synagogue.

Aunt Sylvia thanked the policemen and started to follow the SA man toward the synagogue. The policeman stopped her and told her that she didn't want to go down there. The synagogue was completely engulfed in flames, but luckily, all the archives had been rescued, along with the records from the Jewish Community Center. When Aunt Sylvia asked him who had rescued all the records, he replied, "The Gestapo Geheim Staatspolizei [State Secret Police], of course." Aunt Sylvia felt a cold shiver run down her spine. The secret police had the name and address of every Jew in the entire community. She thanked the policeman for his assistance and returned to the apartment.

Aunt Sylvia went back upstairs to relate what was going on. She decided not to mention the encounter with the drunken SA man. She had no sooner finished her story when there were the sounds of screams from outside. SA men and local citizens were breaking into apartments and dragging male family members from their homes. They were being dragged away, and their families were told they were under arrest. They were not told where their husbands, fathers, sons, and brothers were being taken. There was suddenly pounding at Uncle Abraham's downstairs door. Aunt Sylvia went to see what the commotion was about. There were several men at the door demanding entry to search for Jewish males. The policeman from earlier was blocking entry. He told the gathering at the door that the people occupying this property were American women and were under the protection of the Reich. The SA man from earlier arrived and verified what the policeman said and ordered the crowd to move on.

Aunt Sylvia returned to the apartment and told Uncle Abraham about the synagogue and all the records and archives being confiscated by the Gestapo. Uncle Abraham made the decision to leave Saturday instead of Monday morning alone. Aunt Sylvia said that was ridiculous. It was eight hundred kilometers to Amsterdam, about eighteen hours' driving time, much too far for Uncle Abraham to drive alone. He had to agree, but the two women could not enter Holland without passports. He decided that once on the road, he would call his brother and have him meet him at the border town of Enschede, and Aunt Sylvia and Rachel would return to Berlin in the car. They started packing for the trip. Uncle Abraham split the money three ways, giving Aunt Sylvia and Rachel equal portions. They tried to protest, but Uncle Abraham explained that if somehow they were detained, it might look suspicious if an old Jew had such a large sum of money.

In the morning, things had calmed considerably, and glass littered the streets. A pall of smoke from still smoldering buildings hung over the streets. There was a group of Hitler Youth nailing placards on Jewish homes and those businesses that hadn't been torched. After they had moved down the street, Aunt Sylvia went downstairs and retrieved one from the door. The placard was a decree announcing that in reparation for the assassination of Ernst von Rath, the Jewish inhabitants of the German Reich were hereby assessed a fine of 1 billion reichsmarks. The fine would be collected by all Jews forfeiting 20 percent of all their possessions. Additionally, all insurance claims paid to cover damages to property and possessions would be surrendered to the Reich. Collection of fines would begin on Monday, November 13. Aunt Sylvia showed the placard to Uncle Abraham. They decided to leave before dark today.

Aunt Sylvia said that she would make a trip to the American Embassy, in case their passports arrived, and inform Lieutenant Colonel Mitchell of their plan. It would be a good idea if someone knew where they were going so that they wouldn't "disappear." Lieutenant Colonel Mitchell wasn't available to speak to Aunt Sylvia, so she left him a letter detailing their expected itinerary and returned to the car.

They left Berlin, not knowing if they would return. Uncle Abraham told them that the apartment would probably no longer be available when they returned, and they would have to contact the embassy for a place to stay. They carefully made their way out of Berlin and headed west. So far, they had not encountered any checkpoints or other hindrances to traffic. They considered themselves lucky and settled in for a very long trip.

Chapter 8

The funeral for Oberjunker Dieter Hannauer conducted at Bad Tölz was just a dry run for what was going to take place once his casket was transported to his hometown of Kaiserslautern. All the military pomp had been meticulously orchestrated from the flag-draped casket lying in repose at the cadet chapel with nine student honor guards to the corps of cadets passing in review and the church service that resembled a Viking send-off to Valhalla. It was pure Wagnerian opera. After the ceremony, the casket was loaded onto an artillery caisson, which made its way outside the kaserne to a waiting hearse for transportation to the train station. The honor guard, led by *Standartenjunker* (Cadet Technical Sergeant) Klaus Bergman, boarded a waiting truck that followed the hearse.

At the train station, Scharführer Winter awaited the casket and honor guard. He waited while the cadets ceremoniously transferred Dieter's casket from the hearse to a specially prepared and decorated freight car. After the casket was properly secured, the honor guard formed outside the freight car. Scharführer Winter handed them their train tickets and meal vouchers. He indicated the railcar they would occupy and instructed them that they would not get drunk or indulge in any behavior that would bring discredit on the Fahnenjunker Schule or the Waffen-SS. Any infractions would be rewarded with the opportunity to spend another month chasing tanks at Grafenwöhr.

"Are my instructions clear?"

The group answered with a resounding "Jawohl Herr Scharführer!"

He instructed them to board the train but called Klaus to him. He informed Klaus that although he would be accompanying the honor guard, Klaus would be responsible for the supervision and conduct of the honor guard. Klaus would ensure that they got their meals at the designated stops. They boarded the train on time and behaved like officer candidates at all times.

The trip to Kaiserslautern was uneventful, if not boring. When they arrived at the train station, Klaus formed up the honor guard in preparation for the transfer of the casket to the hearse waiting for them. Scharführer Winter was speaking to the hearse driver, an army corporal. The corporal was relating to Scharführer Winter the plans for the upcoming events. When he was finished, Scharführer Winter briefed the cadets. They would transport the casket to the *Stiftskirche* (collegiate church) in the *marktplatz* (marketplace). The casket would remain in repose for two days. The family would have a private viewing this evening, with a public viewing tomorrow. The funeral would take place on the third day. As access to the church was available twenty-four hours a day, the honor guard would provide four cadets, four hours on and four hours off, until the day of the funeral when all nine guards would be present. Klaus, as guard commander would conduct the changing of the guard every four hours. The church would provide a room where the off-duty guards could rest. The guards would eat in the church rectory with the priests. As there were no questions, they conducted the casket transfers at the train station and the church.

After they had set the casket in place before the altar, Klaus established the watch list, and the first watch was posted. The remainder of the guard followed the priest on duty to what looked to be a barracks room with four bunks. The priest told Klaus that his room was next door. Klaus instructed them to make sure their uniforms were in order and to get some rest. They would go eat before they went on guard. Klaus followed the priest to where his room was and then down the corridor and across the courtyard to where they would be taking their meals. Klaus was informed that the monsignor liked to have dinner at 1800 (6:00 p.m.), so that was when dinner would be served, but they would, of course, make provisions for the guard schedule. Klaus thanked the priest then went back to the church where the guard was posted. He closely inspected the four cadets on duty and discovered that all four needed their uniforms brushed and two needed a shave. He sent the two who needed to straighten their uniforms and shave to the room they were assigned; the other two he posted at the head of the casket. In fifteen minutes, the first two returned, and the second pair retired to straighten their uniforms. He did not write any of them up for demerits as they had come straight from two days on a train. When the entire four-man shift was present, Klaus went to the bunk room to check uniforms and shaves on the other four cadets.

At 1830, the guards were changed, and the first shift went to eat and break time. The second shift had just been posted when a man and woman entered the vestibule and slowly proceeded to where the casket was staged. Klaus recognized them from a picture that Dieter kept next to his bunk. They were his mother and father. Klaus snapped to attention, as did the honor guard. Klaus approached the pair, clicked his heels, and extended his hand first to Dieter's mother and then his father and said, "Mein herzlich Beileid." (My heartfelt condolences.) It was all Klaus could do to hold back a tear as he looked into the eyes of the woman. She appeared utterly devastated. Her only child, still a boy, now lay in the casket before her while other "boys" were dressed up as soldiers. It was one thing to play at soldier. When you were killed in battle, you came back at the end of the fight. Now her boy came back in a box, and she couldn't understand why.

Dieter's father looked at Klaus and wanted to know if Klaus had been with him. Klaus nodded and lied, "He felt no pain. It was very quick."

Dieter's father nodded and mumbled, "That was good."

Klaus led Dieter's parents to the casket and stayed by their side while they had a moment with him. Dieter's mother asked if she could see him one more time. It almost broke Klaus's heart to have to tell her that it was not possible; it was against regulations.

The changing of the guards, meals, rest, and repeat went on until the day of the funeral. On that day, the entire nine-man detachment was present for the entire ceremony. The casket was moved outside to the artillery caisson and, drawn by horses, was moved down the street to the church cemetery. The graveside ceremony concluded with a rifle salute and the playing of "Ich hatte Einen Kameraden" ("I Had a Comrade"). The honor guard marched off to their transport while Klaus paid his last respects to Dieter's parents. His father told Klaus that he had been in the Big War and knew what it was to lose a comrade. Klaus looked down at the man and told him he hoped it would be his last. The man looked back at Klaus and just shook his head. "With the man currently in charge, I wouldn't bet on it." Klaus was shocked that Dieter's father had spoken against Der Führer but chalked it up as grief and decided not to do his expected duty of reporting him to the Gestapo.

Scharführer Winter met them at the train station and performed the same procedure as coming out. He issued train tickets, meal tickets, and assigned them their train car, but this time, he issued each man a beer ticket. "One beer," he said. He called Klaus aside and told him that he had demonstrated outstanding leadership qualities during this assignment, and if he could manage to return this gang of hooligans to Bad Tölz without any of them getting drunk and/or arrested, it would bode well for his early promotion to *standartenoberjunker* (cadet master sergeant). There was only one cadet per class promoted to that rank.

Klaus settled back in his seat on the train and thought about what Scharführer Winter had said, and then he thought about what Dieter's father had said about this not being the last comrade whom he would bury with Adolf Hitler in charge. Klaus just hoped that Herr Hannauer's prediction was wrong. After the grueling schedule for the past week, it didn't take long for the rhythm of the railroad tracks to lull Klaus into sleep.

The train was pulling into the main train station at Frankfurt am Main when the sound of sirens was heard. There were fires burning throughout the city of Frankfurt. When they pulled into the station, they received word that pogroms against the Jews had begun because of the assassination of Ernst von Rath. Kristallnacht had begun. Klaus wondered if this was what Dieter's father was talking about.

*C*hapter 9

Over the past several weeks, Sidney had become quite proficient at Morse code. Paul was really impressed with how quickly he had picked it up and the growing circle of contacts he had developed. Sidney did have a great advantage over the other operators because of his language skills. There were many European operators who communicated in English, but it was always an advantage to be able to communicate in French and German. Sidney had been lucky enough to discover a couple of operators who were not particularly enamored with the current government policies regarding treatment of non-Aryan residents of the Reich. After several weeks of communicating with one operator in Berlin, he had finally broached the subject of Rachel. After explaining the situation to his newfound friend, who would only identify himself by his call sign NN2Z-DE—Sidney called him Z for short—he agreed to venture over to the section of the city where Aunt Sylvia's Uncle Abraham lived. He would check on Rachel and deliver a message from Sidney then send a reply back to him the next day.

After two days in which Sidney spent three to four hours a day attempting to contact Z, he finally received a reply. Z told Sidney that he apparently had not heard the news about the German foreign officer assassination and Kristallnacht in Germany. It was not easy to enter the neighborhood where Rachel was staying unless one came to loot and burn. He found the address that Sidney had given him, but there was no answer. A policeman approached to ask what he was looking for. Z told the policeman he was inquiring about the Americans who were supposed to be staying there. The policeman shrugged his shoulders and simply said, "Gone. This morning sometime, they were in a car." Z told Sidney he had no other information for him other than a neighbor saying that they visited the American Embassy often. Sidney thanked Z for all his help and would contact him again soon.

That evening, Sidney asked his father if he had any news from Lieutenant Colonel Mitchell. His father replied that as a matter of fact, he did. Aunt Sylvia had left a letter for Lieutenant Colonel Mitchell saying that they were driving Uncle Abraham to the Dutch border where he would be met by his brother. They would then return to Berlin and wait for their passports. The delay with the passports was due to a change at the State Department, causing the passports to be sent by regular mail instead of by military courier via diplomatic pouch. The main problem was if the mail went through France. There was presently a longshoreman's strike of all French ports, so everything was being delayed. Lieutenant Colonel Mitchell had already contacted the American Embassy in Paris to see what could be done, but it didn't look good. As far as the trip to the Dutch border, Lieutenant Colonel Mitchell considered the whole trip a crap shoot. He realized Aunt Sylvia's reason for the trip but considered it extremely risky. If they were detained, they could be arrested for not surrendering Uncle Abraham's automobile as part of his 20 percent of property for fines. Although they had American identity cards, they still didn't have passports, and a rural police department might not recognize the identity cards as valid and call for someone, maybe the security service or Gestapo, to adjudicate for them. This would create bigger problems when trying to get them released.

All this did nothing to reassure Sidney that everything was going to turn out well. Lieutenant Colonel Mitchell said that there was absolutely nothing that anyone could do at the moment. Aunt Sylvia had worked out a code where she would call Lieutenant Colonel Mitchell's private phone number at eleven each day, let it ring twice, and hang up, and repeat that. If it rang more than twice, he would answer. If she didn't call, he knew there was trouble. That was the best system that they could work out. When Sidney asked why they didn't just speak every day, his father told him that if the embassy phone lines were tapped, they might be able to trace where Aunt Sylvia and Rachel were calling from. It was all a matter of wait and see.

For the next three days, Sidney continued to reach out to ham operators in Europe, trying to get a feel for what was happening. Every day Sidney would tap out NN2Z-DE in hopes of hearing Z reply. One day his call sign came back, and they started a conversation. It started to turn a little strange when Z began asking questions about where Rachel might be headed, with whom she was traveling, and why. It was then that he noticed the operator's "hand" was not Z's. Sidney realized that either Z's station or his call sign was being hijacked by someone, more than likely one of the intelligence services. Sidney tapped back that he had no idea where she might be going or why. After all, Rachel was there as a tourist, and he presumed she was sightseeing. The fake Z asked what she might be interested in seeing and an entire battery of other personal questions that Sidney didn't think he should know. As he started to tap back to Z, he slowly turned the frequency knob so that it sounded as if atmospherics were interfering with his transmission. Finally, Sidney stopped transmitting.

He switched to an alternate frequency that he and Z had seldom used but thought he might pick him up there. As soon as he heard his call sign, he knew it was Z. He tapped out, "QRU." (Do you have traffic for me?)

Z came back with a very short reply, "Compromised. Don't transmit."

Sidney wondered what he should do now. Did that mean not to try to contact Z ever again or just to monitor for traffic in the future? Sidney felt responsible for bringing the intelligence services down on Z. He presumed he still had his equipment, but for how long?

*C*hapter 10

The trip to Holland, so far, had been uneventful. They were able to travel by *Reichsautobahn* (federal highway) from Berlin to Hannover in a little over twelve hours. They probably could have made better time, but when Uncle Abraham insisted it was his turn to drive, Aunt Sylvia could tell that he was not comfortable behind the wheel. Their speed dropped from 70 kph (kilometers per hour, 40 mph) down to 50 kph (30 mph). They found an inconspicuous hotel near the entrance to the Reichsautobahn that accepted their American identity cards in lieu of passports. Uncle Abraham stayed in the car while they registered so that he didn't have to present his identification, which would identify him as a Jew. Aunt Sylvia found a small grocery store where she was able to buy bread and cheese for their dinner. She also found a phone booth in which to make her call to the embassy.

In the morning, they continued on their way. They would have to leave the Reichsautobahn soon and travel further north to the Dutch border on two-lane highway. This would slow their travel down, and they would be passing through many small towns and villages. Before they left the highway, they came to a gas station / café. They definitely needed fuel, and a good breakfast would be appreciated by all. The service attendant refueled the car; checked the oil, water, and tire pressures; and cleaned the windshield. Aunt Sylvia paid the man, and they went to the café. Luckily, the place was fairly full, so they would easily blend in with the other patrons and not be subject to a chatty waitress with a load of questions. In twenty minutes, they received and ate their breakfast, paid, and left. They all thought that had gone rather well and, with the car and themselves refueled, looked forward to the next leg of the trip, Hannover to Enschede. According to the map, they should be near the Dutch border in about six hours. They had no reason to stop for anything, so they should make decent time.

By 14:30, they approached the sign notifying them that they were ten kilometers from the border. This was where things could get tricky. As Aunt Sylvia and Rachel had no passport, the border agent didn't have to let them cross to the Dutch border. They were not sure what would happen. The zone between the German and the Dutch borders were kind of a no-man's-land. Depending on the whim or special instructions of the customs/immigration official on duty, he could simply wave them through or conduct a full-on inspection. It was strictly a roll of the dice. As they approached the gate, they saw that the official on duty was reading the newspaper and studiously ignoring their approaching vehicle. He glanced up once and waved them through the German control point without a second glance. It was all they could do to control their joy at passing this major hurdle.

At the Dutch control point, the customs/immigration official was very friendly. He examined Aunt Sylvia's and Rachel's American identity cards and explained to them that their documents were not sufficient to cross into the Netherlands. Aunt Sylvia explained that they were here only to escort her uncle to Holland and return to Germany. He smiled and examined Uncle Abraham's documents. He inquired how Uncle Abraham was going to support himself and where he was going to live. Uncle Abraham showed him his wad of reichsmarks, and before he could answer where he was going to live, a man spoke up and said he would be living with him. It was Uncle Abraham's brother, Mordecai. Mordecai's credentials as a federal judge in Holland convinced the immigration official that he should be allowed to take them to the nearest hotel for dinner and a room for the night. The immigration official stamped Uncle Abraham's passport, which allowed him to immigrate into the Netherlands, and issued Aunt Sylvia and Rachel a special twenty-four-hour visa. They left Uncle Abraham's car at the control point and rode with Mordecai to a local hotel. Rooms were arranged for, and it was agreed that they would meet in the dining room at six for cocktails and dinner.

Dinning in Holland was quite different than it had been in Germany. At first, they were very conscious when speaking, looking around to see if other diners were listening or looking suspiciously at them. Mordecai reassured them that this was Holland, a free country where you could think and say what you wanted, not Nazi Germany where the secret police or even the regular citizens were likely to report you for speech against the Reich. After the second bottle of wine, all thoughts of the secret police and the Third Reich were forgotten. When asked for a local specialty, the waiter recommended the *hasenpfeffer* (rabbit stew), a local delicacy, along with *knödel* (potato dumplings) and *rotkraut* (red cabbage). Everyone agreed it sounded delicious, and the dish was ordered all around, along with another bottle of an excellent Mosel Rheinwein.

Mordecai told stories about Uncle Abraham as a child. For the first time in what seemed like months, everyone laughed and felt at ease. Uncle Abraham looked years younger, and a twinkle had returned to his eyes. Aunt Sylvia felt relieved, but then she remembered that she and Rachel had to return to Germany and uncertainty in the morning. It was then that she remembered her scheduled phone call. She told the hotel owner that she needed to make a call to Germany. The hotel owner warned her that the call might be monitored. Aunt Sylvia explained that there would be no conversation. The hotel owner just smiled and nodded his understanding. After her "call," Aunt Sylvia returned to the table for a very enjoyable meal and a relaxing evening. Their trials and tribulations in Germany would wait until tomorrow.

In the morning, they all met for breakfast. The dreaded return to Germany was discussed in detail. They all agreed that the most dangerous part would be crossing back into Germany. True, they had a twenty-four-hour Dutch visa that verified they had been allowed into Holland from Germany, but the fines imposed on the Jews after the Von Rath assassination might still cause them problems because they were in possession of an automobile owned by a Jew and therefore subject to confiscation for sale and payment of the 20 percent fine.

Mordecai had an idea. He would use his influence to execute a bill of sale from a Dutch auto dealer, selling the car to Aunt Sylvia. They would register the car in Enschede, and they would cross the border with Dutch license plates. When they crossed the border, they would have to pay an import tax of 5 percent of the sale price, which the bill of sale would list as 2,000 Dutch guilders (1,200 reichsmarks). The import tax would therefore be only 60 reichsmark. It was a genius plan. That is, if it worked. After breakfast, Mordecai set the plan in motion. It was all a matter of accomplishing everything before three, when the twenty-four-hour visa expired.

By two thirty, Mordecai had accomplished everything. He said the fact that Aunt Sylvia and Rachel were Americans sped things up considerably. All the proper documents were given to Aunt Sylvia, along with a convincing cover story that they had come to visit relatives in Holland and were returning to Germany to continue to wait for their passports. Hopefully, the same German customs/immigration official who was on duty upon their entry to Holland would not be on duty upon their exit from Holland into Germany. It was time to go. Aunt Sylvia and Rachel gave Uncle Abraham and Mordecai a kiss on the cheek, and Uncle Abraham recited the *Tefilat Haderech* (Traveler's Prayer) to protect them on their journey. With a final wave, they drove toward the border and uncertainty.

They arrived at the Dutch control point. The same official was on duty as when they entered. He validated their visa and looked a little quizzically at the car as if he wanted to say something about the registration. He just shook his head and wished them a safe trip. Now came the part that they both dreaded—the German side of the border. As they approached the German control point, they both prayed that everything would go smoothly. The German official stepped from the booth and held up his hand to stop them. He approached the driver's side, looked at Aunt Sylvia and Rachel, and demanded their papers. Aunt Sylvia handed him their American identity cards and Dutch visas. He studied the identity cards, looked at Aunt Sylvia, and said, "American?" Aunt Sylvia told him, in German, that they were American. When he asked why they didn't have passports, Aunt Sylvia pointed to the back of the cards where it explained that the cards were a temporary identification for lost/stolen passports. The official read the back of the card, and that seemed to satisfy him.

Next, he asked about the automobile. Why were Americans driving a Dutch-registered automobile into Germany, and was she aware she would have to pay a 5 percent import tax, refundable when she returned the automobile to the Netherlands? Aunt Sylvia told the story that Mordecai had concocted that they had visited her uncle in Holland and had arranged to purchase this car from a friend to use in Germany and return the car to him before they left to return to America. Aunt Sylvia said she understood there would be an import tax and was prepared to pay the tax based upon the sale price. The official looked at her and informed her that the import tax was 100 reichsmarks. Aunt Sylvia knew that the tax should be 60 reichsmarks but knew when a bribe was being demanded. She calmly handed over a 100-reichsmark banknote. After one last look at their documents, he returned them to Aunt Sylvia and said, "Auf wiedersehen und eine gute reisen." (Goodbye and a good trip.) They started to pull away, thinking the worst was over, when the official called out, "Halt!" Aunt Sylvia felt her heart beating in her chest. What could be wrong? The official approached the driver's side window and said, "Ihre quittung." (Your receipt.) It was her receipt for 60 reichsmark, the official import tax. He waved a casual salute and returned to his booth. Aunt Sylvia drove on. It was going to be an even longer drive back to Berlin.

Aunt Sylvia and Rachel arrived at the American Embassy at six on Monday, November 13. They should have arrived earlier in the afternoon, but a flat tire delayed them until a friendly truck driver stopped and changed the tire for them. Arriving at the embassy at this late hour almost guaranteed that Lieutenant Colonel Mitchell would be gone for the day. Aunt Sylvia had made the prearranged phone call yesterday, but it was past the time for today's call. Still, perhaps Lieutenant Colonel Mitchell had waited for her call. She told Rachel that she would go to the gate and ask for Lieutenant Colonel Mitchell. If he were gone for the day, she would leave a message for him and call his private number for the daily signal that all was well. Lieutenant Colonel Mitchell had said that someone would be listening for their signal every day.

While Aunt Sylvia was arranging to leave a message, Rachel waited in the car. A tapping on the window startled Rachel. Standing outside the car was a German police officer. Rachel lowered the window, and the police officer started telling her something, but of course, Rachel didn't speak German. The policeman kept pointing at the car then pointing at a traffic sign. Rachel tried to explain that she didn't understand. Finally, the policeman held out his hand and told Rachel, "Papieren bitte." (Papers please.) Rachel opened her purse to produce her identity card, but in doing so, she displayed the large sum of reichsmarks she was carrying. She handed the American identification card to the policeman but noticed where he was looking. The policeman examined the identification card closely as if it were going to reveal some secret as to how this young girl had come into such a large amount of cash. A thought entered the policeman's head; he believed he had just stumbled upon a prostitute. He ordered Rachel out of the car, placed her in handcuffs, and led her around the corner to a police call box. In a minute or two, a patrol car arrived, and Rachel and the policeman were transported to the nearest police station.

Aunt Sylvia returned to the car to discover Rachel gone. She began to look down the street thinking she might be looking for a *schnellimbiss* (snack stand) to purchase a bratwurst. It had been a long time since they ate last. As she passed a bus stop, an elderly lady asked if she were perhaps looking for the young girl from the car. When Aunt Sylvia replied that she was, the lady told her that the police had taken her away in a patrol car. Aunt Sylvia couldn't believe what she had just heard. *Arrested! For what reason would the police arrest her? Where would they take her?* The lady waiting at the bus stop offered that the nearest police station to Pariser Platz was the one on Friedrich Str. 219. Aunt Sylvia thanked the woman and returned to the embassy.

She explained to the Marine sentry on duty that she absolutely had to speak with Lieutenant Colonel Mitchell as this was a dire emergency. The Marine told her he didn't have the authority to summon Lieutenant Colonel Mitchell, but he would notify the sergeant of the guard of the situation. While Aunt Sylvia was waiting for the sergeant of the guard to be summoned, she stepped out onto the street and noticed a police officer next to her car. She hurried across the street to ask if he had arrested Rachel. He replied that he had indeed taken her into custody and asked what her relationship was to the girl. Aunt Sylvia produced her identity card and informed the policeman that she was Rachel's aunt. The policeman looked briefly at the identity card and more intensely at Aunt Sylvia. She looked much too young to be anybody's aunt, and the policeman saw this as an entirely different relationship. He informed Aunt Sylvia that she was also under arrest and placed her in handcuffs. When Aunt Sylvia asked what she was being charged with, the policeman replied, "For the same offense as your so-called niece." The German Reich frowned on the crime of prostitution.

When the sergeant of the guard arrived at the gate to handle this dire emergency, the sentry on duty said the women was just there five minutes ago, but now she was gone. The sergeant was about to go off shift and said that he would enter the exchange in the briefing book for the next shift.

Chapter 11

As the train passed through towns, villages, and small cities, Klaus couldn't help but notice the smoke and ash in the air from the fires burning in each one of these areas. Apparently, the rioting was far-reaching and widespread. When the train pulled into the main train station in Frankfurt am Main, they noticed a large group of what appeared to be strictly male civilians being herded into freight cars. After the train stopped, he allowed the cadets to disembark for five minutes with instructions not to wander off. Scharführer Winter approached and told Klaus that they would be slightly delayed. The freight cars they saw being loaded with civilians were being moved from the siding to have those cars attached to the rear of their train. When Klaus asked Scharführer Winter about the civilians, Scharführer Winter replied that they were Jews being transported to the Dachau concentration camp. Klaus knew better than to make further inquiries about the added cars or their passengers.

Early the next morning, Klaus was awakened by the shaking and noise of the railcars as they left the main line and entered a siding. He stared as the train entered a garishly lit fenced-in compound with guard towers every twenty meters. The outer fences appeared to be electrified, and there were guards with dogs on the inside. They rolled past what appeared to be a reception station with a combination of SS troops and personnel in prison garb with triangles of varying colors sewn to the left breast of their shirts. Some wore one triangle; some wore two. When the cars came abreast of the reception area, the train came to a stop. SS guards flung the doors open, and prisoners leaned ramps against the openings. An SS officer ordered the civilians inside the freight cars to disembark and form lines before the tables in the reception area. Those that the SS guards didn't feel moved fast enough were helped along with the cudgels that they applied to the backs and legs of those not moving fast enough.

Klaus watched as each civilian in turn was registered and given a prison uniform and a triangle to be sewn onto their uniform jacket. Klaus noticed that all the new prisoners in this bunch were receiving a yellow triangle. Scharführer Winter stood next to Klaus and watched the procedure. Klaus asked him about the triangles. Scharführer Winter said he had a classmate who applied for and was selected for the SS. One evening, after what was probably too much bier and schnapps, his classmate related the meaning of the triangles. Each triangle, at a glance, identified what type of prisoner the SS was dealing with. A red triangle signified a political prisoner, usually a communist. Green identified a professional criminal. Purple was for the Jehovah's Witnesses. Pink was selected for homosexuals. And yellow was, of course, for the Jews. Some were awarded two triangles. A red and a yellow triangle, one imposed over the other, red pointing down and yellow pointing up, sort of like the Star of David, labeled that particular prisoner as a political prisoner and a Jew. There was one category that received extra recognition. These were repeat offenders, and they received what looked like a bull's-eye sewn below their triangles. The SS guards laughingly referred to this as their point of aim when the time came to get rid of them.

Eventually, the crowd of prisoners were processed and moved from the reception area into the interior of the camp. It was then that the prisoners who had set up the ramps returned to the railcars, carrying stretchers. They went aboard the railcars and removed eight bodies. One body they lay on the ground outside the railcar; the other seven were carried off to the left toward an open lot, presumably for burial. The body they placed on the ground was examined by one of the prisoners who called an SS guard over to them. When the SS guard approached, the prisoner who had summoned him removed his cap and, looking at the ground, pointed to the prisoner on the ground and said something to the guard. The SS guard looked down at the prisoner, drew his sidearm, and fired one shot into the prisoner's head. The guard then holstered his pistol, turned on his heel, and walked away. The prisoner detail quickly picked up the body and moved in the direction of the other prisoner details.

After a few moments, the railcars that had held the newest prisoners of the Dachau camp were uncoupled, and the train pulled out of the camp to continue its journey to Bad Tölz. The cadets were unusually silent for the remainder of the train ride. What they had just witnessed was a sobering testament to what life was to be like in the future. The majority of the cadets realized that this was what they were being taught in their almost daily lectures. The lives and liberties of the Jews were basically forfeit. They were a hindrance to the future of the Reich and therefore must be eradicated. Klaus had attended and listened to the same lectures as everyone else. He just had a difficult time accepting that the cold-blooded execution of a defenseless prisoner was going to further the glory and future of the Third Reich. That scene at Dachau would haunt him for some time. Little did he know that he would witness far worse atrocities in the years to come.

The train arrived in Bad Tölz at 1700. A truck and driver from the school awaited them. Scharführer Winter told Klaus to get the cadets on board. If they hurried, they could make it back to the school kaserne in time for the evening meal. It would be good to have a hot meal after two days of train station sandwiches. Klaus agreed but wasn't really enthusiastic about eating at the moment. After the events of the day, he had lost his appetite. When they arrived back at the school kaserne, Scharführer Winter addressed the honor guard detachment. They had all performed exceptionally well during a difficult assignment made more so by the fact the honoree was a personal friend and comrade. They would all receive a commendation in their records. He then dismissed the cadets for the day.

That night, after much tossing and turning, Klaus awoke from a terrible nightmare. In it, he was the SS guard who was called over to a prisoner lying on the ground. But instead of an unknown Jewish civilian, he looked down to see his best friend, Sidney. Sidney looked up at Klaus and said, "See, like we said, till we meet again." Then here was a flash and a boom as Klaus pulled the trigger. Klaus shot straight up in bed, now wide awake; he recognized the pistol shot as thunder and lightning. Klaus was drenched in sweat as the scene replayed in his head. He wished it were one of those dreams that once you awoke, you couldn't remember the details, but this one remained as vivid as any movie he had ever seen. Klaus didn't want to go back to sleep for fear the dream would return, but he must have dozed off sometime during the night while sitting upright in his bed. He awoke in the morning with a horrendous pain in his neck and back and felt like he hadn't slept at all. Luckily, it was Saturday, and the honor guard detachment was released from the training schedule for the weekend. Klaus showered, shaved, donned a clean uniform, and went to the dining hall for breakfast. Skipping dinner last night had left him ravenous. He had an enormous breakfast of *brotchen* (rolls), ham, cheese, soft-boiled eggs, smoked salmon, yogurt, coffee, and finally, a piece of apple strudel.

Finally feeling human again, Klaus went outside to walk off some of this feast. As he was walking past the headquarters building, Scharführer Winter called out to him. Klaus reported to him in the prescribed manner, and Scharführer Winter told him to follow inside. Scharführer Winter reminded him of their conversation at the start of the honor guard mission, that if Klaus had acquitted himself properly, there could be a promotion in store for him. Scharführer Winter said Klaus had done that and more. Therefore, he was proud to promote Klaus to the rank of *standartenoberjunker* (cadet master sergeant), the senior-ranking cadet in the class. This promotion was normally not awarded until the senior year, and only one student received this promotion.

On Monday morning, it was back to classwork. The first order of the day were lectures concerning the pogroms being conducted and the punishment being meted out to the Jews because of the assassination of Ernst von Rath. Personally, Klaus thought that the punishments and fines were excessive. The punishment of an entire race of people for the deeds of one person were extreme. Of course, the lecturers pointed out the entire German population was being punished for the Great War because, according to Hitler and Goebbels, the Jewish bankers had demanded harsh punishment as reparations by the Allied nations. The German people had a right to visit revenge and demand payment from the Jews. There was no reason for the cadets, future German officers, to feel any remorse or doubt the orders received from superiors regarding the Jews. They were considered enemies of the state, and according to Der Führer, they should and would be eradicated from Germany.

The speeches by the lecturers achieved the desired results—they fired up the cadets. As usual, Klaus forced himself to cheer and feign enthusiasm for the subject matter though he felt just the opposite. Anyone who had studied the history of the Great War couldn't help but see that these pogroms were part of the propaganda program orchestrated by Dr. Goebbels to facilitate belief in the writings of Hitler in *Mein Kampf*. From what Klaus had seen during his brief visit to Dachau, it made him believe that Germany was headed down a dark and dangerous path.

*C*hapter 12

The new sergeant of the guard, Sergeant Kincaid, came on duty and was briefed. During the briefing, the outgoing sergeant, Sergeant Wilson, told him of the pretty dark-haired American woman who was demanding to see Lieutenant Colonel Mitchell. Sergeant Kincaid knew who the man was referring to and asked what had happened. Sergeant Wilson told him that by the time he got to the gate, she was gone. An embassy employee who was coming on shift asked them if they were talking about the woman that the police had arrested just as he was approaching the gate. Both sergeants looked at him and, in unison, blurted, "Arrested!" The employee said that he was walking toward the gate when the young woman crossed the street to where a car was parked, and a policeman was walking around it. They appeared to have a short conversation during which the young woman produced what he presumed was her identification. The policeman glanced at the document and then promptly placed the young woman in handcuffs and led her away.

Sergeant Kincaid hurried back into the guard post and dialed Lieutenant Colonel Mitchell's office number. Lieutenant Colonel Mitchell just happened to be working late and answered the phone himself. Sergeant Kincaid reported what had happened and asked for orders. Lieutenant Colonel Mitchell told him to check if the keys were in the car; if they were, he was to bring the car inside the embassy compound. That would at least prevent the car from being towed and adding to Aunt Sylvia's problems. The next problem was locating which police station the women had been taken. Sergeant Kincaid informed Lieutenant Colonel Mitchell that the nearest police station was on Freiderich Str. 219, about three kilometers from the embassy. Lieutenant Colonel Mitchell was going to ask the sergeant how he knew where the nearest police station was but thought better of it.

Calls to the police station were utterly fruitless. He spoke to who he presumed was the German equivalent of the desk sergeant. The man absolutely refused to provide any information. He would neither confirm nor deny that Aunt Sylvia or Rachel was even in custody or if there were any Americans in custody. He wouldn't even verify if they had arrested anybody that day. His only response to any questions was that if they had anyone in custody, they weren't required to provide any information for up to forty-eight hours. This seemed totally absurd, but further argument was just a waste of breath. His only option was to get the embassy legal chief on the case. Lieutenant Colonel Mitchell contacted the embassy's legal affairs officer and described what was going on. After hearing everything that Lieutenant Colonel Mitchell knew, which wasn't much, he promised him that he would speak to the embassy's German lawyer in the morning. It was obvious that the German police were not going to cooperate with the Americans. They would just have to wait until morning. In the morning, the embassy German lawyer contacted Lieutenant Colonel Mitchell and told him he would attempt to pry some information from a new desk sergeant but couldn't make any promises. He would go to the police station in person and see if he could make a difference.

When Aunt Sylvia was brought before the desk sergeant, she saw that Rachel was handcuffed to an iron pole that ran horizontal to the wooden bench she was seated on. The desk sergeant looked down at her then to the arresting policeman and said, "Wass, Krueger, noch eine strassen madchen?" (What, Krueger, another street girl?) The desk sergeant nodded toward the bench where Rachel was sitting and Aunt Sylvia was handcuffed next to her. Rachel asked Aunt Sylvia what was happening. Why had they been arrested? Aunt Sylvia told Rachel that, for some reason, the police thought that they were "street girls"—prostitutes. Rachel was shocked. What would lead them to suspect such a thing?

Aunt Sylvia had Rachel tell her what had happened up to the time of her arrest. When Rachel got to the part where she opened her purse to retrieve her identification, Aunt Sylvia understood everything. She told Rachel that when the policeman saw all that cash in the purse of an attractive young girl, she must be up to no good. Aunt Sylvia told Rachel that they should get an opportunity to make a phone call, and when they did, she would call Lieutenant Colonel Mitchell, and he would straighten out everything.

Aunt Sylvia and Rachel were moved to a holding cell where they remained until almost midnight without anything to eat or drink for almost seven hours. Finally, at two, they were brought into a small courtroom before a magistrate. He heard the charges against them, saw the evidence of over 2,000 reichsmarks in cash, and pronounced them guilty of prostitution and sentenced them to ninety days confinement in the *bezirksgefängnis* (county jail) and fined them 2,000 reichsmarks. Aunt Sylvia was in complete disbelief. She tried to tell the magistrate that they were innocent and asked why they couldn't have a lawyer present. The magistrate left the courtroom without answering her questions. When the policeman approached to lead them away, Aunt Sylvia insisted that they were Americans and were entitled to a phone call to the American Embassy. The policeman told her that the embassy would be notified of their incarceration in due time. Aunt Sylvia translated for Rachel, who broke into tears. They were led out the back door of the police station and loaded into the back of a police transport for the trip to the county jail.

The county jail was across the street from a large Gothic-looking compound on the Wilhelmstrasse. A sign before the compound identified it as *Spandauer Gefängnis* (Spandau Prison). The building that Aunt Sylvia and Rachel were led into was nowhere near as grandiose. It was a simple three-story stone building with bars on all the windows surrounded by brick walls and floodlights. They were led into the portico where they were transferred to female prison guards for in processing. They were fingerprinted, photographed, and their meager belongings inventoried. They were given a bag in which to place their clothes and shoes.

They were ordered to strip and pointed to the showers. After a cold shower, they were issued a prison smock and paper slippers. They were led to a cell with two thin metal bunk beds and a toilet and sink in the back corner. They would be moved out for meals at 7:00 a.m., 12:00 p.m., and 6:00 p.m. daily. They would have one hour out in the courtyard from 1:00 p.m. to 2:00 p.m. Other than that, they would remain in their cells unless they had a visitor. Visitation time came out of their outdoor time. Aunt Sylvia asked when they could make a phone call. The guard told her, "Anytime, anytime you find a phone in your cell." The guard laughed and slammed the door shut. It was now 4:00 a.m., another three hours until breakfast, but they hadn't eaten since lunch the previous day. Rachel and Aunt Silvia sat on the lower bunk and leaned against each other, wondering how they would manage to get through this ordeal.

Breakfast, a generous term for what was presented, consisted of a cup of very weak coffee, a hunk of black bread, and a thin gruel that was supposed to pass as porridge. It was all very bland and totally tasteless. They were seated at twelve-person metal tables that ensured that both inmates and food were thoroughly chilled through in a matter of minutes. The ten other inmates seated at the table eyed Aunt Sylvia and Rachel suspiciously. One inmate nudged Rachel and asked the usual inmate question of what she had done to be here. As Rachel didn't speak German, she couldn't answer. The inmate became insulted that Rachel wouldn't speak to her and wanted to know if Rachel were too good to speak to her. Aunt Sylvia had to intervene and explain to the woman who asked the question that she and Rachel were Americans and that Rachel didn't speak German. As to what they had done to be here, Aunt Sylvia said that they were innocent and were falsely accused of prostitution. This caused a roar of laughter from the entire table. The inmate who started the conversation just shook her head and agreed with Aunt Sylvia, "Of course, you are. We're all innocent."

At 7:30 a.m., they were marched back to their cell. There would be nothing to do until the 12:00 p.m. meal break and the 1:00 p.m.

exercise break. They discussed what the future held for them if they, in fact, had to remain in prison until at least February of 1939. Aunt Sylvia rationalized that before then, their replacement passports would have arrived and the American Embassy would have managed to establish their innocence, thus gaining their freedom and ultimately returning to the United States.

When the midday meal came and went, they were marched outside to the exercise yard. Aunt Sylvia thought for sure that they would be called inside for a visitor, but it was not to be. The inmate who had spoken to them this morning walked up to them and told Aunt Sylvia that if she were awaiting a visitor, she could forget it. The police weren't required to report their being in custody for forty-eight hours, and they usually were very punctual concerning their reporting. They couldn't possibly expect to see anyone until the day after tomorrow at the earliest. This did nothing for Aunt Sylvia's and Rachel's morale. The inmate finally introduced herself as Gisela and gave Aunt Sylvia the ground rules on living in the cellblock. Gisela told them to listen carefully as infractions of the inmate rules could result in a beating, whereas infractions of the prison rules could result in solitary confinement and/or additional prison time.

* * *

The German lawyer for the embassy appeared at Lieutenant Colonel Mitchell's office at 2:00 p.m. on the day Aunt Sylvia and Rachel were transferred to the county jail. He had managed to bribe the new desk sergeant with an offer of free legal advice for information regarding the two Americans who had been brought in yesterday. He told the lawyer that they had been arrested for suspicion of prostitution. There was a new magistrate on duty last night, and he was trying to make a name for himself by single-handedly ridding Berlin of street crime. The lawyer asked what evidence the police presented and was told that each woman had a large sum of cash, which was indicative of a lucrative street trade. Additionally, they did not have the correct identity papers, i.e., no passports. Although they did possess a temporary identity card, the magistrate was convinced that the document might be a forgery. The magistrate considered the evidence presented by the police and prosecutor and pronounced them guilty of prostitution and sentenced them to ninety days in the county jail.

Lieutenant Colonel Mitchell was thunderstruck. He told the lawyer that they had to get them released and asked what was to be their next step to achieve that end. The lawyer said that he would write an appeal to the magistrate and provide character witness letters vouching for their moral character and explaining the reason for the large amount of cash was their plan to visit other countries in Europe. He mentioned to Lieutenant Colonel Mitchell that being able to provide their replacement passports would help in proving their innocence. Lieutenant Colonel Mitchell was not hopeful about providing the passports anytime soon. There was still the longshoreman strike in France, and the mail was just not moving. The embassy in Paris was trying to negotiate with the French government to get mail released but, as yet, no success. In the meantime, he would get the character witness letters written and see if the ambassador would agree to sign one. The ambassador knew of Aunt Sylvia's and Rachel's plight; it was just a matter of if he would vouch for their moral character. The lawyer said he would begin writing his appeal and include the reasoning why the passports had yet to be received. Lieutenant Colonel Mitchell knew that after he had drafted his letters, he would have to break the latest news to Colonel Bergman. In the meantime, he called the ambassador's secretary to request an appointment. Twenty minutes later, the ambassador's secretary called him back and told him if he could be in the ambassador's office in ten minutes, he would give him thirty minutes. Lieutenant Colonel Mitchell told her he was on his way.

Ambassador Wilson's secretary ushered Lieutenant Colonel Mitchell into the ambassador's office and offered him coffee, which he politely refused; he didn't want to take up much of the ambassador's time. The ambassador entered his office through another door and waved at Lieutenant Colonel Mitchell to keep his seat. He sat behind his desk and looked at Lieutenant Colonel Mitchell, who began to tell the whole story of the arrest of two American citizens and the difficulties he was having with the German authorities. Ambassador Wilson listened intently until Lieutenant Colonel Mitchell had finished giving him all the details. Ambassador Wilson held up a communiqué and told Lieutenant Colonel Mitchell that there was absolutely nothing that he could do for him as he had just been recalled to the United States by order of the president. The recall order was in protest to the treatment of the Jews during and after Kristallnacht. The embassy's work would be taken over by the interim chargé d'affaires until the newly appointed chargé d'affaires, Alexander Kirk, arrived, which wouldn't be until May.

This sounded to Lieutenant Colonel Mitchell like no help would be forthcoming until May 1939, if any. By that time, Aunt Sylvia's and Rachel's jail sentences would be over, and they should be released. His only recourse was to continue to pursue action through the German legal system, which was not looking very helpful. With the recall of the US ambassador in protest, the Germans were not going to be very agreeable to granting any favors for American citizens in their jails.

Two days later, the embassy's German lawyer came to Lieutenant Colonel Mitchell with official notification of the arrests of Fraulein Sylvia Silberman and Fraulein Rachel Silberman for the charge of prostitution. It detailed the jail sentence and the fines that were imposed, where they were being incarcerated, and how and when visitation could be arranged. At first, Lieutenant Colonel Mitchell was going to visit them, but Herr Waldheim thought that as their and the embassy's legal representative, he should visit first to inform them of the appeals process and their legal rights. Lieutenant Colonel Mitchell had to agree with that logic. He wanted to know when Herr Waldheim intended to visit them. He said that he would try to arrange visitation today. He would have to call the prison to request visitation, and the prison would tell him when and where to report. Herr Waldheim would set the wheels in motion and report back to Lieutenant Colonel Mitchell on his progress. Herr Waldheim asked Lieutenant Colonel Mitchell about the character witness letters. The ambassador had signed his letter but was not sure that they would want to submit his letter after being recalled in protest. Herr

Waldheim was unaware of that development and agreed the ambassador's letter might not carry as much weight after his departure. Herr Waldheim said that when he met with the women, he would ask if they could provide any local citizens that might be willing to vouch for them.

Herr Waldheim called Lieutenant Colonel Mitchell's office and told him he had arranged for an appointment for 1:00 p.m. and would let him know what the outcome of their visit was.

* * *

After lunch—this consisted of weak coffee, a hunk of black bread, and some sort of watery potato soup—Aunt Sylvia and Rachel were headed for the courtyard when the female guard on duty directed them to another gate. A second guard informed them they had a visitor and reminded them of the rules; there was to be no physical contact, no exchange of personal items unless inspected first by the guard, and no use of a foreign language between visitors and prisoners. Aunt Sylvia asked if she could translate for Rachel, who didn't speak German. The guard said as long as Rachel did not speak directly to the visitor, Aunt Sylvia could translate. They signed a statement saying that they understood the rules and the punishment for violating the rules. Punishment would be no visitation for thirty days and fifteen days of solitary confinement. They were then escorted into the visitation area. Aunt Sylvia had hoped it would be Lieutenant Colonel Mitchell waiting for them, but it was the embassy lawyer. She had to think a moment before she remembered his name, Herr Waldheim.

They joined Herr Waldheim at the table, and he began by asking about their condition and treatment. He then explained what was going on with their case, what efforts were being taken to gain their release, and if there were any Germans who would write them a character reference. The only person they could think of who wasn't a Jew would be Herr Rheinhaus, Uncle Abraham's business colleague. Herr Waldheim took down all the information for Herr Rheinhaus and then asked the women if they had any questions. Rachel whispered in Aunt Sylvia's ear. Aunt Sylvia turned to Herr Waldheim and asked if he thought that they would get out of jail before February. Herr Waldheim thought for a moment then told them, "Honestly, the way the relations are between Germany and the United States, I wouldn't place much hope on the possibility. On the other hand, the justice system sometimes grants early releases at Christmastime. That is always a possibility." He left the women sitting at the table awaiting escort back inside as he headed to locate Herr Rheinhaus.

Herr Waldheim's interview with Herr Rheinhaus was quite informative. He had located Herr Rheinhaus at his jewelry store and introduced himself as an attorney for the American Embassy. He asked Herr Rheinhaus if he recalled Aunt Sylvia and Rachel. He said he remembered them quite well, and then Herr Waldheim explained the reason for his questions was, they had been arrested for prostitution. Herr Rheinhaus said it was preposterous. He had observed the women for several months as they had cared for the uncle who had been injured in an unfortunate incident. They hadn't displayed any of the conduct one would associate with a person involved in such an enterprise. Herr Waldheim smiled and asked if Herr Rheinhaus would sign a letter attesting to their good character. Herr Rheinhaus just looked at Herr Waldheim in shock and told him of course he wouldn't sign such a letter. Herr Waldheim, totally confused, asked him why he wouldn't. Herr Rheinhaus said, "Didn't you know? They're Jews."

Herr Waldheim burst into Lieutenant Colonel Mitchell's office past his protesting secretary and stared at him and asked him when he was going to inform him that he was trying to defend two Jews in a Nazi court. Lieutenant Colonel Mitchell wanted to know what difference it made. Herr Waldheim said that if they went to court and it came out that Aunt Sylvia and Rachel were Jews, they would be immediately transferred to a concentration camp as professional criminals. They could be held there indefinitely, with no visitation. Their claim to being American citizens would mean absolutely nothing. As far as the American government was concerned, they would have no contact with them. It would be as if they disappeared from the face of the earth. Lieutenant Colonel Mitchell asked what they should do for them. Herr Waldheim looked at him and told him the best thing to do would be to keep a low profile, and hopefully, they could serve out their sentence without drawing any attention to themselves. Herr Waldheim said that he would visit the women tomorrow and explain the situation. If they insisted that he try to get the charges dropped or reduced, he would do his best to achieve that without having to call on anyone who knew that they were Jews. Lieutenant Colonel Mitchell told him to let him know if there was anything he could do to help.

The next afternoon, Herr Waldheim entered Lieutenant Colonel Mitchell's office to report on what the two women had decided as far as their charges were concerned. Lieutenant Colonel Mitchell waved him to a seat, but Herr Waldheim chose to remain standing. Herr Waldheim looked at him and told him that during the night, Aunt Sylvia and Rachel were removed from the county jail and transferred to one of the concentration camps. What he had feared had come true. Someone had reported them to the county magistrate as Jews and that they had aided a Herr Abraham Silberman leave the country with a large amount of cash and jewelry that had not had the required tax and fines paid. Additionally, they had in their possession an automobile that had not had the 20 percent retribution tax paid on it. Herr Waldheim wasn't told where they were taken. They had just disappeared into the black hole that was the concentration camp system.

$\mathcal{C}$hapter 13

Colonel Klein slowly hung up his phone. It had been a long and troubling call from Lieutenant Colonel Mitchell. He could not wrap his mind around the fact that Aunt Sylvia and Rachel first had been arrested for prostitution of all things and now had disappeared into the concentration camps. It was all some horrible nightmare. He had asked George if their parents had been notified, and he said that a telegram would be sent. Unfortunately, it was nothing like the military's casualty notification system where an officer and a chaplain would visit the family and notify them personally what had happened to their loved one. Colonel Klein decided that he would undertake that task. Sidney could accompany him if he were up to it after he was informed. Speaking of Sidney, he decided that he would leave work in time to meet him as soon as he got home from school.

* * *

Sidney was at the ham club, as was his habit for the last few months. He was monitoring a couple of his favorite frequencies when he heard his call sign. He answered the call, and the distant station sent, "QSY Alt." (Change to alternate frequency.) Sidney knew that it had to be Z. He hadn't heard from him in almost two weeks and was anxious to hear what Z had to say. Sidney changed to their alternate frequency and tapped NN2Z-DE. Z answered almost immediately. Things had been quite interesting since their last conversation.

Z gave him the frequency of a BBC (British Broadcasting Company) radio station that provided fairly accurate and up-to-date news from inside Germany. He had to limit his transmissions after his reconnaissance mission for Sidney. Somehow, it had stirred up the interest of one of the intelligence services. He had noticed vehicles equipped with RDF (radio direction finding) equipment slowly patrolling his neighborhood. When he heard the conversation between Sidney and someone using his call sign, he knew he had to lay low for a while before they got a location on his transmitter. He told Sidney that he tried to keep an eye out for Rachel, but things had really changed. In the neighborhood where Rachel had been staying, all the Jews were gone. No one knew where, but there were some rumors of concentration camps, and others said they had all moved away after Kristallnacht. Sidney thanked Z for the information, and they both signed off.

Sidney arrived home and was surprised to see his father home. He normally didn't arrive home until six. Sidney said hello to his father and started up the stairs to his room and homework. His father called him into the kitchen and asked him to sit down. Sidney could see on his face that he was troubled by something. His father told Sidney of the news he had received from Lieutenant Colonel Mitchell. Sidney was completely numb. His father was saying something, but he didn't hear a word. What he had said just couldn't be possible, not to his Rachel. He had to do something to get her back to America. He just couldn't imagine her in a prison camp. He had no idea what a concentration camp was like, but the stories he had heard on ham radio didn't sound good. It was then that he realized that his father was still talking to him. His father had just asked him if he had heard a word that he had said. Sidney shook his head as if to clear the cobwebs from his mind and apologized to his father, but his news had so shocked him that he hadn't heard what he was saying. He told Sidney that he understood how he felt; the news had shocked him too.

He explained to Sidney that the embassy in Germany would send a telegram notifying the relatives of Aunt Sylvia's and Rachel's arrest; it would provide nothing else. He told Sidney that he felt they should notify them before the telegrams arrived if Sidney felt up to facing them. Sidney agreed with his father and would accompany him on this very unpleasant mission. They went first to Aunt Sylvia's house. There was the anticipated tears and rage directed at the Nazis. Then they remembered that they had talked Rachel's parents into allowing Rachel to accompany Sylvia to Germany. They felt immense guilt and believed that Rachel's parents would probably curse them with their last breath. They had a thousand questions, the majority of which Jacob couldn't answer because there were no answers. They spent an hour with Aunt Sylvia's parents before moving on to what promised to be the most difficult part of this mission—notifying Rachel's parents.

Rachel's father sat dumbstruck. The news had hit him as if he had been poleaxed. At first, Sidney thought that Mr. Silberman would fall over. Mrs. Silberman was near hysterical, crying and pulling her hair. About the time that she started blaming Aunt Sylvia and her parents for the loss of her daughter, Mr. Silberman seemed to regain his composure. He grabbed his wife and sat her in the chair that he had been sitting in and said to her, "Mama, you speak as if our Rachel is dead! She is not dead!" His wife wailed that she might as well be dead if she was in one of those Nazi hellholes.

Mr. Silberman went back to asking Jacob more pertinent questions. Was there any way possible to contact their daughter? Could the American Embassy be of any help? Would it do any good to go to Germany? Jacob told them that the American Embassy would continue to try and establish contact with Rachel and Aunt Sylvia, but the current political climate between the two countries were very strained at the moment. He told them that the American and German ambassadors had been recalled. There was the possibility that word could be forwarded through the Red Cross in Switzerland. As far as going to Germany, that would be utter insanity. He could possibly find Rachel by being in the same camp as her. Jacob told Mr. Silberman that they would soon be receiving a telegram from the American Embassy. He just didn't want them to get such catastrophic news in the form of a telegram. Mr. Silberman thanked Jacob and wished him a good night.

On the way home, Sidney asked his father if this was what it was like to bring such news to the family of a soldier killed in the line of duty. His father told him that this was more difficult because you knew them personally and likely felt their pain a lot closer.

Sidney could not sleep that night. He wondered if there was anything he could have done to convince Rachel not to have gone to Europe. No, there was nothing he could have said or done to stop her. She was too strong-willed and determined to go to Europe. He wondered if Rachel ever got to sing in a Berlin nightclub like she had dreamed about. He hoped that she had. If not, everything would have been such a wasted effort for nothing. From what Sidney had been able to learn about German concentration camps, he sincerely feared for Rachel's health and safety. He had learned that the camps were not just a prison. They were labor camps that engaged in brutal manual labor. He was told to imagine the old movies of inmates breaking rocks and multiply that by ten. It weighed heavily upon his heart to think that his delicate Rachel might be forced to do such backbreaking labor. He doubted that Rachel could survive such rigorous work for very long.

Sidney tried to focus on his studies. Midterm exams would be starting soon, and he knew that if he wanted to keep his grades up to the standards required for admission to West Point, he would have to crack the books. That meant more study time and less radio time. With the possibility of contacting Rachel gone, Sidney lost the desire to converse with European operators. He would limit his radio time to Saturday mornings and then only if he could contact his friend Z. Their chats were fewer, but more informative than idle chatter. Z tried to send Sidney any snippets of hard news that he could. His recommendation that he monitor BBC was a fountain of news from Europe and from Germany. Sidney wondered how they managed to get the information, which was definitely not complimentary to Nazi Germany, out without being stopped by German intelligence. Sidney asked Z one time, and his response was not to inquire into the BBC's sources. Many of them had been compromised and paid a heavy price, usually imprisonment at the Sachsenhausen concentration camp.

Midterm exams began in December and didn't seem as difficult as Sidney had anticipated, probably because of all the extra time he had spent studying. His hard work had paid off as he was ranked number 1 in his class when the grades were posted the twenty-first of December before the school Christmas vacation commenced. Sidney's parents were, of course, proud of his accomplishment and had planned a surprise dinner party in celebration. A dinner party was not exactly what Sidney had in mind for a reward, but he would show his appreciation. What Sidney really had in mind was a car. He had been hinting about a car since he had earned his driver's license this past summer, but apparently, no one was listening. He figured he would have to use the money that Uncle Saul had paid him for his work at the deli last summer and try to get some odd jobs on the weekends—mowing grass and shoveling snow—to come up with the money to buy a cheap secondhand car.

Guests started arriving around six, with the first one being his classmate from French and Morse code, Paul. People from his father's office and friends of the family all arrived by six thirty. There was a cocktail hour for the adults where congratulations were wished and small talk was engaged in. The vast majority of the guests were military officers, so naturally, conversations gravitated that way. Sidney did notice that the talk steered away from any mention of events in Germany.

After dinner, Sidney's father asked him to go out to the garage and bring in another bottle of wine. Sidney turned on the garage light to find a red 1934 Ford Coupe parked where his father's car normally stood. As he stood there staring at the car, the garage roll-up door opened, and all the guests, led by his parents, yelled, "Surprise!" This was exactly what Sidney had been wishing for as a reward for his hard work.

Sidney's father presented him with the keys and said, "Congratulations."

His mother said, "Drive safe."

Paul said, "No more waiting for the bus."

Sidney thought, *I'd love to take Rachel for a drive.*

Although not Christian, they tended to celebrate the Christmas holidays, in a fashion. They didn't decorate a tree but did wish people a "Merry Christmas" and would attend and host Christmas parties, as was the traditions of the military service. Sidney's father impressed upon him the importance of such traditions along with unit "dining in" and "dining out" ceremonies. A *dining in* is a formal ceremony in which military members-only attend. This is a time to develop professional relationships and nurture bonds to further one's career. The *dining out* is less formal and includes wives or girlfriends and is intended to be a unit get-together in a more social setting.

Tonight, Sidney's father was attending a dining in for the Command and General Staff College student body and cadre. This promised to be an interesting gathering as there were twelve foreign military students in the class this year. There would be five British, four French, two Dutch, and one Norwegian officers. Undoubtedly, European politics would be a hot topic for conversation. He was not proven wrong. It was not long after the opening of "the punch bowl" that political opinions began to fly. The British officers complained that the politicians couldn't see that the more they submitted to Hitler, the more that he would demand and take. The French were not in favor of antagonizing Hitler by refusing him what legally belonged to Germany and was taken from them after the Great War. Jacob thought that the French could afford to feel that way because they felt secure behind their Maginot Line. The Dutch were concerned because if Hitler decided he wanted the Netherlands, they did not have the military strength to stop them.

The lone Norwegian voiced the opinion that he was told that the German Army was limited to one hundred thousand men and had no armor or airplanes. How were they going to accomplish all of Hitler's threats and demands? All the foreign students along with a goodly portion of the American students and cadre broke out in laughter. The Norwegian student had obviously been so misinformed regarding Nazi Germany's actual military strength to be laughable. He was soon set straight regarding ground troops, armored units, aircraft, and their supposed nonexistent navy. The Norwegian student could hardly believe that his military was so misinformed. He felt embarrassed for Norway's military. Jacob steered the conversation on to other subjects to take the spotlight off the unfortunate officer. The night ended with the usual telling of bawdy tales and war stories as such gatherings seemed to do.

On Monday morning, the last duty day before the Christmas holiday, Jacob received another call from Lieutenant Colonel Mitchell. The news was not promising. The embassy had not been able to get any further information from the German government. Herr Waldheim had spoken with the magistrate who had sentenced Aunt Sylvia and Rachel to the concentration camp. He presented his case for appeal, which the magistrate simply threw back in his face. He told Herr Waldheim that the two criminals he referred to in his appeal case had no legal right for appeal under German law. When Herr Waldheim asked why they couldn't appeal when they were American citizens, the magistrate told him that regardless of their citizenship, they were Jews and therefore had no rights under German law. Herr Waldheim tried to argue that the law only pertained to German citizens. The magistrate reminded him that Jews were not citizens but subjects of the Reich and not afforded the same rights and privileges as German citizens and told him if he continued to belabor the point, he would find Herr Waldheim in contempt of court and have him arrested. Herr Waldheim wisely conceded the point and left to report to Lieutenant Colonel Mitchell. Colonel Klein thanked Lieutenant Colonel Mitchell for the update and for all the time and resources that the embassy had dedicated to this case.

Chapter 14

Klaus had drawn the short straw and was on the duty roster over Christmas holiday. The corps of cadets had to maintain a presence at the school to oversee those cadets who had earned enough demerits or low grades that they were denied leave over Christmas and New Year's. Klaus had drawn duty for Christmas, and as he didn't care too much about New Year's, he volunteered to take another cadet's duty assignment, which allowed that cadet the unusual opportunity to go home for Christmas and New Year's.

It was Christmas Eve, and Klaus had just reported to the cadre headquarters building to begin his watch as cadet duty officer. Scharführer Winter was just leaving to begin his Christmas leave and noticed Klaus receiving his briefing from the cadre duty officer. Scharführer Winter nodded to Klaus and said, "Frohe Weinachten und eine Frohes neues Jahr, Standartenoberjunker Bergman." (Merry Christmas and a Happy New Year, Cadet Master Sergeant Bergman.)

Klaus nodded back and replied, "Danke, Ebenfals." (Thank you and the same to you, Scharführer Winter.)

Klaus's duties consisted of an hourly patrol of the entire barracks area, armory, and the motor park. The last stop was the dining facility where the mess personnel were already starting preparations for the Christmas meal. The smell of baking breads and cakes was mouthwatering, and the mess staff always had a soft spot for the poor devils who caught the duty over the holidays. There was always hot coffee and a *Christstollen* (a classic German Christmas cake) laid out for duty personnel, which was a welcome treat when you were far from home over the holidays.

Klaus grabbed a cup of coffee and a piece of cake and chatted with the mess sergeant about the upcoming meal and what was on the menu. It was the typical holiday meal most Germans ate this time of year. There would be a green salad, bone marrow soup, goose stuffed with chestnuts, boiled potatoes, red cabbage, and finally, coffee and cakes for dessert. Klaus complimented the mess sergeant on the Christstollen and continued back to the headquarters building to make his hourly duty log entry, "All secure. Nothing to report."

During Klaus's 0200 area check, the snow started to fall. He made his rounds through the barracks to ensure that the cadets posted to fire watch duties were awake and performing their duties. Next, he checked on the armory then the motor park. By the time he was headed for the dining facility, the snow was deep enough to leave footprints where he had walked. By dawn, he knew that he would have to organize snow removal crews to clear sidewalks.

Klaus went to each barracks and greeted the sleeping cadets who had not gone home with a cheery "Merry Christmas! Now get outside for snow detail!" Klaus was not greeted with the same spirit of the season by those cadets who were still warm and snug in their bunks. Klaus returned to the headquarters building to make his log entries to the effect that snow removal duties had been assigned and the cadre duty NCO had been awakened and briefed. One of the drawbacks of having the duty over weekends and holidays was the twenty-four-hour shift. His watch ran from 1800 Christmas Eve to 1800 Christmas Day. Klaus and the cadre duty officer would rotate twelve hours on and twelve hours off. Although Klaus's watch would be over at 0600, he had to remain at the headquarters building until 1800 in case the cadre duty officer were to be called away for some emergency. There was a cadre private available to answer the telephone, so either duty officer could sleep when off watch. Still, it was a long day.

Klaus went for a light breakfast of coffee, brotchen, and jam in anticipation of the Christmas meal, which would begin serving at 1400. Klaus walked through the snow to the dining facility for his breakfast. The snow was falling heavier and promised to be a real Bavarian blizzard. The snow removal details were shoveling almost constantly now, and Klaus thought they would have to arrange for additional cadets to avoid keeping the details out too long at a time, risking frostbite or exposure. After breakfast, he assigned those details and reported same to the cadre duty officer before heading to his bunk for some sleep.

Klaus awoke at 1330 and noticed everything was a muffled quiet, except for the sound of the wind whistling outside. He looked outside his window to see mounds of snow. During the time that he had slept, it had snowed over a meter and the winds had pushed snowbanks up to the windows. Klaus quickly shaved and dressed and went outside to observe what was happening. Apparently, every hand had been called into action to handle the snow emergency. The walkways between buildings looked more like canyons with snow piled almost two meters high. While walking on the walkways was bearable, anytime one was exposed to the wind and snow was what it must feel like to be in the Arctic. The wind and snow cut through the thickest winter coats like a knife, and the cold stole your breath away while freezing your nostrils closed. The cadre duty officer had notified the academy commandant of the situation, and he ordered that all snow removal details be limited to no more than thirty-minute shifts outside. The dining facility was of course open continuously with large urns of coffee and hot chocolate.

Well, Klaus thought, *at least the cadets wouldn't suffer from boredom.* Klaus entered the dining facility and encountered snow removal crews in for a warm-up break. He overheard one of the cadets say that he hoped that they would never have to fight in weather such as this. The other cadets agreed wholeheartedly. This had to be the worst weather ever to fight in. The storm finally dissipated after two days. Klaus had two days off before he had another duty watch on the twenty-eighth of December and then two more days off before the shift from December 31 to January 1.

The New Year's Eve duty officer detail was very quiet. There was a new group of cadets at the academy; those who had been off over Christmas were now to celebrate New Year's at the academy.

Although the cadets were not restricted to the kaserne, it was still a couple of days until payday, and they had just returned from leave at home. Long story short, money was tight, so most cadets remained on the kaserne where they could have cheap beer at the cadet's canteen. The canteen was run by a retired *hauptfeldwebel* (sergeant major), who kept a close eye on his boys to ensure they didn't do anything that would get them placed on report and get hit with demerits. He would also let the cadets run a bar tab when it got close to the end of the month, like tonight. At midnight came the usual cheers of "Prost Neu Jahre!" (Toast New Year!) And 1939 officially began. Around 0100, they had the usual spate of a few loud and off-key singers making their way back to their barracks, but otherwise, all was quiet.

With the beginning of March, spring was on the horizon, and the temperatures were becoming quite pleasant. The cadre, having determined that the long winter months had prevented the cadets from engaging in sufficient outdoor physical activities, scheduled a series of road marches of ever-increasing distance, over more difficult terrain, and with heavier loads of equipment. The first few marches were torture. It was hard to believe that they had gotten so out of shape. By the second week, things were starting to improve. The third-year cadets were preparing for the spring field exercises, once again at Grafenwöhr, when suddenly the exercises were canceled. The entire cadet motor park was being requisitioned for another mission until further notice. The cadets were at first disappointed. They were looking forward to getting out of the classroom and their kaserne. That is, until an upperclassman told them what Grafenwöhr was like in the springtime.

"If you happened to be on the first rotation of the spring, things aren't too bad. After the first week of training, the tanks and half-tracks ground everything into a quagmire. Everything is a thick, sticky mud that clings to everything. Your boots weigh twenty pounds each, and you just never get enough time during the day to scrape the mud off. At the end of the training day, you will spend two to three hours cleaning the mud off your half-tracks. Cadets can easily spend that much time cleaning individual and crew-served weapons. Naturally, no one gets to eat until everything is inspected and found to be clean enough for the cadre's inspection. This means that the evening meal is late and usually cold."

After hearing these horror stories from the upperclassman, the cadets considered themselves fortunate to be just heading for another hike through the Bavarian forests tomorrow.

After the evening meal, the cadets were in the barracks preparing their equipment for the road march when the cadet who was assigned the daily duty as messenger at the headquarters building entered the barracks and announced that he knew where all their trucks had gone. Everyone looked at him expectantly until Klaus said, "And where have our trucks gone?"

The cadet smirked and said, "Czechoslovakia. Germany has invaded Czechoslovakia."

Adolf Hitler had already annexed the Sudetenland in September 1938 with the Munich Agreement signed by England and France and granted the Sudetenland to Germany. At the time, Hitler had told British Prime Minister Chamberlain that this was the end of his plans of expansion, and the British and French leaders believed him. Prime Minister Chamberlain had returned to London waving the Munich Agreement and declaring the document would ensure "peace in our time." Now six months later, Germany had invaded and occupied the remainder of Czechoslovakia.

Some cadets wondered if they would graduate early and be sent to combat units in support of the Czech invasion. Klaus quickly put an end to that thought before it became a believable rumor. The conflict in the Czech Republic would be over very soon, long before they could possibly be ready for combat. They should dedicate more thought to their studies and training; they could worry about combat when they were fully trained.

World events were developing rapidly. March 31 brought about the statement issued by England that they would guarantee the independence of Poland. Adolf Hitler was demanding that the Free City of Danzig be returned to the German Reich as it was part of Germany until the end of the Great War when the Treaty of Versailles declared Danzig an independent city-state. The majority of the population was German, and favored annexation by Germany, the Reichsautobahn was prepared to build a highway between the German border and Danzig, but Poland was not in agreement. The Polish Corridor had long been disputed territory and was not going to give Germany a foot inside their borders. England and France were contemplating making Germany an offer of the Polish Corridor in hopes of ensuring peace in the region, but Poland would not negotiate the point.

On the first of May, the cadet vehicles returned to the kaserne from service in Czechoslovakia. The first-year cadets were given the task of getting the trucks ready for inspection under the supervision of Klaus's third-year cadets. Klaus could not believe what he saw. Prior to being requisitioned, they were in perfect condition. The trucks were freshly painted, all the woodwork in pristine condition, a complete compliment of tools and jack. The water and fuel cans had the top portion of the canisters properly painted, red for fuel and blue for water, plus a complete squad-level first aid kit. The trucks now looked like they should be moved to the scrapyard. The trucks were all scraped and dented. They were absolutely filthy, covered in dirt, grease, and oil. Most of the trucks had their spare tires missing, along with their tools and jack. The fuel and water cans were gone. Every single first aid kit had been stolen; they were a very valuable commodity in an infantry unit. Klaus's inspectors came back to him with quite an extensive list of materials they would require to restore their vehicles to their previous condition. Klaus instructed his cadets to have the trucks at least washed and the interiors cleaned before running the trucks by the mechanics for servicing and assessment for further repairs. Klaus would take his inspection sheets to Scharführer Winter for his information. He was quite sure that Scharführer Winter would not be pleased with the condition of their trucks.

As is the case in all armies, every unit has a resupply priority assigned to determine where they are in the pecking order. Units that are engaged in combat or in a high readiness state are higher up the supply chain and have priority when it comes to replacing equipment or receiving necessary supplies. And so it goes down the line. It therefore stands to reason that a school unit that trains officer cadets is pretty far down the priority list. As a result of this priority assignment, the Fahnenjunkerschule did not have their trucks back to 100 percent capability until the fifteenth of July. The cadets, after many kilometers of marching and several bivouac exercises, finally went to another motor park that was near the school's railroad siding and began training on loading their Sd. Kfz. 7 half-tracks onto railcars. This was an exercise not without danger. The Sd. Kfz. 7 had a huge hood, which made locating the front wheels on the railway car almost impossible. Without a ground guide, it was almost guaranteed that a driver would run a front wheel off the railcar, which would cause the eight-ton monster to flip over, almost surely killing the driver. Before the block of instruction began, there was a one-hour safety briefing stressing observance of hand signals by the ground guide. Everyone was trained on proper positioning of the vehicle relative to the railcar and, the most important, and deadly, segment of the exercise, transitioning between railcars.

At this segment, the eight-ton half-track was crossing from one railcar to the next by traversing two ramps. Safety personnel had to ensure that the ramps had not shifted as the half-track moved down the railcar and the driver was lined up correctly on the ramps before committing to crossing over. The first loading required an hour to cross over three railcars. The training sergeant told the cadets that they had managed to accomplish the task safely. The only problem was, they needed to load one half-track every twenty minutes, which meant they had to load all four of the half-tracks in their platoon in eighty minutes. They had a lot of work to do. The cadets practiced this exercise daily for the entire week. For the remainder of the school year, they practiced convoy tactics and classroom work. They had missed out on their Grafenwöhr rotation because of the Czech invasion but knew that somehow it would be rescheduled into the next year's class schedule.

The fifteenth of August brought the usual hustle and bustle of preparing for their summer break. Equipment was placed into storage, and weapons were returned to the armory. The cadets would return on Friday, September 1, to reclaim their weapons and equipment and start the new school year on Monday, September 4.

While on their two-week vacation, the world would change dramatically. On August 23, Germany and the Soviet Union would sign the Molotov-Ribbentrop Pact, a nonaggression agreement, which contained a secret provision for dividing Poland between the two nations. On August 25, Great Britain signed the Polish-British Common Defense Pact as an annex to the Franco-Polish alliance (1921), pledging defense of Poland. On August 29, the Polish High Command ordered a full mobilization of its forces, only to be talked into standing down by England and France, hoping still for diplomatic solutions. On August 30, the Polish Navy sent its entire destroyer flotilla to Britain. On the night of August 31, SS troops in Polish uniforms attacked the Gleiwitz radio station on the German-Polish border. They used executed concentration camp inmates as "casualties" to help make the ruse more convincing. At four forty-five on September 1, *Fall Weiss* (Operation White) commenced, signaling the invasion of Poland.

The cadets arrived back at the kaserne on September 1, unaware of what was going on at the German-Polish border. They reclaimed their stored equipment and weapons to prepare them for the start of training on Monday. At evening meal, the school commandant announced that German forces had invaded Poland in response to an unprovoked attack by Polish Armed Forces on a German radio station in Gleiwitz. German forces under General Gerd von Rundstedt were making great advances toward the cities of Danzig and Warsaw. The cadets joined in a huge round of applause and cheers for the German Armed Forces. On Monday, September 4, England and France declared war on Germany. The Second World War had begun.

Chapter 15

Aunt Sylvia and Rachel were transferred from the county jail to a holding facility near the main train station. They were not told where they were going or how long they would be held here. All they knew for sure was it was late November and getting colder without any real cold-weather clothing. Although they didn't know what time it was, they could tell that it was quite some time since they had eaten last. When the door to the outer room opened, Aunt Sylvia spied a clock across the room. The time was 5:20 a.m. The door hadn't opened to bring them breakfast; it opened to admit four more female prisoners. This happened periodically until about eight, when the cell population reached ten prisoners. Finally, at around eight thirty, four of the prisoners were called out of the cell to bring a basket with hunks of black bread and a tray with cups of coffee. The guard told them they had twenty minutes to eat and be ready to board the train. If they thought they were going to ride in coach cars like real people, they were sadly mistaken. They were loaded onto freight cars like so many cattle. There was nowhere to sit except the floor, and the interior of the freight car was ice-cold. The car door was slammed shut and bolted from outside. There was the sound of a whistle then a sudden jerk as the train started to move. The only light in the railcar was two steel-barred openings on each side of the railcar. It didn't provide much light, but as the train started to pick up speed, they found that an icy wind entered through the openings. The openings worked very well for ventilation as there was nowhere inside the railcar to escape the wind. It was a miserably cold four hours until the train's next stop at Nuremburg.

At Nuremburg, the door slid open, and another twenty women were loaded onto the railcar. And so it continued, through stops at Würzburg, Frankfurt, Kassel, and Hannover, finally pulling into a train siding. The sign over the buildings facing the railcars read Ravensbrück. The railcar door was flung open, and makeshift stairs leaned against the railcar. The railcar was so overpacked with women that as soon as the door was opened, the first two rows of women standing at the door were literally ejected from the railcar. Several were injured, suffering broken arms and legs. The female SS guards showed them no compassion and applied their cudgels to their backs, arms, and legs, forcing them to move toward the induction building. Here, their personal information was entered into camp records. A camp identification number was assigned, and they were photographed. Next, they were ordered to strip naked. Their personal belongings were taken, inventoried, and disinfected prior to being placed in storage until such time as they were to be released. The women were marched naked to the showers where all body hair was shaved off before they were sprayed with disinfectant and sent to shower.

The actual purpose of these procedures was not for cleanliness and to prevent the spread of disease. The entire exercise was to humiliate and degrade the women so that they would begin to believe that they were worthless as a human being. They no longer had a modicum of privacy and personal dignity. After showering, the women were issued uniforms, usually ill-fitting, consisting of a smock, blouse, socks, and a pair of wood and canvas shoes. They had their camp ID number stamped onto their smocks and were issued their identification triangles. Aunt Sylvia and Rachel each received two triangles, a yellow triangle signifying that they were Jews and a black triangle signifying that they were classified "asocial" (prostitutes). This combination of triangles earned them some very disdainful looks from the other inmates.

Aunt Sylvia was becoming very concerned about Rachel. She had developed a vacant stare and had hardly spoken a word in the last two weeks. She simply followed Aunt Sylvia around and followed what she did. Aunt Silvia had already had to intervene when an SS guard had started to beat Rachel when she did not answer the guard when asked a question. Aunt Sylvia explained to the guard that Rachel did not speak German, only English or French. The guard's response was to beat Aunt Sylvia and tell her she had better teach Rachel German, and in a hurry, or she would not survive in Ravensbrück very long.

At 1800, the inmates were called to evening head count. They were stood at attention for more than an hour as all inmates were either physically counted or otherwise accounted for. This first head count took longer than usual because the number of inmates at the evening count was different than the morning count. The reason was that over two hundred inmates were added to the camp population with the arrival of today's trainload of new inmates. Once all the numbers were correct, the inmates were released for evening meal. Aunt Sylvia was surprised at the rations served. They received a meal of a very hearty soup, sausages, bread, margarine, and coffee. These rations were so much better than those of the county jail that Aunt Sylvia was at first a little suspicious. After watching the other inmates eat with relish, she figured it was all right to follow suit. Aunt Sylvia had to push Rachel to eat. She just picked at her food and told Aunt Sylvia that she wasn't hungry. Aunt Sylvia noticed that other inmates near them were eyeing Rachel's tray of food. It wouldn't be long before they snatched the food from her tray and devoured it themselves.

A small voice spoke to Rachel from across the table in French. For the first time in weeks, a light came into Rachel's eyes. Rachel entered into a conversation with the young girl across from her, which became more and more animated, and as the conversation progressed, the food on Rachel's tray disappeared. The two girls continued their conversation on their walk back to the barracks. The French girl, Anne-Marie, was in the barracks next to theirs. They wished each other *bon soir* (good night) and entered their respective barracks blocks. Aunt Sylvia, pleased that Rachel had met someone her own age and seemed to connect with, asked about Rachel's new friend. Rachel proceeded to tell Aunt Sylvia that Anne-Marie was obviously French and had been arrested because she was at a Communist Party rally, protesting the arrest of party members. This explained the red triangle sewn to the left breast of her smock.

When Anne-Marie inquired about the triangles on Rachel's smock, Rachel blushed and looked away in shame. Rachel took a deep breath and explained to Anne-Marie that the yellow triangle was for being a Jew and the black triangle was for being accused of being a prostitute. Anne-Marie told Rachel that she made no judgments regarding her religion or how she earned a living. Rachel looked at Anne-Marie in disbelief and told her that she had been accused of being a prostitute after being arrested with a large sum of cash on her person. She was definitely not a prostitute! She had never even been with a man. It was a completely fictitious charge that had received an even harsher sentence after it was discovered that they were Jews. Anne-Marie asked Rachel what she really did for a living. When Rachel replied that at the moment she was, or had been until recently, a high school student, Anne-Marie just stared at Rachel. She couldn't believe that Rachel was a teenager. She looked to be at least twenty years old. Anne-Marie asked her what she was studying and what she wanted to do. Rachel related the story of her singing in the Berlin nightclub.

Anne-Marie was intrigued. "You'll have to sing for us sometime."

Rachel just shook her head and turned away. "I don't know if I can sing again. There's just no joy left in my heart."

The barracks lights went out. Aunt Sylvia felt such guilt that she had caused this sweet young girl with such a promising career so much pain. How could she ever make things right again?

The inmates didn't understand the reason for the morning head count. They were accounted for last night; there should be the same number of inmates the next morning. That logic did not take into account the human psyche. The fact that during the night, the thought of continuing to live under such conditions could become so unbearable that their only recourse was to take their own life. Such was the case of four of the inmate population. The head count was held up until the bodies were recovered from where they had ended their lives and were placed in the formation where they normally would stand. Once that was accomplished, the head count procedure would begin again until the numbers matched. It seemed ridiculous, but one couldn't fault Teutonic efficiency.

As a result of the delayed head count, breakfast would be curtailed, and the inmates would only receive bread, margarine, jam, and coffee. The inmates were then divided into work details of twenty women each, assigned to an inmate *aufseherin* (female supervisor). This supervisor would march the inmates to the gate and turn them over to a female SS guard for work details. Depending on the inmate's skills, they were assigned to a diverse array of jobs. The majority were assigned to the camp's textile industry, producing prison clothing and uniform items for the German Army. The unfortunate ones were assigned to construction crews engaged in expanding the size of the camp. This was brutal backbreaking work. Rachel was assigned to the textile industry because she knew how to sew. Aunt Sylvia did not and was therefore assigned to the construction crew.

Work on the construction crew was brutal. They were made to construct the roadways and assembly areas. This was accomplished by first removing all vegetation that grew within the designated boundaries of the roadway and assembly areas. Earth was brought in by the wheelbarrow full and spread to make a fairly level area, and then women were assigned to the *Walzkommando* (the road roller). The road roller was a one-ton stone cylinder about two meters wide and one meter in diameter. An axle through the middle and a handle configuration would allow four women to pull this apparatus, which would compact the soil and make for a proper surface. The women assigned to the Walzkommando would perform this work until they died of exhaustion and another crew was selected to continue this work. Assignment to this work was basically a death sentence. All work details were required to work ten-hour shifts. There was no midday lunch break. They received two fifteen-minute breaks during the day. At the end of their ten-hour shift, they were marched back to the main gate where they were returned to their aufseherin for evening meal and final head count.

Final head count usually took longer than morning head count because they had to go through the charade of bringing the bodies of inmates who had died during the day to their place in line to be counted. Once head count was completed, the bodies had to be removed to the transport area to be loaded into trucks for transport to the crematoriums in nearby Fürstenberg. After about an hour and a half of standing at attention, during which around a dozen women collapsed, the inmates were released for evening meal.

When Rachel saw Aunt Sylvia, she was shocked at her appearance. Aunt Sylvia was absolutely filthy, her smock was torn, and she was favoring her left leg. Her hands were scraped and blistered, her knuckles were bloodied, and her fingernails torn. Rachel went to her and helped her limp toward the barracks to wash up before going to eat. Aunt Sylvia told Rachel what a day on the construction crew was like. The crew was divided into four teams of five women each. The first team was charged with removing any bushes and small trees in the designated pathway. The second team dug up and removed large stones or anything that stuck up above ground level. The third team brought soil that was deposited by dump trucks, and they spread the soil over the holes left by team 2. The fourth team operated the Walzkommando. By the end of the day, the five poor souls given that job were at the end of their strength. The other women had to almost carry them back to the barracks. Aunt Sylvia had been assigned to the second team. When they dug up a large stone, they had to carry the stone about fifty meters to a large pile of stones. Aunt Sylvia felt sure that at some time during their time in hell, they would be ordered to move the ever-growing mound of stones to another location. After the evening meal, no one had the strength for conversation, so they went straight to sleep.

The next day was a repeat of yesterday and the day after that and the day after that. Every day was the same nightmare, just an exercise in survival. Try the best that you could to keep pace with the other workers and not draw attention to yourself but also not to work yourself to exhaustion. Survival meant becoming invisible to the guards. If for any reason you managed to draw the wrath of one of the guards, you could count on a beating, at the very least. A few of the more sadistic guards were known to beat an inmate to death because they hadn't bowed quickly enough. One guard passed an inmate and called out to her. When the inmate turned to face the guard, the guard clubbed her in the head, causing her to fall against the guard. The guard looked at the inmate as she struggled to regain her feet, drew her pistol, and shot her through the spine. The inmate was crippled, but the guard refused to allow any of the other inmates to come to her aid. The poor wretch lay there on the assembly area all day until she bled to death. Only then were inmates allowed to remove her corpse to the crematorium transport area.

Christmas morning—a day of joy, happiness, and festivities in earlier times—began with snowfall. By 0500, there was already three centimeters (two inches) of snow on the ground, and the snow was falling hard with the wind beginning to howl. This had no impact on the usual routine of the day. The inmates stood at attention in what was rapidly becoming a blizzard. The inmates' smocks and thin jackets that they wore did nothing to protect them from the icy wind and blowing snow. The inmates had no boots, just the wooden clogs, and the snow was already to the tops of their useless footwear. Just because the inmates were freezing to death was no reason to be slack in the performance of the head count duty. Luckily, there were no deaths during the night, so the head count took just a little less than an hour. The inmates were released for breakfast, and theories began to run rampant regarding the work details for the day. Aunt Sylvia and Rachel, along with Rachel's new friend Anne-Marie, sat together at a table that was close to one of the heating stoves. In no time, a large puddle of melted snow had formed under them. They were shivering so bad they could hardly drink their coffee without spilling it.

One of the more optimistic women at the table was saying that there was no way that they would be sent out to work in these conditions. Almost the entire table broke into laughter, a dangerous thing to do because the guards might want to know what they had to laugh about. Rachel didn't look up from her coffee but told the optimist that if she thought that the guards might be concerned about the inmates catching cold, then she had forgotten that their purpose was to work them to death in the most efficient manner. If one or two thousand of them were to succumb to exposure or pneumonia, then all the better. The optimist refused to believe what Rachel said. Again, without looking up, Rachel told her she would bet her tomorrow's bread ration that after breakfast, they would be formed up for work details. The bet was agreed upon. The work details were marched off right after breakfast. Rachel hoped for one thing for today, that Aunt Sylvia and the optimist would survive the day so that Rachel could share the optimist's bread ration with Aunt Sylvia.

Rachel, Anne-Marie, and the other seamstresses were marched to the front gate by the inmate aufseherin and turned over to their SS guard. The two-kilometer hike to the textile factory was very difficult. The road was covered with at least ten centimeters (six inches) of snow, well over the tops of their clogs. From Ravensbrück to the textile factory was open land that the wind howled through. It wasn't long before the inmates could no longer feel their feet and legs. Several times along the way, inmates lost their shoes and had to stop and retrieve them, standing barefoot in the snow while they readjusted the ties. By the time the inmates reached their destination, their feet and legs had turned blue. The inmates were expected to commence their work immediately, but many could not because they could not move their fingers. Once their feet and toes began to get blood flow through them, the pain was excruciating. The SS guard told them she didn't care about their fingers and toes. If anyone did not make their quota for the day, they would be walking back to camp barefoot.

Aunt Sylvia's work crew was reassigned from construction to snow removal. They cleared snow from the sidewalks and roadways while others marched up and down the assembly area, packing the snow down. By 0900, twenty-five centimeters (sixteen inches) of snow had accumulated with no sign of letting up. In addition to the snowfall, the winds had drifted snow over one meter (thirty-nine inches) deep in places. The inmates had been working for three hours in subfreezing temperatures without a break. Over twenty inmates had collapsed in the snow, and the aufseherin left them lying where they fell. Other inmates were not allowed to go to their aid. By 1400, you could only see mounds of snow where the inmates fell, frozen to death. By 1500, the work details were halted. Sixty-one centimeters (forty inches) of snow had fallen so far. So much snow had fallen that they had nowhere to pile it anymore.

The work detail from the textile factory had just entered the front gate. They looked like walking snowmen. It had taken over an hour to make the trip from the textile factory, normally a twenty-minute walk. Before head count could begin, the inmates had to recover all the frozen bodies. After the first count, there was a discrepancy of four inmates. They were about to begin scouring the assembly area for frozen bodies when the SS guard for the textile factory inmates reported that four inmates had not survived the trip. When the head SS guard asked if she were certain that they were dead, she patted the holster on her hip and just nodded. The inmates were released early for their evening meal, after of course the frozen bodies were moved to the staging area then to the Fürstenberg crematorium. It wasn't until the spring thaw that the four inmates from the textile factory were discovered and sent to Fürstenberg.

The next morning, the snow was still accumulating. The inmates were assembled for the morning head count. So far, the storm had dumped almost seventy-five centimeters (fifty inches) of snow. Even the guards couldn't supervise inmates in these conditions. After morning head count, in which an additional ten inmates had died during the night to either the effects of exposure or suicide, the inmates were told that after breakfast, they would return to their barracks and stand by their bunks. They would not sit or lie on their bunks until released for evening meal. On the morning of December 27, the snow stopped, and hell began again.

On the first of March, after morning head count and their breakfast meal, the inmates were reformed on the assembly area but were not assigned work details for the day. A rumor had started that they were going to receive a visitor, a very important visitor who wanted to see the inmates. They had remained on the assembly area at attention for two hours when a gleaming black Mercedes entered the front gate, preceded by two motorcycle riders. For the first time since Aunt Sylvia and Rachel had been imprisoned at Ravensbrück, they actually saw SS Standartenführer Gunther Tamaschke, the camp commandant. He and his entire staff awaited their distinguished guest. The car stopped before the camp commandant, and an SS officer leaped out of the passenger door to open the rear door. A rather bookish-looking small man with wire-rimmed glasses and a small moustache stepped out of the car. Nazi salutes were exchanged, and introductions of his staff were made. Rachel whispered to Anne-Marie if she knew who the funny-looking little man was. Anne-Marie whispered back to Rachel to keep her mouth shut. The funny-looking little man was Heinrich Himmler, head of the SS and one of the most powerful and dangerous men in all of Germany.

Himmler trooped down the rows of inmates, suddenly coming to a stop in front of Aunt Sylvia and Rachel. Himmler turned to Tamaschke and asked him what the nationality indicator on her smock meant. Tamaschke stared at the letter *A* superimposed on Aunt Sylvia's triangle badges. He turned to one of his staff who replied that the *A* indicated that she was American. Himmler took a step back and spoke to one of his staff. Himmler then noticed Rachel with her *A*. He pointed to his staff officer and then at Rachel. Himmler asked Tamaschke if he had any other surprises and continued his inspection. Himmler met with Tamaschke for about thirty minutes then got into his car and left. The inmates had been standing at attention the entire visit and were relieved when they were finally being assigned their work details for the day.

The senior SS guard came over to Aunt Sylvia and Rachel and told them to report to the commandant's office. She didn't elaborate as to why they were to report, just to go there now. They made their way to the commandant's office with an overwhelming sense of dread in their hearts. Aunt Sylvia and Rachel stood before the door to the headquarters building. As they had never been here before, they had absolutely no idea what the protocol was. Fortunately, before they had to make a decision as to what course to take, a female SS guard came out. She looked as though she were about to beat them to death. Just as she was about to start beating them with her cudgel, she stopped. The SS guard had spotted the *A* on their smocks and said, "Ach, ihr zwei." (Oh, you two.) She pointed to a door and ordered them to wait there. Aunt Sylvia and Rachel went to the door and waited. Soon the door opened, and a young woman in SS uniform told them to come in and sit down. It took a minute for Aunt Sylvia to realize that the woman had spoken to them in English. The second surprise was that she had told them to sit down.

The young woman introduced herself as *Sturmmann* (Corporal) Mueller, and she would be their translator and would handle their records and work assignments. She had their camp records before her and went through them. It didn't take long as there was very little information contained in them. Sturmmann Mueller noted that there was no mention of their nationality in their records. This was very unusual. She asked Aunt Sylvia and Rachel if they had any proof of their American citizenship. They related the story of their passports and the temporary identification cards. Sturmmann Mueller located the identity cards in their personal belongings and said she had overlooked them as she had expected to find passports.

Sturmmann Mueller looked at their records again and then from Aunt Sylvia to Rachel. She did this several times before placing the records on her desk while shaking her head. She looked at the two women and told them she was having a hard time accepting what was listed on their records as occupation. Aunt Sylvia and Rachel looked first at each other then at Sturmmann Mueller and told her that they had never been asked their occupation when their records were completed. Sturmmann Mueller told them that was probably why their records list their occupation as "prostitute." It required a good forty-five minutes for Aunt Sylvia to tell the entire story of how they got to Ravensbrück with the charge of prostitution hung on them. Sturmmann Mueller said that she felt that the charge didn't seem to fit. Unfortunately, there was nothing she could do about the charge. What she could do was change the entry for occupation if they could prove that they had the necessary skills to work in another field.

Aunt Sylvia explained that both her father and uncle were jewelers, and as a young girl, she had been taught to clean, adjust, and repair watches. Sturmmann Mueller made a note and asked Rachel about her occupation. Rachel explained that she was still a student with her major in music. Other than sewing, she had no other skills. Sturmmann Mueller made another note then picked up her phone.

She spoke to someone for a few minutes then hung up. In a moment, an elderly man in prison garb knocked on the door and entered. Sturmmann Mueller looked at Aunt Sylvia and nodded to the old man. "Go with Herr Goldmann. He will evaluate your skills. If he deems you are sufficiently qualified, you will be transferred to his department and removed from the construction crew." Aunt Sylvia left with Herr Goldmann.

Sturmmann Mueller looked at Rachel and sighed. She tapped her pencil on her desk in thought. Suddenly, she jumped up and dashed out the door. Rachel sat alone in the Sturmmann's office for about thirty minutes. Sturmmann Mueller returned with a Scharführer Kolbitz. He was introduced as the man in charge of running the officer's canteen. If Rachel could convince him that she was a singer, they might utilize her in the canteen to entertain the officers. Rachel explained that she didn't know any German songs. Sturmmann Mueller relayed that to Scharführer Kolbitz. Through Sturmmann Mueller, he asked if she knew any French songs and if she could read music and also if she played any instruments. Rachel said that she knew several dozen French songs. She had used them during her French lessons. She could read music and play the piano. Scharführer Kolbitz smiled first at Rachel then at Sturmmann Mueller. He told Rachel to come with him for an audition.

Several hours later, Herr Goldmann returned to Sturmmann Mueller's office with Aunt Sylvia. He reported to Sturmmann Mueller that Aunt Sylvia knew what she was talking about when it came to watch repair or working on fine timing devices. The weeks of work on the construction crew had damaged her fingers, but the precise feelings that were required for the work they wanted would return in a few days. She would be more than acceptable for work in his section. Sturmmann Mueller dismissed him and had Aunt Sylvia take a seat while they waited for the results of Rachel's audition.

While they waited, Aunt Sylvia asked Sturmmann Mueller where she came to speak such good American English. Sturmmann Mueller smiled and told Aunt Sylvia that she learned English in grade school in Milwaukee. She was born there of German parents. They spoke German at home and English when outside of the home. In the mid-1930s, when the Depression made finding work very difficult, they heard stories of what Hitler was doing in Germany, and her parents decided to return to the homeland. Sturmmann Mueller was finishing high school when a recruiter contacted her regarding joining the SS. They had already researched her records and membership in the *Bund Deutscher Maedel in Der Hitler Jugend* (League of German Girls in the Hitler Youth) and found her attendance and participation exemplary. Her family passed the background test for purity, so she was accepted into the SS.

A knock at the door announced the return of Scharführer Kolbitz and Rachel. The scharführer announced that he hadn't heard a voice as pure and sweet as Rachel's in his entire life. He knew of a singing coach who would be glad to instruct her in German music and asked when she would be able to work full-time in the canteen. Sturmmann Mueller told him that she could probably start tomorrow. She would type the orders to change her assignment immediately and have the commandant sign it today. The same would apply for Aunt Sylvia's reassignment to Herr Goldmann's section. After Scharführer Kolbitz left, Sturmmann Mueller looked at Aunt Sylvia and told her that she would be working at a subcamp for Siemens AG, a company that manufactured very delicate mechanical assemblies for the *Luftwaffe* (Air Force). Aunt Sylvia was to never discuss what work she did there.

While Sturmmann Mueller busily typed reassignment orders for Aunt Sylvia and Rachel and *sonder ausweisse* (special identification) for Aunt Sylvia, the thought occurred to both of them that this just might be their chance for survival. Not having to face the back-breaking physical labor of the construction crew and the textile factory, they might just make it through this ordeal. It was a possibility almost too great to contemplate. Could this opportunity be real, or was it just a dream? Sturmmann Mueller completed the paperwork and went to get the required signatures. While she was gone, another young woman entered the office and asked which one was going to be assigned to Herr Goldmann. Aunt Sylvia raised her hand and was told to accompany the young woman down the hall to have a special access badge made. When Aunt Sylvia returned, she had a badge with her picture on it suspended around her neck on a chain.

Sturmmann Mueller returned with their orders. They were told that they would be moved to a special barracks and would be subject to head counts for that barracks only. Aunt Sylvia and Rachel thanked Sturmmann Mueller and left for their new barracks. Outside the headquarters building, the world had an entirely different look to it. It had the look of hope.

Chapter 16

With Great Britain and France declaring war on Germany after the invasion of Poland, Klaus and his senior class of cadets were placed on enhanced exercises. They had been ordered to deploy back to Grafenwöhr for extended live-fire training. There was a flurry of activities as preparations were made. They were told that they would not travel by truck to the training area. They would utilize the training they received before they went on break and use it to entrain their tracked and wheeled vehicles. For the first time, they would use their own equipment on a deployment.

Klaus sent the drivers to the motor park to bring up the Sd. Kfz. 7s to have their basic loads of ammunition loaded. He had the three-ton Opel Blitz trucks sent to load rations, ammunition, tents, water, and fuel canisters. Klaus conferred with Scharführer Winter, and he was told that at least for the foreseeable future, they would have to subsist on field rations. Apparently, there had been no provisions made for a field kitchen unit to be made available. This was supposed to be a school environment, not a possible combat deployment. The predeployment activities continued throughout the day. In order to keep up the momentum and not interrupt critical tasks, such as loading the Sd. Kfz. 7s, the lunch meal was divided into sections. The senior class received first priority for the lunch meal, and the remaining cadets were fed after them. This same procedure was followed for the evening meal.

By 2000, the loading of all vehicles, supplies, and personal equipment was completed. Klaus had the senior cadet class formed on the assembly area and waiting for Scharführer Winter. As he approached the formation, Klaus ordered, "Achtung!" (Attention!).

Scharführer Winter responded with, "Ruht euch." (At ease.) He then addressed the senior class cadets, informing them that the train would be departing at 2100. They would assemble back no later than 2040. He could not tell them what the final outcome of this training deployment would be, but there was a real possibility they could be placed into corps or division reserve. They were, therefore, to consider this a wartime deployment. If ammunition was issued, it would not be training ammunition but live ammunition. All usual safety protocols were to be observed at all times. Until assembly time, they were dismissed.

Klaus called the cadets to attention, and after Scharführer Winter left, he dismissed the cadets. The cadets mainly milled around the assembly area, talking in small groups, discussing what was happening. Would they see action? How long would this deployment last? A few cadets headed away from the assembly area, walking with purpose to some destination on the kaserne.

Unknown to Klaus, these enterprising cadets were headed to the canteen to procure some liquid courage to help this deployment go a little easier. At 2040 hours, the senior class of cadets was assembled on the assembly area with weapons and field packs. They were marched out of the kaserne to the railroad siding where they boarded the train cars that would take them to Grafenwöhr and possibly beyond. It was a four-hour train ride to the training site's railroad siding. Arriving at 0100, there was the usual banging and crashing as railcars were decoupled and moved to different sidings. The troop train cars were pulled up to a small station-like loading platform. The cadets disembarked and were moved to a small warehouse in which they would temporarily store their weapons and field packs while they went back to the switchyard and off-loaded their vehicles.

Klaus noticed that there was not the usual amount of lighting in the rail yard. When another cadet made the same observation about the lack of lighting, Klaus turned to the cadet and said, "Kriegs seit." (Wartime.)

The lack of lighting had impacted the time it took to off-load their vehicles. Although they had practiced these tasks in the dark, it hadn't been this dark. It took until 0400 to get their vehicles off-loaded and moved to the fueling point. Safety regulations at the time prohibited vehicles to be fully fueled while being transported by rail. It had something to do with fuel being sloshed from side-to-side, causing the freight cars to become unstable and subject to derailing. The vehicles had the bare minimum amount of fuel necessary to load, unload, and proceed to the fuel dump to be filled up. The fueling process added another two hours to their time. At 0600, the cadets broke out field rations for breakfast. A few kind souls from the Grafenwöhr field kitchen had brought them several thermos containers of hot water so the cadets could at least have hot field ration coffee.

The next task on the morning's schedule was erecting tents so they wouldn't have to sleep under the stars. The cadets moved on this task rapidly, as they were well aware of the fickle weather of Grafenwöhr. It could be sunny and warm one minute, and a blizzard or torrential rains the next. By 1000, the tents were erected, and the cadets had their cots and field packs moved in. Sanitation facilities, latrines, had been dug and signs posted. After lunch, another field ration, briefings were held regarding the training schedule for the next few days. They would be trained in fighting in built-up areas, towns, and cities. This was an area where tanks were extremely vulnerable and counted on the panzer grenadiers to protect them.

The training range at Grafenwöhr was unique in that within its confines were several towns and villages that were confiscated by the Reich when the training area was expanded from 96 kilometers to 230 square kilometers. The residents were evicted, and the structures, including several churches, were left standing to add realism for training exercises. The remainder of the day was used to discuss the tactics that would be used over the next week.

They would not have any tanks available for training; they were otherwise engaged, most likely being held in reserve for the Polish invasion. In lieu of Panzer IIs, they would use their Sd. Kfz. 7s to simulate tanks. They utilized blackboards to draw out the maneuvers they would practice and sand tables to visualize the maneuvers within the village. At 1800, they were dismissed for the day to look forward to another cold field ration for dinner. The cadets were formed up at the bivouac area, but instead of being released for evening meal, they were marched 500 meters to the main compound of the training facility. There, to the cadet's great surprise and relief, they could smell food cooking. Scharführer Winter had struck a bargain with the training facility dining hall to prepare meals for the cadets. The cadets just had to provide the rations, and the cooks would prepare the food, with a little incentive of a couple bottles of cognac, which Scharführer Winter had provided. The cadets were dismissed from formation and allowed to eat.

Klaus, always interested in how the "real" army functioned, went to Scharführer Winter and asked him how he managed to talk the cooks into performing this task. Scharführer Winter took Klaus aside and explained to him that it wouldn't be long before he would be an officer. The mark of a "good" officer was one who worked with his sergeant, learned from his sergeant, and built a bond of trust between them. A good officer knew when to let his sergeant take care of "sergeant's business." In this case, a good officer would have mentioned to his sergeant that it would be a great boost to the morale of "their" soldiers if hot food could be arranged then let the sergeant do what sergeants do and arrange for hot food. The officer would not question how the sergeant had arranged for hot food; he would just accept that "his" sergeant had understood "his" officer's wishes and had accomplished the task. Klaus immediately understood what Scharführer Winter was telling him. He wasn't going to explain how he knew what to do; he was teaching Klaus what an officer needed to do.

The next two weeks were spent conducting training in movement through a built-up area. This was a different set of skills from open country and sandbag bunker emplacements. They had to survey the area ahead of them, on either side of them, and even above them. They learned about snipers in church towers and anti-tank guns hidden in the rubble of bombed-out buildings. There were machine guns hidden in haylofts and even tanks hidden inside buildings. The first week of training in this environment resulted in horrendous simulated casualties. The first run-through resulted in 85 percent casualties. The cadets ran the exercise usually five times per day. Each time, it was a different scenario, so they couldn't simply memorize where the opposing force was deployed. By the end of the first week, they were down to 35 percent simulated casualties. At the end of each day, the cadets were soaked with sweat and more tired than they had been the entire three years previously.

Klaus was walking by a group of cadets during a reset of the scenario when he heard one cadet say that 35 percent wasn't too bad. Klaus called the entire cadet company into formation. He addressed the cadets by saying that he heard someone say that 35 percent casualties weren't too bad. He pulled out the company roster and called off thirty-five names and had them lay down in front of the formation. He then turned to the company formation and asked them how they would feel having to write condolence letters to each of the parents of the thirty-five comrades who lay before them. He reminded them of his own experience of writing a letter to the parents of cadet Oberjunker Dieter Hannauer, escorting his body home, and delivering that letter to his father and mother. Thirty-five percent casualties, simulated or not, was an extremely high price to pay when the way to reduce that number was more training. For his liking, they would continue to run these exercises until they were under 5 percent simulated casualties. The cadets shouted in unison, "Jawohl Standartenoberjunker Bergman!" (Yes, Cadet Master Sergeant Bergman!) Klaus ordered the cadets back to their training exercise.

Scharführer Winter had been watching from the tent area and was impressed with Klaus's dressing down of the cadet company. He was sure that Klaus would make a decent officer, with a little more training.

On Wednesday of the second week, the cadets were just finishing the second assault of the day when they were called from the training area to the assembly area. Scharführer Winter ordered the cadets to strike the tents and prepare the vehicles for railcar loading in three hours. They were moving to the Polish border as soon as railcars arrived and were loaded. They were not to drain fuel from the vehicles as was normal protocol; this was an emergency deployment. Klaus assigned the platoons the jobs they needed to perform. The cadets moved faster than Klaus and Scharführer Winter had ever seen them move before. By the time that the railcars arrived, the tents were struck, and all vehicles were staged for loading. The cadets set an all-time record of twelve minutes per vehicle loading time. The cadets had cut so much off the load-out time that they were forced to wait for their assigned track time from the Reichsbahn. They had to wait forty-five minutes before they could leave their siding and proceed northeast to the Polish border. When one's future lies in the balance, forty-five minutes can seem like an eternity.

Each cadet was deep in their own thoughts. If this were to be combat, how would they react? They all wanted to act like soldiers and not to shame themselves. They tried to remember everything they had learned so far, but it all seemed too much to recall. Klaus walked among the cadets, reassuring them that as long as they followed the orders of their squad leaders and the cadre, everything would be all right. Besides, they were probably going into reserve status and would not be needed. Did they think that their leadership was going to waste all the training invested in them on a bunch of Poles? This was just more of their training. They had eleven more months before they would be real officers and fit to lead others in combat. They should just relax and enjoy the scenery.

Klaus continued walking through the train car, speaking words of encouragement to the cadets, until he reached the enterprising cadets who had made the last-minute visit to the cadet canteen on the kaserne. He caught them in the process of passing a flask among them. He gave each one an icy stare and held his hand out for the flask. The senior ranking of the group looked guiltily at Klaus and handed him the flask. Klaus tipped the flask up and took a sip from it. Handing it back to the senior cadet, he pronounced it as "not bad" and moved on down the train car without another word.

On Saturday morning, they arrived at the Polish border town of Leszno. The cadets were ordered to disembark their vehicles and equipment and establish a bivouac about twenty meters from the train siding. While they were setting up their bivouac area and motor park, there was almost a never-ending series of trains moving past their area. All manner of rolling stock passed by with freight cars, tanker cars full of fuel, flat cars with tanks, trucks, and artillery pieces. Among the cars heading back into Germany were too many cars marked with the red cross of medical cars carrying wounded back to Germany for treatment. There was an air of excitement in the camp. Everyone wondered if they would get near the front. Many cadets looked forward to the opportunity to test their mettle; others were content to be where they were.

Klaus had a detail of cadets up on the rail siding sorting supplies that had not been available when they packed out of Bad Tölz. A train coming from the east pulled slowly into the siding and hissed to a stop in a cloud of steam. The cadets noticed it was a medical evacuation train returning from the front. They tried very hard not to stare at the wounded soldiers inside the car nearest to them. A door at the rear of the car opened, and a soldier emerged; he was using crutches to compensate for the loss of his left leg. He asked the cadets if anyone had a match. He couldn't smoke on the train because some patients were on oxygen, and the medical personnel became apoplectic if he tried to light a match around them. A cadet offered the soldier a light and could not help but to stare at the missing appendage. The soldier didn't seem offended and told the cadets that he had stepped on a land mine. He was fortunate; the man next to him had his head blown off from the same mine.

Klaus's mind immediately went back to the horrific wounds suffered by Dieter during training. The soldier told of the combat he had witnessed so far. He was a panzer grenadier assigned to the First Panzer Division, the spearhead for the Sixteenth Panzer Corps, the strongest panzer corps in the German Army. They made great strides in pushing the Polish Army back until they reached the Vistula River, where the Polish Army had dug in. It was during an assault on these positions that the German soldier had stepped on the mine. The soldier said that one of the most amazing sights he had seen so far was that the Poles still used mounted cavalry. They were very good at moving reserve forces quickly behind the lines to another part of the battle. The trench emplacements that the Poles had constructed were very well dug in and, as a result, inflicted many casualties on the German tanks and infantry.

Before the cadets could ask any questions, an express freight train headed east raced through the station; that was the reason the medical evacuation train was halted. The train headed to the front had priority over a train loaded with wounded headed home. The conductor's whistle sounded, and the wounded soldier hobbled back onto to his train. As the train pulled out of the siding, the soldier waved and called out to the cadets, "Viel gluck!" (Good luck!) The cadets continued with their detail and eventually moved off the loading dock.

On the morning of September 17, Klaus and ten other senior-ranking cadets were summoned to the headquarters tent. Scharführer Winter said that he had received authorization to take them to the front lines so that they might see actual combat in person. They were to assemble with full field gear, basic load of ammunition, and field rations for three days in thirty minutes. They were not to tell the other cadets where they were off to. They boarded an Opel Blitz and made the five-hour trip to the outskirts of Warsaw. There, they observed the power of the German Luftwaffe as it repeatedly bombed and strafed the city. After twenty minutes, they were moved to a field artillery unit to observe that combat arm perform its function in the application of joint arms. Scharführer Winter stressed upon the cadets the training they had received in calling for artillery support and the importance of being able to plot their position and that of the enemy on their maps. A mistake in map reading could easily result in calling artillery fire on their own positions—a deadly mistake.

The next day, they moved closer to the suburbs of Warsaw. They observed a company of SS troops escorting a group of twenty Polish civilians to a berm. The civilians were lined up facing away from the German SS troops and were summarily executed. As the SS troops were marched away, Klaus took notice of the sleeve insignia that was sewn onto the cuff of their coats, "Leibstandarte SS Adolf Hitler."

(SS Bodyguard Adolf Hitler.) Klaus turned to Scharführer Winter, mouth agape; Scharführer Winter shook his head as if to say, "Not now." The cadets were moved away from this area before they drew too much attention to themselves.

Their next stop was to a battalion headquarters for a panzer unit. The unit's operations officer briefed the cadets on the disposition of the tanks and their assigned mission. Klaus was not hearing a word the officer was saying. All he could see was the twenty civilians falling facedown after being murdered by the SS troops. All the cadets had received training on the laws of land warfare and the Geneva Convention, and what he had just seen constituted a war crime. As soon as the opportunity presented itself, he would have to ask Scharführer Winter to explain what he had just seen and why that had been allowed to happen. It made him question his oath to the German Army, the Führer, and his country.

The five-hour ride back to their bivouac area was made in silence. Klaus could tell that the other cadets were also deep in thought. He would like to have known their thoughts on the execution of civilians that they had all witnessed but decided to keep quiet until he had spoken to Scharführer Winter. They arrived back at the bivouac area at 2300. Everyone went straight to their tents, except for Klaus; he desperately needed answers. He went to Scharführer Winter's tent and requested permission to speak to him. Scharführer Winter invited him in and told him to sit. He looked at Klaus and offered him a beer. Klaus accepted gratefully. He looked at Scharführer Winter and asked him what they saw today. Scharführer Winter took a long pull on his bottle of beer and told Klaus that what they saw today was German soldiers following orders. The Poles, like the Jews, were considered *untermenschen* (subhuman) and therefore needed to be eradicated to protect the pure Aryan race. Klaus looked at Scharführer Winter and asked him if he really believed that. He looked at Klaus and said, "If you don't believe that, you had better not let anyone find out. The two options are ending up with a bullet in your neck or assignment to a *bestrafungsbattalion* [punishment battalion], which is considered worse than the concentration camps." Scharführer Winter could see the troubled look in Klaus's face. He said that with any luck, he would be assigned to a Waffen-SS Panzer Division and not one of the SS Panzer Divisions. Klaus didn't see much difference.

On the seventeenth of September, the cadets were ordered to return to Bad Tölz. With the Soviet invasion of Poland, the German Army considered hostilities to be at an end, and the occupation and administration of Poland was to begin. The majority of the German units in Poland were withdrawn to their home bases for refitting and training of replacements.

The cadets returned to Bad Tölz Kaserne on the twentieth of September. After they had off-loaded their vehicles and equipment, the cadets were ordered to stow their personal equipment and weapons and to reassemble at the cadet canteen. The first round of beer was on Scharführer Winter, after which all senior class cadets were granted a two-day pass.

*C*hapter 17

With the start of what was now being called the Second World War, Sidney was seriously considering dropping out of high school and enlisting in the Army. He went so far as to actually go to the local recruiting office. The army staff sergeant at the recruiting station asked him his age. Sidney considered telling a lie that he was eighteen but knew that he would have to provide a birth certificate eventually, so he told the recruiter that he was seventeen years old. The recruiter told Sidney he would need a letter from his parents giving their permission to enlist in the Army since he was underage.

The staff sergeant took another long look at Sidney and said, "Aren't you Colonel Klein's boy?" Sidney just nodded. The recruiter told Sidney that he thought he recognized him. "If your father found out you were down here trying to enlist right now, he'd have a seizure for sure. As I recall, you're supposed to be headed off to West Point next fall." He told Sidney to go ahead with his plans for West Point. An enlisted man in a peacetime army was no place for someone like him. The monotony would drive him crazy. Sidney thanked the staff sergeant for his time and left the recruiting office.

That night at dinner, the conversation turned to world events, as it usually did lately. The war in Poland was declared over by the end of September. There had been a few minor skirmishes on the French-German border at the beginning of September, but nothing since. Publications were calling it *Sitzkrieg* (Phony War). Aside from a French incursion into the German Saarland, which fizzled out, the only action had been from German aircraft attacking British shipping and the sinking of HMS *Courageous* by German submarine U-29 on September 17. Although there were no major military actions by England and France, they had begun economic sanctions against Germany via naval blockades.

Sidney decided against telling his parents of his attempt to enlist in the Army. There was no sense in causing a confrontation over something that wasn't about to happen. Instead, he announced that he had sent his application for nomination letter to the state representative for their district, as well as both senators and the vice president of the United States back in April. He had also received six letters of recommendation. He had already completed his physical exam and candidate fitness exam and provided his official transcripts with endorsements from his JROTC (Junior Reserve Officer Training Corps) training cadre and the high school principal. Everything had been submitted well before the deadline on January 31, 1940. If all went well, he would be enrolling as a member of the "long gray line" of cadets in September of next year.

On April 9, 1940, Germany invaded Denmark. From start of the invasion at 0415 to the surrender of the Danish king Christian X (the Tenth) at 0834, the incursion lasted a total of four hours and nineteen minutes. At the same time, Germany invaded Norway. The invasion of Denmark was to support the invasion of Norway, which was the main attack. Germany needed the Norwegian port of Narvik to secure shipments of iron ore to produce German steel. The invasion of Norway concluded with Norway's surrender in June 1940. Germany invaded France, Belgium, Netherlands, and Luxembourg beginning in May 1940.

Sidney devoured all the news articles he could get hold of. He listened to BBC until late into the night and monitored Z's frequency as often as he could. On May 30, 1940, Sidney received a letter from the United States Military Academy at West Point congratulating him on his acceptance as a cadet to this esteemed body. He had received a rather thick packet of instructions, which included a statement that had to be signed and notarized attesting that he was not married, had not been married, and was not responsible for the support of a woman or child. His orders to report to the academy were enclosed, along with a voucher for railway transportation and meals. The arrival of this packet brought great joy to the Klein household. Sidney's father insisted that they have dinner at the officers' club to celebrate the good news.

Sidney's mother insisted that the "men" should celebrate this news together. Jacob went upstairs to change into a dress uniform and Sidney into a suit and tie. Sidney's mother let out a sigh, and a tear ran down her cheek as she thought that her only child would be leaving, not to be seen again for almost a year, if not longer. Then he would be entering a career that had an almost certain aspect of danger attached to it, in peace or war. She finally realized he was no longer her little boy. On June 26, Sidney would leave to start his training. She might see him again in a year. Her "men" came downstairs and asked if she was sure she wouldn't accompany them. She kissed them both and said this was a man's celebration and sent them out the door.

Jacob bought several rounds at the club that night, and the sergeant who served as bartender looked the other way when patrons bought Sidney celebratory alcoholic beverages. At eighteen years of age, he could consume alcohol if he were in uniform. The sergeant figured that if the kid were going to West Point, he had earned a drink or two. It was the first time that either of the Klein men had witnessed the other drunk. They found it hilarious. Upon arriving home, Mrs. Klein didn't see the hilarity in the situation and told them so repeatedly.

The night of the celebration, Sidney had received a great deal of advice from West Point alumni. Advice ranged from ways to survive Beast Barracks to which bars to avoid off the West Point reservation. He was warned of the Hudson River girls. These were young ladies looking to marry a soon-to-be army officer. They were aware of the rules and regulations regarding marriage before graduation, so they knew how to string the young cadet along, getting them to promise their undying love till graduation day. There were several wedding chapels outside the main gate that would be backed up with cadets and their Hudson River girls just waiting to tie the knot. When that bit of advice was offered, Sidney's thoughts went immediately to Rachel. He suddenly realized that he hadn't thought of her in weeks. Had he given up on her? Was he consigned to the fact that he would never see her again? He promised himself that he would try to contact Z between now and until he left for West Point to get any information regarding concentration camps. He thought he would ask his father if he could ask Lieutenant Colonel Mitchell if he had uncovered any new information regarding Rachel.

One week before Sidney was to depart for West Point, he managed to connect with Z. He posed the question of which concentration camp would female prisoners be sent to. Z sent back, "QSY to primary +2." That meant he was to change to their primary frequency plus 2 kHz (kilohertz). Sidney retuned his radio and tapped in his call sign. Z sent a one-word reply, "Ravensbrück." Sidney couldn't make any more inquiries as Z had cleared the frequency and wouldn't respond to Sidney's signals. At least Sidney had a good lead as to where Rachel could be. He just didn't know what he could do with the information other than to forward it to Lieutenant Colonel Mitchell.

Sidney made the trip to his father's office and gave him the information he received from Z. Unfortunately, because of the hostilities in Europe, telephone service was restricted to high-priority calls, and even they couldn't be guaranteed to go through. Even if they did go through, they were almost 100 percent guaranteed to be monitored by the SD. Sidney's father called over to the communications center at Fort Leavenworth and spoke to the post's communications officer. He explained that he had information regarding two US citizens being held in a concentration camp in Germany, and he had finally ascertained where they were being held. He needed to pass this information to the US military attaché in Berlin. The communications officer said that they could only send it as routine traffic and could not encrypt the message. He was pretty sure that Colonel Klein didn't want German intelligence to find out that two of their prisoners were receiving so much attention from the US military. Colonel Klein saw the communications officer's point. He thought a moment and asked the communications officer if they could send the following, "Girls staying at the large black bird's bridge. Jacob."

At first, the communications officer didn't understand the message. Colonel Klein explained "the girls" were the two Americans they were searching for, "the large black bird" was a raven, and "the bridge" in German was *brück*. The two Americans they were searching for were at Ravensbrück concentration camp. The communications officer read the message again and declared it brilliant. He would get the message out immediately and would notify Colonel Klein when the message was received and if there was any reply. Colonel Klein thanked the communications officer and hung up the phone.

Sidney looked at his father, shrugged his shoulders, and said, "I guess that's all we can do for now." His father nodded in agreement.

The twenty-sixth of June arrived quicker than Sidney thought. His parents accompanied him to the train station to wish him well. Sidney made his father promise three things: to pass on any information he received about Rachel, to drive the '35 Ford at least once a week, and to not let his mom drive his car. He received hugs and kisses from his mother and a firm handshake from his father, then he climbed aboard the train to Chicago then on to New York City's Grand Central Station. From there, it was a one-hour-and-twenty-minute train ride to West Point. From Fort Leavenworth to West Point, it would take about two days' travel time.

Sidney settled in for the long ride. Sitting across from him was a young man, about his age, so they struck up a conversation. It didn't take long to determine they were headed for the same destination and for the same reason. His new traveling companion, Thomas Coyle, was not a military brat; in other words, his father was not in the military. Sidney asked him why someone with no military background would want to go to West Point. Thomas said he had two reasons. The first was that the Military Academy offered one of the best engineering degrees in the country, and it was free. Sidney reminded him of the minor stipulation that he had to serve in the United States Army for five years after he received his "free" engineering degree. Thomas agreed that there was that minor stipulation. But he was looking forward to being offered the opportunity to travel the world. Sidney told Thomas that travel certainly was in the cards. He had spent his junior high school years in Berlin, Germany.

As soon as Sidney brought up Germany, Thomas was all ears and full of questions. How were the people? What was the food like? Was everyone a Nazi? Sidney related many stories of his travels throughout Germany and Europe, the castles he had seen, the various festivals, especially the *Kristkindle's Markt* (Christmas market) in Nuremburg with their famous Nuremburg bratwurst, gingerbread, and wooden Christmas decorations. Sidney didn't believe that all Germans were Nazis. For the majority of the population, the Nazis were a political party. For the minority, it was more of a religion, a calling, the reason for and the answer to all things. There were some Germans who were absolutely fanatical concerning the ranting of Adolf Hitler. On the one hand, he had done great things economically for Germany. On the other hand, his racial and secular condemnations were causing a great upheaval within the country. His persecution of Jews, Gypsies, communists, and the physically infirm were extreme, to say the least. And now he had just led Germany into a world war that would cost thousands and thousands of lives.

Thomas noticed that when Sidney began talking about the Jews in Germany, he became very passionate. He asked Sidney if his passion was due to himself being Jewish. Sidney told Thomas about Rachel and her Aunt Sylvia. Thomas understood Sidney's feelings right away. Although he didn't know Sidney, he hoped they would become friends and Sidney would be able to concentrate on the trials that they were about to face.

The train from Grand Central Station pulled into the small train station of Garrison, New York. Almost all the passengers on board disembarked, meaning they were most likely *plebes* (freshman) cadets. There were several regular army NCOs (noncommissioned officers) waiting on the platform. The senior NCO, a master sergeant, announced to the new arrivals that if they were here to attempt to become officers in "his" army, they were to move smartly onto the busses behind him. If they were here to attend a four-year college and have fun, they were to reembark on the train, which would carry their sorry asses to Maryland, where the Naval Academy ran their school for wayward boys, feather merchants, and ne'er-do-wells. With that, the master sergeant bellowed, "Now move! I don't wanna see anything but assholes, elbows, and a cloud of dust leaving this platform! Move, move, move! If I catch any of you lollygagging, I'm gonna stick my boot so far up your ass you'll be spitting Kiwi for a week!" With those poetic words of endearment, they were welcomed to the first day of what the next year of their life would be like.

The busses arrived at a courtyard of what looked to be an ancient fortress. In fact, West Point was first occupied in 1787, making it the longest continually occupied post in the United States. The Military Academy was founded in 1802 by President Thomas Jefferson, who was originally against the establishment of a service academy because the Constitution made no provisions for the establishment of a military academy. Inside the walls awaited a large group of men who would come to be known as upperclassmen. Over the next three years, they would be called many other titles, hardly any of them flattering or uttered in mixed company.

The busses disgorged the plebes out onto an assembly area that was decorated with the imprints of yellow footprints. The plebes were directed to stand on the yellow footprints. The senior upperclassman instructed the plebes on how to assume the proper position of attention at West Point called the brace. It was an exaggerated position of attention in that the cadet tucked his chin down to his chest. Once that had been practiced and inspected, with push-ups for performing the move incorrectly, to the satisfaction of the senior cadet, facing movements were taught. With successful learning of that task completed, the senior cadet gave the plebes the order, "Right face. If you are taller than the worm in front of you, move forward. Keep moving until you encounter a worm taller than you or you reach the head of the line. Move!"

After this maneuver was completed, the cadets were given the command, "Left face. Perform the height maneuver again. Quickly, ladies. We have much to do today, and the Army only gives us twenty-four hours every day to do it in." Next, the cadets were instructed on the commands of "Parade rest" and "Stand at ease, or at ease." The cadets were placed at ease and told to look at their position in the formation, to take notice of the cadets to the left and right of them. This would be their position in all future formations unless instructed otherwise. Failure to be in their proper position would result in punishment.

"In order that you might better respond when I ask you a question, you will address me as Cadet First Sergeant. Is that understood?"

As one, the cadets responded, "Yes, Cadet First Sergeant!"

"Cadets, attention!" The cadets snapped to attention. The cadet first sergeant performed an about-face and announced to the waiting upperclassmen, "They're all yours."

The upperclassmen descended upon the plebes like a hoard of banshees, screaming orders, asking questions, and pushing plebes in the direction they wanted them to go. Sidney, having gone to a military school, was much better prepared for the chaos that was befalling them. He knew that the only correct answer to the upperclassmen's questions were "Sir, yes, sir"; "Sir, no, sir"; and "Sir, I don't know the answer, but I will find it." With that grain of knowledge, he was able to deflect a lot of grief long enough to determine what were the important orders being screamed at them and which ones were just to add confusion.

The plebes were first sent to draw bedding, which consisted of a mattress cover, pillow, two sheets, and two blankets. The trick was to transport all this to their barracks room without dropping anything while performing any combination of exercises demanded by the upperclassmen. One of the tidbits of knowledge that Sidney had picked up at the officers' club was to take all his bedding and place it inside his mattress cover. This simple process kept the rest of his bedding from being scattered all over the parade field while having to perform calisthenics between the supply room and his barracks room. Once the bed was made to the satisfaction of the upperclassman that Sidney was assigned to, they returned to the supply room to be issued uniforms, shoes, boots, and accoutrements, such as belts, bayonet and scabbard, dress and field caps, and overcoat. All this was to be packed strategically in a duffel bag. There was a specific order in which to pack everything, or there was no way it would all fit. This was evidenced by the trail of clothing between the supply room and the barracks and the mob of plebes trying to jam all their equipment into their duffel bags while their upperclassman berated them and had them doing push-ups. Once again, Sidney had an edge in having attended a military school and receiving training from a graduate of West Point.

When the cadet first sergeant said that they only had twenty-four hours in which to get the plebes ready for their first day of training, he meant twenty-four continuous hours. The plebes were instructed in setting up their wall lockers for inspection. Each uniform item belonged in a certain place. Underwear and T-shirts were folded a certain way. Socks were rolled and stored just so in a footlocker, along with toiletries. When and only when everything met upperclassman approval were they moved to the arms room to withdraw their Springfield Model 1903, a .30-06-caliber rifle, from the arms room for storage in their barracks weapons racks. The majority of the cadets were glad to hear that they would be receiving brand-new rifles. Sidney knew that to mean that the rifles would be heavily preserved in Cosmoline, an extremely thick and sticky grease used to prevent corrosion in weapons in storage. The Cosmoline was packed into every opening of the rifle. It was packed into the barrel, the bolt, and the magazine well. It was said that many a good soldier had gone mad trying to remove the Cosmoline from his rifle to satisfy his upperclassman or drill sergeant. Once again, Sidney and a few other plebes had been taught how to clean the Cosmoline from their weapons in less than a lifetime.

At 0200, the upperclassmen left the plebes to attempt to clean their rifles. The plebes would be assembled on the parade field, on their yellow footprints with their clean rifles at 0600, which meant that the upperclassmen were going to catch a few hours' sleep while the plebes cleaned, or attempted to clean, their rifles. Once the upperclassmen had left, Sidney called the cadets in his barracks together and determined which cadets had prior experience with the removal of Cosmoline from weapons. Several of these cadets wanted to use the quick but unauthorized method of soaking the rifles in gasoline. This quickly removed the Cosmoline but also allowed corrosion to start almost immediately. The second method, which the Army never taught, was to remove the stocks from the rifle and take it into a hot, soapy shower and, using a toothbrush, scrub the rifle down. This process took a couple hours but removed all the Cosmoline and got the cadet clean too. Sidney instructed the cadets to use the toiletries that they had left home with because once they were finished, the toothbrush and towels would be put in the trash. If they used their military-issued items, they wouldn't be able to pass inspection.

By 0430, the rifles were cleaned and lubricated. Sidney inspected each rifle and told each cadet what he had found wrong. The discrepancies were corrected, and then they prepared their uniforms for the morning, which was an hour away. Sidney allowed the cadets to rest for forty-five minutes as long as they did not lie down on their bunks. They could lie down on their footlockers. At 0545, Sidney, who had not slept, roused the cadets and ran them outside for their 0600 formation.

The upperclassmen began their inspection and were not happy. First of all, the worms were all in their assigned positions, braced at the position of attention. They carried their weapons at left shoulder arms, which was the correct position, although they had not been instructed to do so. The cadets were then ordered to present arms, holding their rifle vertically in front of them, with the front sight aligned with the brim of their cap. They performed the maneuver much better than expected. The upperclassmen then trooped the line looking for oil or grease stains on the cadet's tunics caused by dirty rifles. Again, nothing to be seen.

The final inspection, the one that would surely result in demerits, was rifle inspection. This inspection normally took about thirty minutes for one hundred cadets because every rifle was filthy. After seventy-five minutes, the last weapon was inspected, and the upperclassmen were dumbstruck. As far as they knew, no class of plebes had ever come through the first rifle inspection without demerits. When the upperclassmen were down to the last twenty-five cadets in the fourth platoon, they started making up discrepancies and issuing demerits. Each demerit resulted in one-hour marching on the square. Sidney had told the fourth platoon that they would probably receive a made-up punishment, and the other cadets would make it good by making their bunks or caring for their uniforms while they were on the punishment yard. This arrangement worked well, and they thought it didn't draw too much attention to their successes.

The upperclassmen, however, thought that there was a rat somewhere. The plebes' first inspections had gone far too well. There was either a cadre member or another upperclassman providing inside information. They would have to keep an eye on this group to see if they established a pattern of excellence. The plebes were released for breakfast, which meant they had to hurry back to the barracks and store their weapons, return to the parade field, and in company formation, march to the mess hall. After breakfast, they assembled in company formation and were moved back to the barracks where they were instructed to change into field uniform and report back to the parade field in fifteen minutes.

Once reassembled, they were informed that they would partake in the standard army physical fitness test. This consisted of push-ups, sit-ups, inverted crawl, overhead bars, and one-mile run. They were marched to the physical training field, and the test was administered. Everyone could tell which cadets had goofed off over the summer and which had read the course syllabus regarding physical fitness. Sidney, who was always engaged in sports and track, had no problem with the test. There was a small group of cadets who were going to struggle through the physical training. They were easily recognized as the ones who were along the track throwing up their breakfast or lying along the track gasping for breath. If they didn't spend most of their free time, what there was of it, improving their physical fitness, they wouldn't be here long.

After a month of physical training, followed by classwork and then sports, the cadets finally got to do something that they thought would be more entertaining. They were marched out to the rifle range for, what would be for many, their first encounter with firearms. Learning how to shoot from your dad or older brother was nothing like learning how to shoot "the army way." In the Army, everything was done by the numbers. There was no room for individual ideas on how this should be done. Violations of safety protocols were punished swiftly and severely. The firing ranges were run by regular army sergeants with one range safety officer. Sidney and a few other army brats were familiar with the safety protocols and range procedures and passed them on to the other cadets. Basically, don't do anything unless you were specifically told to. The morning was spent on safety briefings, followed by learning the army method of marksmanship. They were taught the meaning of sight picture, sight alignment, and the importance of squeezing the trigger, not jerking it. They learned the three positions for target acquisition: standing, kneeling supported, and prone supported (the latter being the best position for accuracy).

In the afternoon, the cadets fired to "zero" their weapons. Each cadet would fire three rounds from twenty-five yards at a target that would appear to be three hundred yards because of its size. After they had fired their three rounds, they would safety their rifles and proceed down range to check their targets. The goal was to have the three bullets strike the target as close together as possible. They didn't have to be in the center or bull's-eye of the target as long as they were fairly close together. Once the cadets could place their shots in a good group, they worked on adjusting the rifle's sights to move the strike of the bullet to the bull's-eye. It was easy to tell which cadets had previous marksmanship training. They usually zeroed their weapon within nine rounds. There were also a few "natural born" marksmen. These were cadets who had hunting experience before or just had an affinity for the art of marksmanship. Either way, these cadets all fired for qualification on the first attempt.

To qualify as a *marksman*, one had to fire twenty rounds at two hundred yards and score between 161 and 175 out of 200 points; to qualify as *sharpshooter*, between 176 and 185; and to qualify as *expert*, a cadet had to fire between 186 and 200. Sidney qualified as expert with an impressive score of 198 points. For those cadets who did not qualify on the first round, it was back to the range for another chance. They would continue to fire for qualification until they qualified or it became too dark to safely fire. The cadets who had qualified were allowed to start cleaning their weapons. Cadets waiting their turn to refire were assigned the tasks of "policing up" (picking up) brass from fired cartridges or reloading five-round clips of ammunition for firers. Fortunately, by the end of the day, all cadets had qualified and could clean their weapons. They would march and train with the weapons almost daily but would not fire them again until they fired again for qualification next year. The Army didn't have the budget to fire that much ammunition more than once per year. After today, their time would be occupied with schoolwork, calisthenics, and military drill.

Chapter 18

Klaus went home for Christmas this year. He was looking forward to seeing his parents and getting a feel for what the people back home felt about Germany getting involved in another world war. He got a good feel as to how the average citizen felt. Several train passengers brought him beer and schnapps and toasted his health as a soldier of the Reich. Klaus didn't bother to tell them that he wasn't a soldier yet. When he finally arrived home, he was just a little bit tipsy and a little unsteady on his feet.

Normally, he would have walked the two blocks from the train station to his parents' home, but he decided to catch a taxicab. The driver refused to take any money for the fare no matter how Klaus argued. The driver said that his son had just returned from Poland, and he was very glad to have him home for the holidays. Klaus thanked him for the ride and wished him and his family a "Froehliche Weihnachten" (Merry Christmas) and climbed the stairs to the front door of his parents' house.

His father answered the door, and it was all he could do to keep his voice down so that they could keep the surprise for Klaus's mother. He whispered to Klaus that his mother was in the kitchen mixing up a batch of *glühwein* (spiced red wine), a traditional mixture of red wine, oranges, lemons, cinnamon, cloves, and sugar, which was heated to the temperature of a hot tea and served in a large ceramic mug. For Klaus, this was one of the most memorable things about Christmas. Klaus's father went into the kitchen and called out,

"Liebling, Ich habe eine geschenk fur dich." (Darling, I have a present for you.)

She turned to see Klaus standing in the kitchen door. Her hand went to cover her mouth, and she said, "Ach, Klausie." (Oh, Klausie.) It was a name she hadn't called him since he was in grade school. His mother ran to him and threw her arms around his neck and hugged him to her. Next, there came a barrage of questions: "Are you hungry? How long will you be staying? You look too thin. Are they feeding you enough?" Klaus just let his mother babble on; he knew she had to get this out before they could have a normal conversation. Finally, she calmed down, let out a sigh, and smiled. Klaus said he had eaten on the train but could do with a cup of coffee. His mother jumped up and went to work preparing it. Klaus's father said that he could drink a cup of coffee if she could work it in.

Klaus and his father went into the parlor and sat by the fireplace. Klaus's mother brought three cups of coffee and three snifters of shots of cognac. She poured her cognac into her coffee. The men raised their glasses, and Klaus's father offered a toast to Der Führer and the continued success of the German military. Klaus's mother cleared away the coffee cups and brought the cognac bottle, left it with her two men, and went upstairs. Before she left, she told Klaus that his room was prepared just as he left it, then she kissed him and her husband on the cheek and wished them good night.

Klaus's father poured them each another shot of cognac and asked Klaus how things were going at Bad Tölz. Klaus told his father about the deployment to Poland and the meeting with the wounded German soldier. Klaus's father was not happy with Klaus relating the story of the civilian execution. Klaus's father explained that there were certain missions assigned to the *Sonderkommando* (special squads) that had nothing to do with regular army units, and the less they had to do with them, the better. Hitler had already determined that certain people were "untermenschen" and needed to be removed in order that Germany could have its Lebensraum. The German soldier was to claim that land, and the Sonderkommando were to clear the unwanted people from that land.

Klaus had already heard the speeches in his political education classes. He just still had a problem with cold-blooded extermination of unarmed civilians and prisoners of war. Granted, he had seen hundreds of Polish POWs marching to the rear headed to POW camps, but he had also seen enough being lined up in the drainage ditch along the road and gunned down. He personally didn't care why they were being executed; it was still against the Geneva Convention and the *Laws of Land Warfare*, which all officers were taught to obey and enforce. Klaus could tell that he and his father would never see eye to eye on this point and decided to let the subject go.

Klaus's father asked if he had heard anything concerning his first assignment when he finished school. Klaus said that the only thing he knew for certain was that he would be assigned to a panzer grenadier unit. He had no idea which panzer division, except that it would be an SS panzer division. Klaus poured them each another cognac and asked his father what he thought was going to be the Führer's next move. His father opined that Germany was going to have to protect its supply of iron ore, which came from Norway. Moving it by sea would be subject to interdiction by the much larger English and French fleets, so there would have to be a land route. The most obvious land route would be through Denmark, so a pact of some sort would have to be negotiated with Denmark to allow the iron ore to be shipped from Norway through Denmark to Germany. The big question was how Norway would react to pressure from England and France over exports of iron ore to Germany. Klaus's father thought that in a worst-case scenario, Germany would have to invade Norway in order to secure its iron ore. He also believed that would be the tipping point for the Sitzkrieg. Either England and France would invade Germany, or Germany would invade France. If the second scenario came first, it meant that the Germans would have to conquer Belgium, the Netherlands, and Luxemburg in order to protect the right flank of the invading German Army.

Klaus listened intently and couldn't fault his father's logic and hypothetical battle plan if it weren't for a seminar at Bad Tölz taught by a very interesting tank officer named Heinz Guderian. *General-Major* (Major General) Heinz Guderian was considered the creator of armored and mechanized tactics in the German Army. He discussed the fictitious invasion of France by showing the accepted military concept of attacking through the low countries to avoid the French Maginot Line—a system of heavily reinforced concrete fortresses that ran from the German border to the Swiss border and were considered almost impregnable. Guderian proffered a different, if not a radical, strategy to attack France through the Ardennes Forest and advance rapidly westward to the English Channel, cutting the French forces in half. Many, if not all, conventional officers considered this strategy impossible, considering the steep terrain and thick forest of the Ardennes to be impossible for tanks and mechanized infantry to traverse. General-Major Guderian felt very strongly otherwise. Klaus agreed with Guderian; his father agreed with the other conventional officers.

The remainder of Klaus's Christmas leave was rather pleasant. His mother continued to spoil him, making his favorite meals and baked goods. He met up with some old friends, some of whom were now in uniform. They had felt the call of National Socialism after the invasion of Poland. After all, the Poles had attacked Germany first, and they felt duty bound to join the Army in defense of the Reich. Prior to entering the military themselves, they had teased Klaus that he was going to waste his future. Now they respected him, and some were a little jealous of his standing in the military. After all, in five months, he would be an officer, while they would still be privates.

By New Year's, Klaus was itching to get back to Bad Tölz. Oddly enough, he missed the camaraderie and the military atmosphere. As his friends had said, in five months, he would be commissioned an untersturmführer in the Waffen-SS and would undoubtedly see real action soon afterward.

Klaus returned to Bad Tölz on January 3. Almost everyone who had received Christmas leave had already returned even though they legally had two more days authorized leave. It seemed the other cadets were also looking forward to the end of their schooling and getting to the real purpose of the last four years. One of the first things that Klaus did was to check in with Scharführer Winter. Since he had been off for Christmas and New Year's last year, he had the duty this year. They made small talk about the holidays and where each one thought the war was going, although at the moment, it didn't seem to be going anywhere, therefore the name Sitzkrieg. Scharführer Winter figured after the spring thaw started and the units involved in the Polish invasion had time to rearm and reequip, things would start to heat up. Klaus told Scharführer Winter of his discussion with his father and his theory that Norway would be the next target for the German Army. Scharführer Winter nodded and agreed that would be his guess also, except he didn't think that Der Führer would want to tip his hand by engaging in negotiations with Denmark about passage through their land to attack Norway. Scharführer Winter guessed that there would be a two-pronged attack against Denmark and Norway before England and France could mount defensive maneuvers to help Denmark and Norway.

As April came to a close, several rites of passage were taking place. The senior-class cadets were fitted for their black Waffen-SS uniforms. Their ring sizes were measured for their SS rings, and the next-to-last item to be performed was the tattoo of their blood type under their left arm. The final rite would be performed on graduation day when they received their official insignia of rank as untersturmführer and the presentation of their SS dagger with the inscription "Meine Ehre Heisst Treue" (Loyalty is my honor.) It was after they received their dagger that they received their unit assignment.

Scharführer Winter's prediction that Denmark and Norway would be attacked simultaneously came true, although no one anticipated the Danish government would capitulate in only four hours. Norway was a little harder nut to crack and was still holding out. They had received assistance from England, France, and Polish forces that had evaded capture in Poland.

As graduation rehearsals progressed in May, word came that the Sitzkrieg was definitely over. Germany had invaded the low countries as the conventional generals had predicted. But General Guderian had set the perfect trap. As the British Expeditionary Force (BEF) raced toward the low countries to cut off the German advance at the French border, General Guderian launched his main armored force through the Ardennes Forest just as he had drawn up at Bad

Tölz three years before. Blitzkrieg was being unleashed on the French Army and elements of the BEF. Guderian's panzer and mechanized infantry divisions raced for the coast, cutting off the retreating BEF. If he could reach the French coast before the BEF, almost the entire English Army would ultimately be captured or destroyed on the continent, leaving England mostly defenseless.

There was much talk among the cadets of early graduation and immediate postings to field units currently engaged in France. Scharführer Winter quickly put an end to those rumors. He told Klaus to get word back to the cadets to drive that thought from their minds. The combat situation in France and Norway was so fluid at the moment that any replacements being fed into the field units would come from reserves already in the field. The cadets' assignment right now was to complete their graduation ceremony and fill their parents and fellow cadets with pride. As Klaus was about to leave Scharführer Winter's office, he called Klaus's name, pointed to a document at the top of a stack on his desk, and turned away.

Klaus paused and then glanced at the paper that Scharführer Winter had indicated. It was Klaus's assignment orders. He was being posted to the Fortieth Panzer Grenadier Regiment, Second SS Panzer Division Das Reich, currently near Dunkirk, France. This was the assignment that Klaus had hoped for. Klaus clicked his heels together and left Scharführer Winter's office.

The days left until graduation seemed to drag on. Nothing left to do but rehearsals and turn in equipment. The day before the graduation ceremony, Klaus was informed by Scharführer Winter that his parents had arrived and were staying at the VIP quarters on the kaserne. After the day's duties were completed, Klaus could go and visit them. Klaus joined his parents at the Bad Tölz Officers' Club for a nice dinner. Soon, Klaus would be authorized and required to become a member of an officers' club. Klaus wanted to tell his father of his impending assignment but felt that it would be a betrayal of Scharführer Winter's trust by allowing Klaus to see the assignment orders unofficially. His parents would have to wait until Friday when they were read at the graduation ceremony.

Klaus's father asked him what his plans were following graduation, to which Klaus explained that his plans depended on his orders. Usually, they included a period of leave, normally seven days, but with the war going on, that might all change. Klaus felt a little bad about not being able to tell his parents that he knew that he had seen on his orders that he had been given a ten-day delay en route before having to report to his unit, but he had to maintain the ruse that he knew nothing of his orders. After dinner, Klaus accompanied his parents to their room and then returned to his last night in his barracks.

Graduation day arrived with a beautiful, sunny weather with just enough of a breeze to keep everyone cool and keep the flags waving. The program was set to have the class of cadets raise their right hands to be sworn into the German Army. They would pledge their allegiance to Adolf Hitler, the German Reich, and the Waffen-SS. As each cadet's name would be announced, he would approach the dais where the school commandant would pronounce him an untersturmführer and present him with his SS honor dagger and new insignia of rank. Next, Scharführer Winter would give them their orders and SS ring and announce their assignment.

The first cadet to be announced was Untersturmführer Klaus Bergman. As the first cadet to be announced, he had the additional distinction of being the class honor graduate. As an additional reward for this honor, Klaus received from Scharführer Winter a Walther P38 officer's pistol engraved with his name, in a wooden presentation case with holster. Klaus stood before Scharführer Winter as he read out Klaus's orders. "Untersturmführer Klaus Bergman, you are hereby released from Student Company, Fahnenjunker School Bad Tölz, and reassigned to Fortieth Panzer Grenadier Regiment, Second SS Panzer Division in the field in France." Scharführer Winter handed over the pistol as the last item, looked Klaus in the eyes, and smiled. "Bis wir uns wieder treffen [Till we meet again], Herr Untersturmführer Bergman." He shook Klaus's hand and saluted. Klaus returned his salute and marched off the stage.

Klaus's ten-day delay en route was actually about seven days at home. The remaining three days included travel from Berlin to Paris and then arranging for ground transportation to the Fortieth Panzer

Grenadier Regiment near Dunkirk. Klaus quickly realized that a second lieutenant, even in the Waffen-SS, didn't have much pull. He begged rides on troop and supply trucks headed toward the front. He soon learned that there wasn't much fighting going on at the moment. The Panzer Army had finally stopped to allow the infantry to catch up to them and then to give them a break to recover. The infantry was practically exhausted, and the tanks needed some maintenance and refitting too. Klaus finally caught up to the Fortieth Regiment about fifteen kilometers (ten miles) east of Dunkirk. The familiar sound of artillery raged nonstop into the beach area where English and French troops were awaiting evacuation back to England. The all too familiar howl of Stuka dive bombers could be heard when the artillery paused to let their guns cool while they waited for shells to be brought up from supply trains.

Klaus was introduced to Sturmbannführer (Major) Gruber, the regiment's operations fficer. Klaus came to attention, saluted, and reported to Sturmbannführer Gruber. Klaus almost reported using his academy cadet rank but caught himself in time and used his correct rank.

Sturmbannführer Gruber smiled and said to Klaus, "First time reporting as an officer, Herr Untersturmführer?"

"Jawohl, Herr Sturmbannführer," Klaus replied.

"You'll get used to it eventually, Untersturmführer." Sturmbannführer Gruber went over Klaus's records from the academy. "Very impressive, Untersturmführer Bergman. I see you had Scharführer Winter as your class adviser. How is Scharführer Winter these days?"

Klaus was rather surprised at the question. "Scharführer Winter is doing well, Herr Sturmbannführer, though I imagine he would rather be here than at the academy."

Sturmbannführer Gruber nodded as he looked through a roster on his desk. "Yes, I'm sure he would rather be here." Sturmbannführer Gruber called out for the operations sergeant, *Hauptscharführer* (Master Sergeant) Kraus, to come into the office. He instructed the hauptscharführer to assign Klaus to the Third Company of the First Battalion. They showed they were short a platoon leader. The company commander should send up an officer to escort Klaus to the battalion headquarters to meet the battalion operations officer then to the Third Company area. Sturmbannführer Gruber shook Klaus's hand and welcomed him to the regiment. Klaus saluted and followed the hauptscharführer to his office to await his escort.

Presently, a Scharführer Lindermann arrived from the Third Company to escort Klaus to the First Battalion headquarters. He picked up Klaus's duffel bag and led him to a *Kübelwagen* (German Jeep) parked outside. The scharführer tossed Klaus's bag in the back and asked him if he was armed. Klaus tapped the holster on his hip, indicating his Walther P38 pistol.

"We'll have to remedy that with an MP [machine pistol] as soon as we get to the company, Untersturmführer. Although fairly quiet now, this is still a combat zone. Actually, that's why you are here, to replace the First Platoon's commanding officer. He was killed on patrol two days ago."

Klaus drew his pistol and made sure there was a round in the chamber and the safety was off. He didn't want to fumble with that if he had to use it in a hurry. They didn't spend much time at the battalion headquarters area. Klaus dropped off a copy of his orders and his personnel and pay records. Klaus and Scharführer Lindermann proceeded down the line to the Third Company where he was introduced to Hauptsturmführer (Captain) Becker, the company commander. Hauptsturmführer Becker gave Klaus a briefing on the status of the First Platoon. An incident two days ago, when the previous platoon leader led his platoon on what should have been a routine patrol in a "pacified" area, turned into a deadly ambush that resulted in the platoon leader, the platoon sergeant, and three other soldiers getting killed and two wounded, although not seriously.

Hauptsturmführer Becker looked at Klaus and asked him, "What went wrong, Herr Untersturmführer Bergman?"

"Herr Hauptsturmführer, I wouldn't want to cast aspersions on the abilities or decisions made by a fellow officer."

"Untersturmführer, he won't complain. He's dead! Why do you think he and his men are dead?"

"In my opinion, Hauptsturmführer, there were several errors made. First, I think the platoon leader assumed the area they were patrolling in was devoid of enemy forces. Second, the platoon leader had his command element in the lead of the platoon. He should have had a scout element in the lead, but this goes back to the first mistake. And third, the platoon leader and the platoon sergeant were apparently in close proximity to each other, allowing the enemy to eliminate the entire command element with the first burst of fire."

Hauptsturmführer Becker stared at Klaus for a full minute before he said, "I presume that such a spot-on assessment as you just presented had a great influence on you being selected as the honor graduate of your academy class. I just hope that I don't have to have a similar conversation with your replacement because you repeated mistake number 1."

Klaus was given back to Scharführer Lindermann, who took him down to the First Platoon bivouac area. Klaus took over the platoon leader's tent. The personal belongings had already been removed to the company supply room for shipment to his next of kin. Klaus inherited a practically brand-new MP-40 and seven thirty-round magazines of nine-millimeter parabellum ammunition and the harness and belt with first aid pouch and canteen. Klaus made a note to himself to see the supply sergeant and get a new canteen. He didn't relish the thought of drinking from a dead man's canteen.

During the course of the day, Klaus met the remainder of "his" platoon. He had Scharführer Lindermann, who was the acting platoon sergeant, bring the key members of his platoon to his tent for an introduction, starting with his platoon RTO (radio telephone operator). It was imperative for the platoon leader and the RTO to be able to understand each other clearly. If either party had a speech problem, they would have to work closely with each other until they became accustomed to their manner of speech. In the heat of battle, there could not be misunderstandings that could lead to mistaken orders or missed map coordinates. Sturmmann (Corporal) Andreas was a well-spoken, easygoing young man who appeared to be perfect for the job. When Klaus asked him how long he had been the platoon's RTO, he grinned sheepishly and said, "All day, Untersturmführer."

When Klaus asked him to explain, Sturmmann Andreas replied that he had been assigned as the platoon RTO this morning. The previous RTO had been killed along with the other members of the command element.

"Well," Klaus replied, "I guess we'll train each other, won't we?"

Next to be introduced was Oberschutze (Private First Class) Groenig, the platoon medic. He, like the RTO, had been assigned to the platoon as of this morning for the same reason as the RTO. Klaus hated to speak ill of the dead, but he was having serious doubts about his predecessor's ability to command. He had indeed lost his entire command element and, as he found out later, the First Squad leader as well. If it hadn't been for Scharführer Lindermann filling in for the Second Squad leader that morning, the entire platoon could have been lost. Scharführer Lindermann had rallied the men and laid down a heavy fusillade of fire that drove back the enemy troops. Hauptsturmführer Becker had submitted Scharführer Lindermann for award of the Iron Cross Second Class.

Klaus then met his squad leaders, Unterscharführer (Sergeant) Gross, First Squad, new to the platoon as of today; Unterscharführer Fisch, he had been with the platoon since Poland; Unterscharführer Dieckman, also with the platoon since Poland; and finally, Unterscharführer Iselborn, who joined the platoon at the start of the Ardennes offensive. Except for the command element, less Scharführer Lindermann, the entire platoon had been together for several months and seen action together. Klaus was going to have to ensure that he got his command element up to standards, and quickly.

Klaus started his training the next morning. He asked Scharführer Lindermann to set up a patrol along the front line with two squads—the First Squad as the lead element and the Second Squad in reserve. He would go with the First Squad, and Scharführer Lindermann would accompany the second. Scharführer Lindermann asked what the purpose of this patrol was. At first, Klaus was incensed that his instructions were being questioned. Normally, Klaus would not tolerate having his instructions questioned. But this was not a training exercise, and Klaus had no actual combat experience. Klaus explained to Scharführer Lindermann the inequity in combat experience between his command element and the rest of his platoon. He needed to get the new men, especially himself, up to speed as quick as possible. Scharführer Lindermann nodded and said he would get the squad leaders together and have the patrol ready to move out in forty-five minutes. He told Klaus that before they could go outside the bivouac area, they would have to get clearance from Hauptscharführer Becker and the battalion operations officer so that nobody accidentally called artillery fire on an unknown unit in the woods. Klaus thanked Scharführer Lindermann for the pointers and went to get his gear ready.

When Scharführer Lindermann forwarded the patrol request up the chain of command, he got the same comment from the company commander and the battalion operations officer, "Don't let him get himself killed." He said he would do his best to not let that happen. The patrol went without any problems. Klaus achieved the training he wanted to accomplish, and Scharführer Lindermann didn't have to report the tragic and untimely death of Untersturmführer Bergman.

Upon returning from the last of the patrols that Klaus had requested, the division received orders to move into garrison in Paris. The Dunkirk pocket had closed, and the French government had finally signed the armistice with Germany on June 25, 1940. The division was moved into garrison duty outside Paris until April 1941.

Chapter 19

September 3, 1939. The Ravensbrück camp was in a heightened state of activity. The usual work parties were suspended, and a new task was assigned. Truckloads of building supplies were delivered, and the work details were set to constructing additional barracks. The workers were ordered to construct ten barracks buildings by the end of the month. An almost impossible task with the number of inmates assigned to the construction crew, every available inmate was reassigned to construction. That meant all the inmates from the textile works, kitchen personnel, and maintenance workers became carpenters, plumbers, and roofers. This provided an additional two hundred workers for this seemingly impossible project. Eventually, the reason for this rushed construction came out. The additional space was going to be necessary to house an influx of Polish prisoners. Unknown to the current inmates, Germany had declared war on Poland and was accumulating a large contingent of prisoners.

The thirtieth of September arrived and all, but the last barracks building were completed. The prisoners fully expected there to be punishment handed out for this failure, but to their surprise, there was no punishment. The additional workers were sent back to their usual details, and the construction crew continued working on the last barracks until completed. There was no sign of Polish prisoners until two weeks later when the usual delivery train arrived. When the train arrived, there were many more armed SS guards. The prisoners were herded off the trains and forced into somewhat of a formation. It was immediately apparent that there was a language problem between the German guards and the Polish prisoners. The prisoners didn't or wouldn't understand German, and there were too few Germans who spoke passable Polish. Either way, there were problems getting the Poles to follow directions. It would not be long before German guards would lose their tempers and start beating or shooting the prisoners.

It just so happened that Rachel was returning to the dining hall when the Polish prisoners were delivered. She could see that German tempers were flaring, and it wouldn't be long before punishments would be meted out. Rachel approached Sturmmann Mueller, who was observing the off-loading of the Polish prisoners. "Permission to speak, Sturmmann Mueller." Sturmmann Mueller turned to Rachel and nodded permission. "Sturmmann Mueller, I speak fluent Polish. Maybe I could help translate before things get out of hand."

Sturmmann Mueller looked at Rachel and said, "You may regret trying to help these prisoners. They are likely to consider you a collaborator and kill you if they can. These women are Polish resistance fighters. But if you are certain you want to do this, I can speak to the hauptaufseherin [head guard]." Rachel said she would like to try and help. Sturmmann Mueller spoke to the head guard, who stared at Rachel first with contempt on her face and then disbelief when Sturmmann Mueller told her that Rachel didn't speak very much German. She obviously was not pleased with this announcement. Yet there was a silver lining to this cloud; the head guard spoke French, so they had a common language.

Rachel went to the front of the crowd of Polish women and spoke into the microphone for the public address system, "Ciska! Stanac na bacznasc! Posluchaj mnmie!" (Silence! Stand at attention! And listen to me!) The women formed into a semblance of order and were quiet. Rachel looked to the head guard for instructions. The head guard gave orders to Rachel in French, which she translated into Polish. The women were to follow the usual in-processing routine of proceeding to the disinfection building, removing their clothing, having their hair shaved, showering, and receiving uniforms. Rachel would await them outside the shower building where they would receive instructions for barracks and work assignments. With only a little bit of grumbling, the Polish women moved to perform their assigned tasks.

Rachel started to walk to the end of the shower building when the head guard stopped her and asked where she was going. Rachel said she would await the women at the shower building as she had told them. The head guard smiled and told Rachel to return to her duties. Rachel turned to the head guard and said, "Et les femmes?" (And the women?).

The head guard said, "Ils sont partis maintenant." (They are gone now.)

Rachel could not believe what she had just heard. She had just spoken to over three hundred women; they could not be "gone."

The head guard was walking away, but over her shoulder, she said to Rachel, "Je te reverrai." (I'll see you again.)

Rachel stood on the siding, not knowing what to do, when one of the female guards hit her across the back with her cudgel and asked if she needed a place to be. Rachel bowed to the guard and headed back to the kitchen.

After evening meal, Rachel met up with Aunt Sylvia in their barracks building. After the usual "How was your day?" exchange, Rachel related her encounter with the Polish prisoners and their "disappearance." Aunt Sylvia slapped a hand over Rachel's mouth and hissed, "Don't ever repeat that story again." Because the head guard knew that Rachel had seen the Polish prisoners go into the showers and not come out, an annotation would be made in her records that might ensure her termination if they thought she might be a witness at a later date. A cold chill ran down Rachel's spine as she thought of the possible consequences. She asked Aunt Sylvia what she should do. Aunt Sylvia pondered the predicament for a while. She couldn't decide if it were better to try to avoid the head guard or to become more of an asset to her. Rachel felt that there would be more Polish prisoners coming, and therefore, her services as an interpreter would be more in demand, so avoiding the head guard would be impossible. Aunt Sylvia had to agree with that logic. So Rachel would have to make herself indispensable to the head guard. Rachel said she would rather be indispensable to Scharführer Kolbitz, as she much preferred working in the kitchen and singing in the officers' and sergeants' club than tricking Polish women into thinking they were going for a shower and never coming out alive.

Rachel asked Aunt Sylvia how her work with Herr Goldman was going. Aunt Sylvia replied that it was a subject that was better left alone. Aunt Sylvia looked around the barracks to make sure that no one was within earshot and told Rachel that they weren't fixing or building watches. Leave it at that.

Over the next two months, eleven more trainloads of Polish prisoners were delivered. Rachel was called upon to translate at the rail siding with the same welcome speech and instructions. The main difference was that these prisoners exited the shower building and were issued uniforms. It was quickly determined that Rachel could not spend her day translating for every group of Poles who entered the camp. Rachel had to seek out Polish prisoners who spoke German in order to lighten her workload. As the number of Polish prisoners increased, soon by the thousands, it became evident that the quantity and quality of the food rations decreased. It appeared that even though the population increased, the amount of food appropriated for the camp remained the same. The prisoners became very aware that their rations were growing smaller every day, yet the work details remained the same.

At the evening meal one day, a Polish prisoner, who wore the red triangle of a communist, raised a complaint about the size of the food ration. One of the *kapos* (prisoners appointed as a supervisor) told her to take her ration and move along or face punishment. The Polish prisoner said that she would continue to protest. The head guard approached and asked what was going on, and when the kapo explained that the prisoner was complaining about the reduced ration, the head guard spun the prisoner around, jammed her pistol in her mouth, and said, "Iss dass, du bolschewistiche Schlampe!" (Eat this, you Bolshevik bitch!). Then she pulled the trigger. There was immediate silence. The head guard turned around and looked at the other prisoners. She waved her pistol at them and asked if anyone else was unsatisfied with the food. There was already one extra ration for the evening, and she was willing to make more available. Not a word was uttered from the prisoners. The head guard pointed at two prisoners and said, "Nimm sie weg." (Take her away.) The head guard went on about her business, and the prisoners went about consuming their evening meal.

By June 1940, the camp was reaching the point of overcrowding, and another emergency building program was started. Prisoners were arriving from Norway, Denmark, Holland, Belgium, Luxemburg, and France. This was a result of Germany's conquests in those countries. Reports from women of those countries painted a very bleak picture of what the world was beginning to look like. Germany appeared to be taking over the whole of Europe. As more prisoners arrived, opinions flew like the leaves in fall. Some said that once the war was over and peace was negotiated, they would be returned to their homelands. Others said that they would remain in Germany as slave labor until they died. Still others, the most pessimistic, felt that because they did not fit the definition of the Aryan race, they would face the same punishment as they had seen the Jews face. They would be systematically eradicated. The majority being optimists didn't want to conform to that line of thought. Then there was a tiny group that thought of escape. Almost everyone thought that they were just insane. How would they escape, and where would they go? They had no clothes, they had no papers, and they had no money. Plus, they all looked like death warmed over. Once on the outside, they would stick out like a sore thumb. They might just as well jump on the electric fence. Still, hope was difficult to extinguish in the human psyche.

Eventually, there were enough German-speaking Poles available so that Rachel could return to her regular duties and be away from the head guard. It was quite clear that the ratio of foodstuffs to prisoners was not keeping pace. The rations continued to get thinner, and instances of prisoners dying of starvation and exhaustion were increasing. The prisoners devised a plan where if a prisoner died during the night, they would carry the body out for morning roll call so that the barracks would still receive the prisoner's ration. It didn't take the Germans long to figure this scheme out when two hundred were counted at roll call and only one hundred ninety-five showed up for work details and their bodies were discovered in the barracks. The kapos were instructed to physically touch each and every prisoner to ensure that they were alive before being counted. It didn't take long before rations were being taken from the weaker prisoners and fighting over food became commonplace. It was difficult to believe that a person would kill another human being for 150 grams (5 ounces) of bread, but it was occurring daily.

One Friday night, as Rachel was singing in the officers' club, she suddenly fainted. When she regained consciousness, she was in the camp hospital. A prisoner doctor and Scharführer Kolbitz were standing over her. The doctor was telling Scharführer Kolbitz that Rachel was suffering from malnutrition. Scharführer Kolbitz said that he would take care of that problem by transferring Rachel from the camp kitchen to the officers' club kitchen where he would ensure that she received better rations. After all, he couldn't afford to lose his star performer. The camp commandant had become quite a fan of Rachel's and would be disappointed if she were unable to sing.

After a day of rest and an extra ration of food, Rachel was able to report to the kitchen at the officers' club. She couldn't believe the varieties and amounts of food on hand. There were meats and fresh vegetables that the prisoners only dreamed about. There were cakes and other desserts, breads, and brotchen that made the mouth water just smelling them fresh from the ovens. Just the aromas made Rachel dizzy with hunger. She thought to herself, *How can so few people have so much food and so many people have so little food all in the confines of one camp?*

Rachel was introduced to the head chef of the officers' club. She would work directly for Chef Diehl. Her duties were to follow Chef Diehl and make notes of work that needed to be completed or supplies that needed to be ordered. Basically, she would be Chef Diehl's secretary. As part of her duties, she was required to dine with Chef Diehl, a duty she was happy to perform. By December 1940, Rachel was back to good health and had become quite popular at the officers' club.

A few months earlier, Scharführer Kolbitz called her into the club and took her backstage. He pointed to a door; it had Rachel's name on it. "Every star has to have a dressing room. This is yours." They entered the room, which was outfitted with a makeup table, including makeup. There was a *kleiderschrank* (armoire) full of evening gowns and shoes. Scharführer Kolbitz said he had Sturmmann Mueller arrange for the clothing and makeup as she was better suited for such a task. When Rachel asked where all the expensive clothing came from, Scharführer Kolbitz shrugged and said, "Gespendet." (Donated.) Rachel didn't want to consider who had "donated" the expensive clothing or how the donation was made. Scharführer Kolbitz went on to explain that Rachel was to change from her prison garb into one of the evening dresses before her performances at night. The dressing room even came with a private shower fully equipped with shampoo and linen.

Later that day, Sturmmann Mueller stopped by the officers' club kitchen to inform her that she would be moving from her present barracks to one that was located outside the main camp by the officers' club and administration buildings. This was being done to ensure that the officers would not be exposed to the diseases, which were prevalent among the prisoners inside the camp. This meant that she would be housed in the same barracks with Aunt Sylvia.

Rachel and Aunt Sylvia hadn't had a chance to talk in almost three months. They had seen each other when Rachel had been escorted to the officers' club and Aunt Sylvia was standing for evening head count but had been unable to talk. That first night, they had talked until long after lights out, whispering to each other in the darkness. Aunt Sylvia was very concerned about Rachel. "You look to be in great shape for a concentration camp inmate. People might get the wrong impression that you are collaborating with the Germans." Rachel explained how she got to be where she was and why. Aunt Sylvia told Rachel that she believed her but wouldn't blame her if she was collaborating with the Germans. After all, the US wasn't at war with Germany like the countries of all the other women, and she had to do what she had to do to survive this hellhole.

For a short time, Rachel was drafted to serve as an interpreter again when a large influx of French prisoners were delivered to the camp. The barracks spaces were not expanded. Winter was upon them, so the Germans just put more prisoners in each barracks. "The better to keep each other warm." From the French prisoners, they found out the French and British Armies had been defeated and France had signed an armistice with Germany. When the French women were moved from their prisons in France, all male prisoners were being relocated to the coast of France to begin construction of massive beach defenses all along the French coast. Germany intended to build up the coastline in preparation for their invasion of England. Already large Luftwaffe contingents were being staged at former French airfields, and the construction of new airfields were progressing at a fever pace. It was quite apparent that Germany intended on keeping its conquered lands and expanding. Hitler still needed Lebensraum for Germany's people.

For Aunt Sylvia and Rachel, life was not overly severe compared to the poor souls in the main camp. It was determined by the camp administration that the female prisoners would simply be worked to death instead of wasting bullets executing them. The meager rations, about four hundred calories per day, were barely enough to keep a small dog alive, let alone an adult woman doing hard labor. Rachel and Aunt Sylvia were both warned to keep their distance from the other prisoners. This went for the other prisoners in the "special" barracks. The warning was twofold, to prevent the spread of disease and possible retribution for them receiving preferential treatment. The head guard was instructed not to use Rachel for any translating duties.

December 1940 gave way to spring of 1941. Beginning in May of 1941, a new crop of prisoners began arriving. The new prisoners were Croats, Serbians, and Yugoslavians. It was soon discovered that they had to be kept apart as they hated one another almost more than they hated the Germans. With the arrival of these prisoners, Germany was widening its reach throughout Europe and increasing the strain on the limited resources of the camp even further.

Chapter 20

Walking punishment rounds during a cold December night in New York was not the average cadet's idea of entertainment, but for every circuit a cadet walked around the quad reduced his demerit count by one. Sidney didn't have many demerits, but he didn't really have anything else to do this evening, and the fewer demerits one had, the higher one's class standing. Sidney was aiming to graduate in the top 5 percent of his class, which would almost guarantee his choice of assignment upon graduation. In five more months, his plebe year would be over, and as an upperclassman, he would no longer be the lowest thing on the food chain.

He looked forward to the four-week summer training class that would be conducted with the Regular Army. The cadets would get the opportunity to integrate with an active-duty army unit actually performing the same training as the "real" army. Sidney was hoping the rumors were true and they would train with armored forces. Sidney was keen on becoming a cavalry officer even more than an infantry officer. This training wouldn't occur until they returned from their summer break, a two-week furlough in June. He intended to spend his two weeks with his Uncle Saul and Aunt Miriam in New York City. If he made the trip back to Kansas, he would spend one whole week just traveling.

The end of the plebe year finally arrived. There were quite a few cadets who had practically worn out a pair of shoes walking punishment tours. The cadets in the bottom 5 percent of the class would not be going on leave. Those who were in the bottom of class for academics would take remedial classes. Those who had too many demerits for other infractions would remain and do various punishment details in addition to marching the quadrangle. Sidney was ranked number 2 in his class. The cadet ranked number 1 was ahead by 5.6 points. Sidney would try harder next semester.

Sidney's two weeks in New York City were enjoyable but went by far too quickly. He helped out in the deli and ran errands and made deliveries for Aunt Miriam. His aunt and uncle did not want him to work; they thought he deserved time to socialize and relax, but Sidney insisted on helping out. Sidney refused any money when Uncle Saul tried to pay him for his work. He told Uncle Saul he had nowhere to spend the money and the Army provided everything he needed. He kissed each of them goodbye and headed for the subway to Grand Central Station and the "milk train" back to West Point.

Sidney arrived back to school on Sunday, June 22. He was passing through the cadet recreation room, and a group of cadets was listening to the radio quite intently. "What's the news?" Sidney asked.

One of the cadets turned and said, "Hitler just invaded the Soviet Union."

Sidney just shook his head and said, "That man is totally insane. To attack Russia this late in the year is a grave mistake. Winter will be upon them soon, and nobody beats the Russian winter."

Another cadet turned to Sidney and sarcastically said, "Well, thank you, General Klein. I'm sure the German general staff would've appreciated your assessment prior to launching their attack." Everyone laughed, and Sidney continued on his way.

After the July 4 holiday, the second classmen were notified that they would be participating in the Louisiana Maneuvers for their summer training exercise. This would add an additional week to the training schedule because of travel time. It also appeared that Sidney was going to get his wish for training with an armored unit. His section of the class was being attached to the Second Armored Division. The class was divided into four sections of 118 cadets each. The four sections were attached to one of the approximately nineteen divisions used during the exercise. Within the units, the cadets would be paired with a platoon leader and follow him throughout the exercise.

On September 5, the 472 cadets of the class of '44 boarded the train for Louisiana. Two days later, they arrived at Fort Polk. They received their initial briefings and were given over to the platoon leaders they were to train with. Sidney's section was taken to the command post for the Second Armored Division, where they were briefed by the division operations officer and received a greeting from the division commander, Major General George S. Patton. General Patton promised them that they would see how armored warfare should be conducted. It would be quick, violent, and stunning for the enemy. This division had three objectives: attack, attack, and attack. With that, the cadets were released to their platoon leaders. Sidney was surprised to discover that the platoon he was attached to actually had tanks. Only one platoon per company had tanks; the other platoons used trucks to simulate tanks. The reasoning was that by using simulated tanks, they wouldn't damage the Army's short supply of tanks and they wouldn't tear up road surfaces with tank treads.

Training with armored forces was an eye-opening experience. The combined arms tactics being taught at the academy were nothing like what Patton was teaching his units in the field. The units kept moving forward all the time. The opposing force was never given a chance to reconsolidate and prepare to repel the next attack because the attacks were constant. When an attacking unit needed relief, the unit just allowed the following unit to pass through their lines and continue the assault. It was very demoralizing for the defending forces. General Patton was a tough commander and pushed himself as hard as he pushed his commanders. By the end of phase 1 of the exercise, 40 percent of the tanks were down for repairs. Of those, 10 percent would need complete overhauls of their drive train components. The commander of the First Armored Corps wasn't happy with the status of his Second Armored Division at the end of phase 1, but he couldn't complain about the success achieved. The briefing after the end of the exercise indicated that the aggressive tactics by the Second Armored Division was the leading cause of the Red

Force success during the exercise. The vehicles weren't the only tired components after the exercise. The cadets slept almost the entire way back to New York.

Sidney thought, *I guess it's true what they say. War is hell, even when it's just an exercise.*

After Thanksgiving and of course the Army-Navy Game, which the Midshipmen won, 14–6, their third straight win, there were the Christmas holidays to look forward to. Sidney's parents were coming out to New York so they could visit over Christmas. They all planned to go into the city and visit Uncle Saul and Aunt Miriam and catch a show at Radio City Music Hall. They would be arriving on the eighteenth of December, and the cadets would be released on the nineteenth.

It was just after 1530 eastern time, December 7 when the first radio reports started coming in of the Japanese attack on Pearl Harbor. The news was just unbelievable. All the cadets were gathered around radios to listen. A few seniors actually owned shortwave radios and were receiving international broadcasts that indicated that the Commonwealth of the Philippines was also under attack. By later on in the evening, it became clear that the surprise attack had caused a great deal of damage to the US Pacific Fleet as well as numerous shore facilities and Army Air Corps installations. Commercial radio stations attempted to contact affiliates in Honolulu and Manila, to no avail. This meant the United States was at war with Japan. Would Germany be far behind? The president scheduled an address to the Congress in the morning, no doubt to ask for a declaration of war. The next day, December 8, 1941, President Roosevelt delivered his Day of Infamy speech to a joint session of Congress. An hour later, Congress voted to enact a declaration of war against the Empire of Japan.

The commandant of cadets addressed the corps at the evening formation. He notified the cadets that on January 20, 1942, the class of 1943 would be graduated early in response to the state of war presently in effect. Many cadets were so eager to serve that they were considering resigning from the academy and enlisting in the Army immediately.

On Thursday, December 11, Adolf Hitler declared war on the United States in support of his ally, Japan. Once Germany was in the war with the US, Sidney was strongly contemplating a similar decision. The cadets of the class of 1943 were given leave immediately and instructed to return no later than January 5, 1942, for graduation and acceptance of a commission in the United States Army.

Sidney met his parents at the Thayer Hotel on the nineteenth of December. Sidney was actually surprised that his father made the trip, considering the circumstances. They met for dinner in the main dining room where at first conversation centered on school and academic standings. Eventually, the elephant in the room became the center of conversation. Sidney's father was looking forward to a combat command somewhere. He would never achieve flag rank (general officer) without a combat assignment. Sidney told his parents of the accelerated graduation schedule. Sidney's father agreed that the Army was going to need officers to lead the multitude of divisions that would be mustered to prosecute a world war being fought on both sides of the country. He had heard talk that certain congressmen were in favor of the abolishment of the military academies and converting them into Officer Candidate Schools that would graduate a class of second lieutenants every ninety days. Sidney's father hoped that there were enough alumni in high places to prevent that from happening. Sidney told his parents that with his present class standing, his intention was to request assignment to the Second Armored Division, which was sure to go to Europe. He was still intent on finding and rescuing Rachel. Sidney's parents gave each other a look that indicated that they didn't hold out much hope for Sidney finding Rachel. After three years of captivity in a German concentration camp, they didn't think that Rachel could have survived this long. They had heard some of the stories of treatment of Jews in the camps, and it was not good. They decided that they would not tell Sidney what they had heard.

The next day, they took the train into the city to meet up with Uncle Saul and Aunt Miriam. The plan was to tour Times Square and take in a show at Radio City Music Hall. On the way to Times Square, they passed by an Armed Forces recruiting station. Sidney was impressed by the number of young men who were lined up waiting to enlist. As he passed by, he was bombarded with questions by the men standing in line. What was military life like? How long had he been in the Army? When would they be able to fight the Japs? Sidney explained to them that he was a cadet at West Point, and they might be fighting the Japs or the Germans before he did. Once they found out he was going to be an officer, they lost interest in him.

Sidney and his parents continued down Times Square to meet with Uncle Saul and Aunt Miriam. They decided to grab a bite to eat before they went to the show, so Uncle Saul recommended a restaurant near the music hall. Uncle Saul said it was probably the best German restaurant in the city. He highly recommended their sauerbraten and either the knödel or spaetzle. When Sidney heard those menu items, his mouth began to water in anticipation.

As they approached the restaurant, they noticed a group of young men dressed as Brownshirts with Swastika armbands. When Sidney's party went to enter the restaurant, one of the men approached them and said, "You don't want to patronize this establishment. I would recommend you go somewhere else."

Sidney's father looked down at the young man and asked, "Why wouldn't we want to patronize this establishment?"

The leader of the group leaned in to Sidney's father and said, "It's owned by Jews."

Sidney's father turned and looked at the rest of the party and said, "Jews!" Then he looked back to the leader and said, "That's all right with us. We're Jews too."

They started past the Nazis when the leader said, "That can't be true." Pointing at Sidney, he said, "He's a cadet at West Point. They don't allow Jews in there."

Sidney's father just looked at the leader and said, "One of the reasons my son is there is because I graduated from West Point. Now step away from the door. This is still America and not Nazi Germany!"

Just as the confrontation looked as though it would get violent, one of New York's finest, a very large, very Irish police officer rounded the corner. He looked at the group of Nazis and said, "Aye,

I think it best if your sort moved along before I'm forced to cite you all for littering."

The leader of the Nazis responded by saying that they had a right to free speech. The police officer told them the other people had the right to choose the restaurant of their choice. The officer then went nose to nose with the Nazi leader and said to him, "How dare you bring up rights under the Constitution of the United States while trying to deprive those same rights from another citizen. Now move along before I run you all in for creating a nuisance."

The Nazis moved away from the restaurant. The police officer turned to the Klein's and said, "Me cousin fell at Dunkirk, so I have no love for their like, but I do enforce the law. Please enjoy your evening."

Jacob Klein thanked the police officer, and the family entered the restaurant.

Uncle Saul knew the owner of the restaurant and asked him if the incident that just happened was a common occurrence. Mr. Rabin, the owner, said that it was becoming more common since Germany's declaration of war against the United States. But the police were patrolling more often, and there were more and more young men in suits observing the "Nazis." It was said that the "young men" were FBI agents.

The Kleins enjoyed the sauerbraten as recommended by Uncle Saul and proceeded to Radio City Music Hall for the show. There was a dark-haired female soloist singer that reminded Sidney of Rachel and caused him to wonder how she had spent her Hanukkah. Then he thought, *What a stupid idea. The Nazis would hardly allow the Jews to celebrate their holidays.* After the show, the family went to Rockefeller Center to see the official New York City Christmas Tree. A tradition since 1931, it was always a must-see attraction when in New York. The Kleins stopped at a street-side café for coffee and cake before heading home for the night.

A last cognac found the three men alone in the parlor. Uncle Saul was disturbed over the encounter with the "Nazis" outside the restaurant. "Do you think that things are that bad in Germany?"

Jacob looked at his brother and said, "I have it on good authority that what we experienced tonight is nothing like what life is like not only in Germany but also in the vast majority of Europe. In fact, if German police had arrived on the scene, they would either have allowed the Nazis to assault us or would have arrested us."

Uncle Saul just shook his head and said, "It's hard to believe that a nation that has produced such brilliant minds as Schiller and Mozart could also produce Hitler and Himmler."

Sidney reminded his uncle that Hitler was actually Austrian. Uncle Saul asked them what the future held for them in the Army. Sidney said he would graduate early and go on to Fort Benning for infantry training. Jacob said he would soon be receiving orders for, he hoped, a combat command assignment, preferably command of an infantry brigade. He preferred an assignment to Europe, but the Army didn't know yet which way the military was going to go. It seemed more logical to go against Japan first as they had attacked them, but there was talk that Roosevelt had made promises to Churchill to back England first. Sidney made it very clear that his intentions were to get into liberating Europe as fast as possible. His father understood his desire to "rescue" Rachel, but it would be years before the United States and its allies were anywhere near ready to launch a campaign against the coast of Europe. In the meantime, Germany would be actively engaged in erecting fortifications against such a campaign while simultaneously mounting attacks against England with the intent of invading and occupying that island, thereby preventing any hope of liberating Europe.

After the Christmas and New Year holidays, there was a great deal of activity. West Point had never graduated a class in January, so many of the traditional ceremonies had to be revamped. The weather forecast for graduation day promised unusually cold temperatures and snow. The ceremonies would be moved indoors, and instead of the entire Corps of Cadets passing in review, as was the normal practice, only the graduating class would perform this ceremony. Additionally, because of the size of the auditorium, only a representation of the Corps of Cadets would attend graduation to allow for invited family and friends of the graduating class to attend.

Upon the departure of the senior class, the remaining cadets settled back into their normal routines. Sidney's class knew that their class was to be shortened by one year so that this time next year, they would have less than six months before graduation. There was a noticeable increase in field training. Land navigation, tactics, logistical training, and radio communications were stressed. It was during their radio class that Sidney got the opportunity to operate a radio again. It was during a break-in training that Sidney received permission from the instructor, a regular army technical sergeant, to change the frequency on one of the radio sets. He tuned to the frequency that he and Z had frequently used, and to his surprise, he recognized Z's hand. He said to the technical sergeant, "I wish I had a key set. I know who this operator is!"

The sergeant said to Sidney, "You can send and receive?"

Sidney nodded and replied, "I even have a valid license."

"Hold on a second." The sergeant reached into a desk drawer and removed a key set, handing it to Sidney. He said, "I like to keep my hand in between classes."

Sidney hooked up the key set and started tapping away. Soon, he was receiving a reply. Sidney had sent his call sign, and Z had replied back, wanting Sidney to prove who he was. He wanted to know what their last conversation had been. Sidney sent back "BBC news." It seemed to assure Z of Sidney's credentials. They exchanged niceties and news tidbits, but Z still seemed to be more reserved than he had been. Z said that communications were being monitored more than ever before. There was a great amount of concern that enemy agents throughout the Reich were reporting sensitive intelligence to England and the United States. Z knew of several operators who were no longer on the air and were supposedly arrested by the SD. No one knew of their current whereabouts or condition. Z asked what Sidney was doing these days, and Sidney simply replied that he was in "college." They both agreed that they would try to keep in touch, but Sidney didn't place much hope in that sentiment. They both signed off.

The technical sergeant told Sidney he was impressed with his speed on the key set, although he couldn't say if Sidney was accurate because he couldn't pick up a word. Sidney told him that his friend was in Germany, and so they conversed in German. The sergeant told Sidney that Army Counterintelligence would love to have a conversation with him. Sidney just laughed and said, "Thanks, but my career goals are pointed to the infantry."

The sergeant said, "So, so." The cadets returned from their break, and class resumed.

Several weeks after the radio class, Sidney was summoned to the office of the cadet adviser where he was shown into an office and told to wait. A gentleman in civilian clothes entered the office and introduced himself as a lieutenant commander in the United States Navy. He was extremely interested in Sidney's linguistic capabilities. He proceeded to conduct a conversation in German. After about fifteen minutes, he seamlessly switched to Polish and then to Russian. Going back to English, he remarked, "Your language skills are quite impressive. You speak each language like a native, including a recognizable dialect for each language. You didn't learn these languages in school, did you?"

"No sir," Sidney replied. "I learned them from maternal and paternal grandparents."

Lieutenant Commander Wallace explained to Sidney that he represented an organization within the Joint Chiefs of Staff that was tasked with intelligence gathering. Sidney's language and radio skills would be a great asset to this organization known as the Office of Strategic Services or OSS. Lieutenant Commander Wallace went on to explain that the OSS was a joint service that accumulated intelligence gathering efforts from all branches of the military and analyzed the intelligence for dissemination to the joint chiefs and president of the United States. Assignments to the OSS were strictly voluntary, and after OSS training, he would be assigned to one of the European detachments. Sidney asked how soon he would be sent to Europe and, more importantly, to Germany. Lieutenant Commander Wallace couldn't say exactly when that could happen, but he did hint that the OSS might have agents actively engaged in intelligence gathering missions right now.

Sidney thought for a moment then asked, "If I were to be captured wearing civilian clothing, wouldn't I be considered a spy and therefore not afforded the rights under the Geneva Convention regarding prisoners of war?"

Lieutenant Commander Wallace looked Sidney in the eyes and said, "If your question is if you would be shot as a spy, the answer is not only yes, but you would more than likely be harshly interrogated prior to being shot. Does that answer your question?"

Sidney replied, "Yes, sir, it does. I guess that's the reason for voluntary assignments." Sidney thought for a while and then asked Lieutenant Commander Wallace when he would have to provide his decision. This was, after all, a very important career decision.

Lieutenant Commander Wallace said he would need to have Sidney's decision no later than six months prior to graduation. It would require six months to perform all the necessary background checks in order to obtain a top secret security clearance. This gave Sidney almost a year to make up his mind. Plenty of time for Sidney to decide if he would remain an army officer or become a spy.

Chapter 21

On the third of April 1941, Klaus was ordered to prepare his platoon once again for embarkation onto railcars. Their destination was Yugoslavia and then Greece. The invasion of Yugoslavia commenced on the sixth of April with the usual aerial bombardment, followed by armored units attacking on several fronts. The Second SS Panzer Division was routed through Bulgaria, where it pushed through the southern tip of Yugoslavia on its way to Greece. The attack through Yugoslavia was slowed by destroyed roadways, mines, and mud. Still, the division achieved its assigned objective.

The next day, Klaus's platoon was the advance scouts for the division. They encountered resistance from Yugoslavian units, which were easily repelled. It appeared that the Yugoslavian Army was ill-equipped and poorly trained. Klaus's platoon came through the action with only minor casualties. The most severe wound was to an assistant machine gunner who tried to change a hot barrel without his asbestos glove and severely burned his left hand. Oberschutze Groenig treated the soldier and reported to Klaus that the man would be restricted to duties as ammo bearer for two weeks until the blisters healed. He would check on him daily to ensure the wound did not become infected.

Klaus met with Scharführer Lindermann to go over the platoon's performance during the latest engagement. Scharführer Lindermann said that aside from the overzealous assistant gunner burning his hand, the platoon had acquitted itself quite well. They then discussed their orders for the next day, which was to press on into Greece. The next few days would be difficult and dangerous as they had to traverse the mountains that formed a natural barrier along the Greek border. They would be supporting a company from the Fifth Mountain Division. A platoon of Mark IV panzers would accompany them as mobile artillery. It had been reported that the Greek Army had very few modern tanks, much like the Yugoslavian Army.

Crossing over the mountains had been difficult. The Greeks had constructed a series of pillboxes along the roadway along with many land mines. The usual practice for defeating the pillboxes was just as they had trained at Bad Tölz. Machine gun and rifle fire suppressed fire from the pillbox while an assault team flanked the pillbox, and hand grenades or other demolition charges were tossed into the firing port. Once the pillbox was silenced, it was on to the next one. Fortunately, the terrain did not often allow for interlocking fields of fire to support the pillboxes. When the terrain did allow for support fire, taking out a pillbox became even more dangerous. It was during one such assault that Klaus's First Platoon incurred its heaviest casualties so far.

It was Scharführer Lindermann's turn to lead the assault teams. As the First Squad took up its position to engage the pillbox, Scharführer Lindermann was bringing up the Second Squad to provide support. The Second Squad was almost in position when a second machine gun opened fire, catching the Second Squad in the open. Unterscharführer Fisch (Second Squad leader), two riflemen, and Scharführer Lindermann were cut down before they could reach cover. Now the First Squad had to divide its base of fire between the two enemy machine guns. The remaining seven members of the Second Squad were pinned down, unable to retreat or set up their machine gun and provide suppressing fire. The Greek machine guns were firing more rounds into the downed members of the Second Squad and Scharführer Lindermann even though they were obviously dead. Klaus brought the Third Squad over the embankment where the firefight was taking place, which allowed them to outflank the second machine gun, which was not in a bunker. Two well-placed hand grenades destroyed the gun position, and then the Third Squad took the pillbox under fire until the First Squad eliminated the pillbox.

As soon as firing ceased, Oberschutze Groenig was tending to the casualties. It was as they had feared—all four men were dead. Oberschutze Groenig did the only thing he could do for them. He removed the lower half of their identity disk and any personal belongings they had on them. He then removed their blanket from their field pack and, with the help from squad members, wrapped the bodies. Because the mountain roadways were so narrow, they could not transport the bodies to the rear for proper disposition. They would have to move the bodies to the side of the road and wait until the end of their column passed them and a smaller vehicle could be dispatched to collect the dead for removal to the rear. Oberschutze Groenig brought the items removed from the dead to Klaus. He would need the items to prepare his report up the chain of command and to write the notification letters. It would be several days before Klaus got the opportunity to write those letters. The First Platoon was pulled off point security and sent back to the Third Company area.

Klaus went to the company headquarters area to ensure that the bodies and their belongings had been taken care of. Klaus gave the company clerk the four letters he had written and asked if replacement requests had been submitted. The clerk assured him that the requests had been sent up the chain of command, but there was no indication of when they would be acted on. Klaus asked if the company commander was available and was told that he was at battalion headquarters but was due back in about an hour. Klaus thanked the clerk and said he would come back later.

Klaus returned an hour later and reported to Hauptsturmführer Becker. They discussed the overall state of Klaus's platoon and their combat readiness. Klaus reminded his commander that he was now short a platoon sergeant and three men out of a ten-man squad, one of which was the squad leader. This made the squad combat ineffective, and he would have to temporarily attach them to the platoon's command element. Hauptsturmführer Becker said that the First Platoon would be pulled back into the company reserve until replacements could be brought up. In the middle of May 1941, the entire division was ordered to Vienna for replacements and equipment refit. The division would be moved by ship from Greece to Italy and then by train to Vienna. On May 21, during the sealift to Italy, two transport ships with the bulk of the division's tracked vehicles were sunk by a British submarine. The loss would render the division combat ineffective for several months.

Klaus's platoon was assigned their barracks within the kaserne in Vienna. The next few weeks would have the men employed in weapons maintenance and replenishment of equipment. As their Sd. Kfz. 7s were at the bottom of the sea, it would be several weeks, if not months, before they saw replacements. Everyone was concerned that the division might be converted into an infantry division because they had lost their panzers and tracked vehicles. Klaus felt that the idea made perfect sense and couldn't offer any reassurances to his men that it would not happen. But contrary to rumor, new Sd. Kfz. 7s began arriving by train on the seventh of July. Klaus's platoon was instructed to go to the railhead and take possession of four brandnew vehicles. Aboard the same train was the first shipment of the division's replacement PzKw 4 tanks. The Sd. Kfz. 7s were taken to the battalion motor pool area, and the appropriate unit markings were stenciled onto the vehicles. Each squad sent a detail to battalion supply to collect the necessary equipment to make the vehicles combat-ready. This equipment was such items as shovels, picks, axes, tow cables, and water and gasoline canisters. The vehicles came from the factory with spare tracks, hydraulic jack, and fire extinguishers. Klaus inspected the vehicles and found them to be combat-ready.

Word reached the platoon that the replacement soldiers were waiting at the company headquarters. Unterscharführer Gross, as acting platoon sergeant, was dispatched to bring the new men to the platoon area. Klaus would have gone but was involved with signing requisitions and various other reports. Klaus was elbow deep in paperwork when Unterscharführer Gross knocked on his office door and announced, "Untersturmführer Bergman, our replacements are here."

Without looking up, Klaus replied, "Show them in, Unterscharführer."

Klaus heard boots on the floor as the men came to attention; he looked up just in time to see the ranking sergeant announce, "Oberscharführer [Sergeant First Class] Martin Winter with three replacements reporting as ordered, Herr Untersturmführer!"

Klaus could hardly believe his eyes—Scharführer, now Oberscharführer Winter from Bad Tölz! This was indeed quite a surprise. Each man, in turn, introduced himself and presented a copy of their orders assigning them to the First Platoon. Klaus welcomed them to the platoon and then summoned Unterscharführer Gross back into the office and instructed him to take Unterscharführer Steiner and the other two replacements to Sturmmann Boehmer, who ws acting squad leader of the Second Squad.

After the other men had left, Klaus came from behind his desk to warmly shake Oberscharführer Winter's hand. They spent about an hour catching up. Klaus related the combat actions the platoon had engaged in, especially the action that had resulted in the need for replacements. Klaus asked Oberscharführer Winter how he managed to get reassigned to his platoon.

He said, "I kept harassing the school staff until they finally got tired of me. The division has recently been sent to Vienna for refit, and I have an old friend who works at division personnel. It just so happens that the Third Company, First Battalion of the Fortieth Panzer Grenadier Regiment has a requirement for a platoon sergeant, and so here I am. Besides, I told you when you left the academy, 'Till we meet again.'"

Klaus said he didn't care what magic Oberscharführer Winter had used to get here; he was damned glad to see him. Winter asked Klaus what kind of shape the platoon was in. Klaus said that for the exception of the three new replacements, the entire unit was tested combat veterans; some had been in the platoon since Poland and the rest since France.

They continued their conversations well into the evening. They established the platoon's training schedule and discussed the possibility of leave time. Klaus said they would have to go over the platoon records with the company clerk and establish a merit roster for leave. Klaus was sure that some soldiers in his platoon hadn't received any time off since France, and he knew no leaves had been granted in the fourteen months he had been platoon leader.

On June 10, a company formation was called. Klaus and two other platoon members were called to the front of the formation and were presented with the *Eiserne Kreuz 2 Klasse* (Iron Cross Second Class) along with the *Infanterie-Sturmabzeichen* (Infantry Assault Badge). The soldiers killed in Greece all received the *Verwundetenabzeichen* (Wound Badge) posthumously.

June 22, 1941. A battalion formation was called to announce the invasion of the Soviet Union. Training tempo was doubled. As the division had yet to receive its full complement of Mark IV panzers, they would not be deployed to the Eastern Front yet. The Fortieth Panzer Grenadier Regiment was up to full strength with personnel and equipment. All training goals had been met and combat drills successfully completed. Division headquarters had decided that the regiment might release 20 percent of its personnel over a ten-day period. Every ten days, a different contingent of the regiment would be granted leave until the entire regiment had received a ten-day leave or the regiment was ordered to move out. Klaus's name was on the first list and quickly packed a light bag. Oberscharführer Winter was left in charge, and Klaus told him how to reach him. Winter threw Klaus's bag in the Kübelwagen and drove him to the train depot. Klaus had a Category II train ticket, which was fairly high priority and allowed him to get on the first train leaving Vienna for Berlin. With luck, he should be in Berlin tomorrow afternoon.

Frau Bergman answered the doorbell to find her son standing before her. She was overcome with joy to see her son again. She ushered him into the kitchen and began to prepare coffee. She asked Klaus if he would go down the street to the *backerei* (bakery) and pick out some sweet rolls for their coffee. When Klaus left, she went to the telephone and called her husband to pass the good news that Klaus was home. Standartenführer (Colonel) Bergman told his wife that he would get home just as soon as he could. Standartenführer Bergman was now on the staff at *Oberkommando der Wehrmacht* (OKW, High

Command of the German Forces) located in Wünsdorf, about an hour south of Berlin. He had been hoping for a combat command, but his abilities as a logistician were greatly appreciated at the headquarters and appeared as though he would be there for the foreseeable future. He was truly looking forward to seeing his son again. Now that he was a combat veteran, he was eager to hear how much the art of war had changed from his war of 1918 and today's modern warfare.

Klaus's father was able to make it home before dinner, which gave Klaus and his father time to have a glass of sherry before dinner. Secretly, Klaus would have preferred a cold Pilsner, but his father favored sherry on such occasions. He immediately took notice of Klaus's Iron Cross and Infantry Assault Badge and congratulated his son on his success in combat. He asked Klaus about the actions he had been involved in, the tactics used, and because he was the chief logistician of the Wehrmacht, how the supply chain was functioning. At first, Klaus was going to just glaze over the combat and relate the actions in general terms, but then he realized that his father needed to hear the whole story. His father was going to experience modern combat through his son because he might never see it himself. To that end, Klaus told the stories as if they were an after-action report that would be provided to higher headquarters. The engagement that resulted in the deaths of Scharführer Lindermann, Unterscharführer Fisch, and the two rifleman of Second Squad he described in such detail that afterward, his father said he felt as if he could hear the machine gun fire and grenades exploding. He wholeheartedly agreed that Klaus was indeed deserving of his Iron Cross.

Klaus went on to tell how Oberschutze Groenig collected the identity disks and personal belongings of the men killed and how he had laid these things on his desk as he wrote the condolence letters to their families, gazing at photographs of wives, children, and parents that these men had left behind. Klaus suddenly realized that his father had tears in his eyes, something he hadn't seen since his grandmother died. They just stood there and looked at each other in silence. Klaus's mother announced that dinner was ready. Klaus's father nodded. They finish their sherry and went in to dinner.

Upon Klaus's return to the platoon, Oberscharführer Winter reported that they had received large amounts of rations, ammunition, and spare parts. Oberscharführer Winter said to Klaus, "Herr Obersturmführer, something is afoot."

Klaus looked at Winter and replied, "Quite. The first thing is, you seem to have forgotten my correct rank, Oberscharführer."

"No, sir. You are simply unaware of your promotion. If the Obersturmführer had not been out sightseeing in Berlin, he would have been present for his promotion."

"Oberscharführer Winter, have you been drinking on duty?"

"No, Obersturmführer. Your promotion orders and new insignia of rank are on your desk. You are to report to Hauptsturmführer Becker in order to make it official. And may I be the first to congratulate you. Oh yes, Herr Obersturmführer, you did mention drinking. I believe it is customary that new insignia of rank be 'wet down.'"

Klaus looked at Oberscharführer Winter and instructed him to assemble the platoon in the enlisted men's canteen after duty hours. Oberscharführer Winter snapped to attention, saluted, and barked, "Zum Befehl, Herr Obersturmführer!" (At your orders, Lieutenant!)

At the company headquarters, Hauptsturmführer Becker officially promoted Klaus as obersturmführer. They toasted his promotion with a glass of Steinhäger. Hauptsturmführer Becker told Klaus that with his promotion, he would normally move him up to company executive officer, but with his combat experience with the First Platoon, he would prefer to leave Klaus there. Klaus could request that he be moved up. Klaus said that he agreed with Hauptsturmführer Becker and would prefer to remain with the First Platoon. With that decided, Hauptsturmführer Becker told Klaus that he had summoned the other platoon leaders for a meeting at the battalion headquarters. He presumed that this would have to do with the division's upcoming deployment to the Eastern Front. Klaus made a mental note to have Oberscharführer Winter start requisitioning, scrounging, or stealing winter clothing and other supplies. He had read that the Russian winters could be brutal, and although he knew the Wehrmacht had an excellent officer in charge of the supply system, his father, he never liked leaving such things to chance.

Klaus received several phone calls from supply channels wanting to know why he was requisitioning winter uniforms, sleeping bags, and overboots in the middle of July. Klaus simply asked if he was or wasn't authorized to request such items. He was told that he was authorized to order them; it just seemed strange to the supply personnel to be ordering winter equipment in the middle of summer. Klaus told the supply officer to just please process the request.

By the end of July 1941, the Second SS Panzer Division had completed refit and training. Klaus, and everyone else, knew that they would soon be posted to the Eastern Front. News of the fighting in Russia was very encouraging. The German assault was advancing rapidly with little to no resistance. The division was placed on alert for shipment to Army Group Central, and the process of loading railcars began again. Once loaded, the first of many trains left the Vienna Hauptbahnhof, headed to Russia via Czechoslovakia and Poland, arriving in Minsk, normally a trip of around thirty hours. The trip would be about twenty-four hours longer because of switching all the vehicles from German freight cars to Russian freight cars at the border. This was required because the German and Russian rail systems were of different gauges. The Russian railroad tracks were narrower than the German tracks. Once the vehicles were transferred to the Russian freight cars, a process of about twenty-four hours, the train continued on to Minsk. Upon arriving in Minsk, the First Platoon detrained and took up position along the main road toward Smolensk. The immediate objective of the division was to take and hold the heights of the town of Yelnya, which were considered strategically important for operations against Moscow. By the first week of August, German forces had captured Yelnya. A defensive perimeter was established, and reconnaissance patrols were sent out to probe for enemy activity.

Klaus met with the First Platoon to brief them on tonight's patrol. Klaus would be taking Unterscharführer Iselborn and his Fourth Squad. He showed their position on the map and described where the patrol would be maneuvering. Their objective was to determine where Russian positions were and if they could establish unit designation and unit size. The patrol would be departing at 0200.

After the evening meal, he would perform an equipment check, and then they should all get some rest. They would meet at the north machine gun position at 0145.

After Klaus dismissed the platoon, Oberscharführer Winter approached and asked which squad he wanted on alert in case they ran into trouble. Klaus thought for a moment then said, "Unterscharführer Steiner and his Second Squad."

Oberscharführer Winter nodded, looked at Klaus, and said "Viel Gluck heute nacht." (Good luck tonight.)

At 0145, the patrol assembled at the north machine gun position. Klaus checked the men one more time and asked if they had any questions. With no questions, Klaus led the patrol through an opening in the barbed wire and headed in the direction of the suspected Russian positions. It was a very warm, moonless night. Off in the distance, Klaus could see what appeared to be either artillery fire or lightning. After a minute, he determined that someone was on the receiving end of a major artillery barrage. They were approaching an old farm building that should be about two hundred meters from their line. The building had already been registered as an artillery reference point. If Klaus had to call for artillery support, he would give range and direction from this reference point instead of having to pull out his map and provide map coordinates to where he wanted the artillery rounds dropped. There were several more reference points that were already plotted for the regiment's artillery batteries, which allowed for quick fire support.

At five hundred meters out, there was a small grove of trees. Klaus stopped the squad there for a short break and to quietly observe their surroundings. About one hundred fifty meters further, there was another grove of trees. Suddenly, Unterscharführer Iselborn whispered, "I smell cigarette smoke, that cheap Russian tobacco. You know, sir, the stuff that smells like cow shit." Klaus nodded in agreement. He motioned for Unterscharführer Iselborn to gather the squad together. Klaus pointed at the two fire team leaders and then told Unterscharführer Iselborn to set the machine gun here. He and the two fire team leaders would infiltrate the Russian position to see what kind of intelligence they could gather.

Klaus instructed the two fire team leaders to leave all their gear except for their MP-40s, two thirty-round magazines, and their trench knives. Klaus and the two men began low-crawling toward the Russian position. The remainder of the squad found cover within the trees and waited. After twenty minutes, Unterscharführer Iselborn thought he heard something from the other grove of trees. It was so dark that they couldn't make out any movement from the other side. Another thirty minutes passed when he heard and sensed movement to his front. He raised his MP-40 and issued the agreed upon challenge and received the appropriate password. Obersturmführer Bergman crawled into their position. Klaus was covered in blood. Before Unterscharführer Iselborn could reach for his first aid pouch, Klaus stopped him and said, "Not my blood." The two fire team leaders crawled in next, dragging someone between them. Trussed up like a pig was a Russian soldier. Klaus looked at Unterscharführer Iselborn and told him to get the squad moving back to the German lines before their prisoner regained consciousness and began raising hell.

Klaus and the Fourth Squad were at the Third Company headquarters being debriefed by Hauptsturmführer Becker and the battalion intelligence officer Sturmbannführer Schuler. Klaus described the action that netted their prisoner. The patrol had successfully reached the Russian position without detection. Klaus ascertained that there were four Russians present; all but one appeared to be asleep. Klaus signaled to his two fire team leaders that he would take out the lone sentry with his trench knife, and then they would fall on the other three. They drew their knives and moved silently into position. Klaus crept up to the sentry, clapped his hand over the sentry's mouth, and slit his throat. Klaus lowered him to the ground without a sound. He signaled for the other two men to attack. Within thirty seconds, it was over, except for Klaus's next intended target. Just as he was about to cut the man's throat, Klaus used the built-in brass knuckles of the handle and hit the man squarely between the eyes, rendering him unconscious. Klaus figured that a live prisoner for interrogation would be more useful than another dead Russian. They tied and gagged the Russian and brought him back. In the dark, they were unable to see his uniform, but once back at the company head-quarters, they were able to determine that he was an artillery lieu-tenant, no doubt a forward observer ready to direct Russian artillery on their position. Klaus and the two fire team leaders were praised for their actions and returned to the platoon area.

During the first week of October, the division was relieved from the Yelnya salient and repositioned for Operation Typhoon, the Battle of Moscow.

Chapter 22

By the end of May 1941, the population of Ravensbrück had grown to five thousand prisoners and counting. It seemed that the construction of barracks was a never-ending project. One would think that with the number of prisoners that were dying, it would offset the new prisoners arriving daily. The duties that Aunt Sylvia and Rachel now performed spared them not only from the murderous work but also from the starvation rations and rampant disease consuming the general population. By working in the officer's mess, when not singing in the officers' club, it had enabled Rachel to regain her strength with the special rations she was provided. Aunt Sylvia had proven to be a very valuable asset to the Siemens AG work. She had no idea what she was assembling, but it took a great deal of patience and manual dexterity.

Starting at the beginning of July, there was a massive influx of prisoners from the east. This was when they found out that Germany had invaded Russia. Herr Goldman asked Aunt Sylvia if the Nazis knew that she spoke Russian. She told him that they know, but there should be enough Polish prisoners in the camp who speak Russian to perform any translation duties. Herr Goldman told Aunt Sylvia that the Nazis would have their hands full keeping the Poles and Russians from killing each other. There was no love lost between those two people.

True to Herr Goldman's words, not a week after the arrival of the Russian prisoners, a full-scale riot broke out between the two factions. The SS guards broke up the conflict swiftly and brutally. One woman from each nationality was selected and was summarily executed before the assembled prisoners. The rest were warned that another such display would be met even more harshly. There were daily harsh words between the two groups, but no outward displays of aggression. This didn't mean that there wasn't a woman or two who showed up for morning count with a black eye or missing teeth. There was one more riot situation in front of the dining hall in October of '41. It was estimated that over one thousand five hundred Poles and Russians took part in this "battle." The female SS guards called for reinforcements from a nearby Wehrmacht unit to quell the riot. The rioters were surrounded and segregated in the middle of the camp compound. There were thirty Polish and twenty Russian bodies lying on the ground. This was not what caused the retribution that was soon to follow. Among the bodies was that of a female SS guard. She had been stabbed over twenty times with a homemade blade.

The camp commandant called for all prisoners to be assembled in the head count area. The Poles and Russians were segregated, and the commandant walked down the lines of prisoners, randomly selecting prisoners, who were brought to the front of the formation. When he had selected twenty-five Poles and twenty-five Russians, they were lined up, facing the formation. He announced that he had promised them that he would not tolerate unrest in his camp and that the next time, punishment would be more severe. He nodded to the SS guards who proceeded to walk down the line of the fifty selected prisoners, firing a single round into the back of their heads. After the last shot was fired, the commandant faced the prisoners and told them that another such incident would result in all participants being placed on the next train to a camp called Auschwitz. The formation was turned over to the female SS guards, who directed Polish and Russian prisoners to remove the bodies for cremation. This had been the largest outright execution of prisoners to date.

So far, prisoners coming from Russia reported that Nazi forces were unstoppable. In every engagement, the German forces rolled over the Red Army as if they were schoolboys. Complete armies were rolled up and captured, resulting in hundreds of thousands of prisoners. Russian civilians were sent to the concentration camps, while the military prisoners were sent to prisoner of war (POW) camps or labor camps. When asked about Jewish prisoners, the Russian women said that there were what were called *Sonder Einheiten* (special units) tasked with rounding up all the Jews and eliminating them as quickly as possible. No one had to ask what "eliminating" meant. Every day, hundreds of Russian prisoners arrived. It was quite obvious that rations were not keeping up with the prison population. Deaths from starvation, overwork, and disease were increasing. The death rate increased from around fifty per day in 1940 to four hundred per day in 1941. Of course, by October of 1941, the prison population had doubled to ten thousand prisoners.

December 11, 1941. Adolf Hitler declared war on the United States, in a move of solidarity with his Asian ally, Japan, after their attack on Pearl Harbor and subsequent declaration of war.

Aunt Sylvia's and Rachel's treatment was different now. Not only were they Jews but they were also from a combatant country opposed to the Third Reich. Rachel arrived at the officers' club for her nightly appearance and was met by Scharführer Kolbitz. He informed her that the camp commandant wished to hear some American music. He believed it would be good for his officers to hear American music so they would become accustomed to it when they invade and occupy the United States. Rachel told him that she didn't know if the band could play any American music. Scharführer Kolbitz told her he would find out and, if necessary, arrange for some sheet music to be procured. This was how Rachel discovered that Nazi Germany and the United States were at war. After she finished at the club, Rachel went back to the barracks and told Aunt Sylvia of the war news.

In January 1942, the Wannsee Conference was convened to discuss and determine the *Endloseung den Juden Frage* (Final Solution to the Jewish Question). This conference was to determine how and when Nazi Germany was to eliminate the eleven million Jews of Europe. As deportation was no longer an option, it was decided that extermination was the only answer. To that end, Jewish prisoners would be relocated from concentration camps to the death camps of Auschwitz, Treblinka, and Sobibor. Other camps were being converted to death camps with the addition of gas chambers and crematoriums. The relocation of Jews was to begin immediately.

In the following weeks, daily formations culled Jewish prisoners from the general population and herded them onto trains. The trains were bound for the "death camp" at Auschwitz in occupied Poland. The prisoners were not being sent there for slave labor purposes; they were being sent for extermination. The prisoners estimated that between eight hundred to one thousand Jewish prisoners were sent to Auschwitz each day.

At night, Rachel and Aunt Sylvia discussed their chances of avoiding the death train. Rachel figured that Aunt Sylvia was performing valuable war work for the Nazis and would be one of the last to be sent away. Maybe she would be kept on indefinitely. Rachel, on the other hand, knew that cooks were a dime a dozen, and she would not be spared just because of her voice. Deep inside, Aunt Sylvia had to agree with Rachel's assessment of the situation but had to try and put a positive spin on the facts. Rachel still had value to the officers. As long as they continued to enjoy her singing, they would forget that she was a Jew. Rachel was not so optimistic and was once again overcome by depression. Aunt Sylvia reminded her of how important it was for Rachel to present a bright and entertaining facade while in front of the Germans. "You don't want to remind them of a cranky old wife waiting at home. You need to make them wish you were the one waiting at home for them." Rachel considered this and realized that this was her only hope for survival. Still, having to be "nice" to the very men who had decided that one had no right to exist just because of their religion was a very tough pill to swallow.

At the Siemens AG plant outside the camp, Herr Goldman came over to Aunt Sylvia's workstation and pretended to inspect some of the devices she had been working on. As he performed his "inspection," he talked to Aunt Sylvia. He asked her how Rachel was getting along. "Is she getting along well with her workmates and other prisoners? How are things at the officers' club?" Aunt Sylvia was confused by this line of questioning and asked why Herr Goldman was so concerned for Rachel's well-being. Herr Goldman looked around to ensure that no one was within earshot and told Aunt Sylvia that he had overheard the facility directors that they would be relocating this operation to the concentration camp at Dachau within the next month. All essential prisoners would be transferred to that camp. That would mean that Rachel would remain here, while Aunt Sylvia went to Dachau.

Aunt Sylvia's heart dropped into her stomach. She feared for Rachel's survival without Aunt Sylvia's morale-boosting support. She looked at Herr Goldman. "Are you certain we are moving?"

"It is what I heard. They are sending an advance party next week to select a facility at Dachau and begin preparations to relocate the equipment and personnel."

She told Herr Goldman that she couldn't leave Rachel behind. There must be some way for her to come with them. Herr Goldman could deem her an essential worker. Herr Goldman looked at Aunt Sylvia as if she had lost her mind. "I could no sooner deem Rachel essential than I could deem you queen of Sheba! You forget. She knows absolutely nothing of the work here, and explaining what we do to someone not working on the project is punishable by death! She would never pass an inspection by the project supervisors, and you and I would be shot after being interrogated about what details we had passed on to her. Then Rachel would be interrogated and shot."

Aunt Sylvia looked away from Herr Goldman and muttered bitterly, "At least we would remain together." She turned back to Herr Goldman and said, "What if I won't go?"

Herr Goldman looked at her, shook his head, and walked back to his desk.

That night, Aunt Sylvia pondered how she was going to tell Rachel the news. She decided that the time wasn't right yet. She needed more time to choose the words; it would be difficult. She was feeling immense guilt for having placed Rachel in this predicament. If she hadn't convinced Rachel to accompany her on this "wonderful" vacation to Europe, she wouldn't be in this hellhole facing imminent death. There had to be a way to arrange for Rachel to be included in the move to Dachau. As tired as Aunt Sylvia was, she couldn't sleep that night, and it showed the next morning at her work. Normally, she turned out faultless devices, but this morning, it was one mistake after the other. Herr Goldman brought three devices back to her that had failed inspection and said, "If this is your idea of how to be left here when we move, keep it up. Just remember where the nonessential Jews go from here." Aunt Sylvia requested and received a five-minute break to wash her face and get a breath of fresh air. After rubbing some snow on her face and neck, she returned to work, renewed.

Scharführer Kolbitz appeared in the officer's kitchen to relieve Rachel from her cooking duties. She was told that she would not be reporting to the kitchen for at least the next week. He had received the sheet music and lyrics that he had requested, and they had been approved by the Reich Ministry of Public Enlightenment and Propaganda. Certain forms of music, jazz and swing, were censored in Germany as being degenerate and so were banned. Still, Scharführer Kolbitz managed to find a dozen or so pieces of music that were acceptable. Rachel would meet with the band every day for at least the next week to rehearse the new music. When Rachel told Aunt Sylvia the news, she was grateful that this would keep Rachel occupied and Aunt Sylvia wouldn't have to burden her with news of leaving. Rachel and the band rehearsed and arranged the new music into a credible "nightclub" act. They would start at 0900 and work until 1700. At the end of the week, Scharführer Kolbitz and the camp commandant stopped by to watch the show's "full dress rehearsal." At the conclusion, the camp commandant and Scharführer Kolbitz applauded.

Scharführer Kolbitz said jokingly to the camp commandant, "And next week, we'll be taking the show on the road." The camp commandant didn't smile at this comment. Scharführer Kolbitz snapped to attention and said, "Just joking, sir!"

The camp commandant looked at Scharführer Kolbitz and said, "Stick to music and leave out the comedy routine. Although, I'm sure a comedy routine would be appreciated on the Russian front." He then turned and left the club.

Scharführer Kolbitz took a deep breath and shuddered at the thought of the Russian front. He would have to watch his mouth in the future around the commandant. Back to Rachel and the band, he congratulated them on their outstanding performance. As today was Wednesday, they could, at their option, either go back to their regular duties or continue to rehearse the show until Friday when they would perform it for the first time at the officers' club. It didn't take them long to decide to continue rehearsing as opposed to their "regular" grueling tasks at the camp.

On Friday evening, Rachel was preparing for that night's show when there was a knock on her dressing room door. Rachel opened the door to find Scharführer Kolbitz standing there with a black sequined gown by Christian Dior with matching shoes. Rachel stared in stunned silence. She had never seen such a beautiful gown before. Scharführer Kolbitz presented it to Rachel and said, "A star should look like a star." Along with the gown and shoes, he presented her with a pair of silk stockings, something Rachel hadn't seen in years, and a case that contained a diamond necklace. Rachel was speechless. "Well," he said, "put them on." Rachel looked at Scharführer Kolbitz and then glanced around the room then back to him. There was nowhere in the room where she could change clothes without him watching her. Suddenly, Scharführer Kolbitz realized Rachel's embarrassment and excused himself, telling her to call him when she was dressed.

A short time later, Rachel called Scharführer Kolbitz. He entered the room and was dumbstruck by the transformation. Rachel was absolutely stunning! Her jet-black hair, cobalt-blue eyes, and red lips made her an absolute beauty. Scharführer Kolbitz noticed that she had not yet put on the necklace. He placed the necklace around her neck and affixed the clasp—the crowning touch to a picture of beauty. "My dear," he said, "even if you didn't sing like an angel, I don't think anyone would notice. You are absolutely breathtaking." Rachel blushed at Scharführer Kolbitz's compliments. "That necklace is very special. It belonged to Elizabeth de Rothschild. I am certain it looks better on you than it ever did on her." Rachel immediately recognized the name, and an icy chill ran down her spine when she realized how she came to be wearing it now. Scharführer Kolbitz announced he was going out to the stage to introduce her and would see her after the show.

Rachel sat and looked at herself in the mirror. Who was this woman who looked back at her? On one hand, this was what she had always dreamed of—a star performing on stage. On the other hand, it was a nightmare performing on a stage surrounded by so much death and degradation. It made her feel as though she were entertaining in an insane asylum. Just as tears were welling up in her eyes, she heard her intro music. "Well, the show must go on, even in an insane asylum."

Rachel took her mark on the stage and waited for the spotlight to come up. There had been the usual background of conversation, glasses clinking, and the occasional "Prosit" (Cheers) until the spotlight illuminated Rachel. There was immediately dead silence. The audience had never seen such a beautiful creature. And then she started singing. It was the first song she had sang in Berlin so very long ago, "Summertime." At the conclusion of her number, the audience at first sat mesmerized by the songstress and the song, then they burst into tumultuous applause. The applause lasted a good two minutes before the crowd would allow her to go on to her next song. That was how she was received for the remainder of the night. She was called upon to sing three encore songs at the conclusion of her regular show. Scharführer Kolbitz escorted her from the stage to the head table to present her to the camp commandant for compliments and to be introduced to his guest of honor, a high-ranking SS officer from Berlin, Reichsführer Heydrich.

For some reason, Rachel got the feeling she were looking at death incarnate. When he looked at her, she felt she knew what it was like to be a head of cattle being sized up for the slaughter. After she was dismissed and headed back to her dressing room, Heydrich looked at Scharführer Kolbitz and commented, "Beautiful young woman. Too bad she won't be around much longer. She'll be going with the others soon to Auschwitz."

Scharführer Kolbitz was stunned. In all his dealings with Rachel, he had actually forgotten she was a Jew. The thought of her going to the death camp was unacceptable. He decided that he had to do something to save this young woman from her horrible fate. But what could *he* do, a lowly scharführer? He was certain that the camp commandant enjoyed having her entertain his soldiers and would delay her departure as long as possible. The question was how long he would be able to keep Rachel safe. This was a question that would occupy his mind day and night for the foreseeable future.

Scharführer Kolbitz knocked on Rachel's dressing room door. She called for him to enter. He praised her on the night's performance and passed on additional words of praise and congratulations from many of the officers present. They all could not wait until the next show. Rachel thanked him for the many compliments and handed him the necklace, gown, and shoes. He told her to keep them here in her dressing room, but Rachel declined, saying that she feared someone would steal them. Scharführer Kolbitz agreed and told her he would have them delivered to her each week before the show. The officers would expect her to be dressed as a star when she sang for them. He said that he would have some more evening gowns delivered for her to choose from. After all, she couldn't wear the same frock every week! That just wouldn't do for a star! Scharführer Kolbitz wished her a good night and left.

Rachel changed into her prison uniform and walked back to her barracks. The princess was once again Cinderella, the scullery maid. Rachel had to tell Aunt Sylvia about the beautiful evening gown, diamond necklace, and the applause she had received. Aunt Sylvia hung on every word, trying to keep the tears from ruining Rachel's evening. If only she hadn't brought her along with her to Europe, Rachel might be enjoying a singing career that didn't end up in a gas chamber or the end of a rope or a bullet in the back of her beautiful head. Eventually, Aunt Sylvia would have to tell Rachel about her moving to Dachau. Unfortunately, it was going to have to be sooner rather than later. She had learned that they would be packing their equipment at the end of next week, with half of the workers traveling to Dachau with the equipment to begin setting up the workshops and the second half remaining to finish closing the facility here. Tonight would not be the time to break the news to

Rachel. She let her enjoy the euphoria from tonight's performance a little longer. Rachel finished telling the story of her night, and Aunt Sylvia wished her good night.

C hapter 23

The end of May 1942 brought about the completion of Sidney's second year at West Point. With graduations being stepped up, it meant that his class would be graduating in thirteen months. For his summer training class, Sidney had chosen something completely out of the ordinary. He had seen a demonstration of parachute tactics and signed up for parachute training. He was told that normally he would have to commit to serving in the Eighty-Second Infantry Division, which was to be designated as the Eighty-Second Airborne Division, but because he was still number 2 in his class, the school would make an exception to the rule.

Sidney had spent quite a bit of time talking to the demonstrators from the Switlik Parachute Company of Trenton, New Jersey. They gave very detailed instructions in the handling of the parachute and the types of survivable failures they had encountered and how to recover from them. They had already certified a platoon at Fort Benning, Georgia, to be parachutists and were now the cadre for the Army's Parachute Training School. Sidney was looking forward to this training. Most of his classmates considered him insane for wanting to voluntarily jump out of an airplane. Sidney told them that he heard that officer parachutists received an extra 100 dollars per month. Everyone agreed that wasn't enough money to jump from an airplane.

Sidney reported for training at Fort Benning. It should be noted that summers at Fort Benning were simply miserable. In addition to miserable weather and mosquitoes the size of B-17s, the Army had apparently banned walking anywhere on Fort Benning. The trainees ran everywhere all the time. Even when stopped, you ran in place. The only time you didn't run, you were doing push-ups. In the three weeks of "airborne" training as it was known, Sidney estimated he ran one thousand miles and did at least as many push-ups. Training started with learning how to properly perform a PLF (parachute landing fall). You were taught how to evenly distribute your weight down the side of your body upon impacting the ground so as to avoid injury. The second week, you were taught how to wear the T-10 parachute and how to use the straps, called risers, that went from the harness up to the canopy to steer the parachute. This was practiced on a zip line and then on 34- and 250-foot towers. The third and final week, trainees conducted five parachute jumps from an aircraft, one of which was conducted at night. After the fifth jump, the trainees were presented with their "Jump Wings."

After graduation, the newly trained airborne soldiers left for their regiments. Sidney could either go home for a week or return to West Point. As he was sitting in the train station making up his mind, a gentleman sat down next to him and said, "Those Jump Wings put you three weeks closer to going to Europe." Sidney looked over to see the face of Lieutenant Commander Wallace.

Sidney looked at Lieutenant Commander Wallace and said, "Excuse me, sir? What does that mean?"

"Well," the OSS man said, "that would reduce your OSS training by three weeks."

Sidney asked what brought him to Fort Benning. Lieutenant Commander Wallace replied that he had a few trainees of his own going through the Army's airborne school. Sidney asked if they had just graduated too.

Lieutenant Commander gazed up at the ceiling and said, "Possibly." Sidney asked where they were headed after they left here. Lieutenant Commander Wallace said, "Some will head for overseas assignments, some for additional technical training with private industry, and some will return to the country club for additional training."

Sidney looked at Lieutenant Commander Wallace and asked, "The country club?"

Lieutenant Commander Wallace explained that because of the war, a large and exclusive country club had been made available to the OSS for the training and billeting of new agents. All the previous members had been notified by the club management that the facility would remain closed for the duration of the war.

Sidney was going to ask why the OSS had commandeered a country club for their training facility but decided against it.

"So, Sidney," Lieutenant Commander Wallace asked, "headed back to West Point or taking a delay en route?"

"No, sir, I'll be headed back to the Point. With graduation being stepped up, there is still a lot of information to cover."

Lieutenant Commander Wallace stood up and offered Sidney his hand. "Remember the six-month window for application to OSS."

"Yes, sir, I remember."

Lieutenant Commander Wallace shook Sidney's hand and then left.

Sidney thought for a second then called out, "Commander!" Sidney walked up to him and asked, "After graduation in June, how long before I could expect to be sent to Europe?"

Lieutenant Wallace looked at Sidney and said, "I remember now why you are in such a rush to get to Europe and, more importantly, Germany. Your girlfriend is there, correct?" Sidney nodded. "She has quite the singing voice. I understand."

Sidney looked at Lieutenant Commander Wallace and said, "I never said anything about her singing ability. How do you know she sings?"

Lieutenant Commander Wallace grinned and said, "Let's just say a little bird told me that Rachel sings every weekend in the SS Officers' Club at Ravensbrück concentration camp. I wouldn't mention that tidbit of information to anybody, especially Mr. and Mrs. Silbermann. It would be very embarrassing as to how you would explain how you came by that information. We'll just consider this a preliminary test of your ability to safeguard classified information." Sidney could not believe his ears! He had a thousand questions for Lieutenant Commander Wallace, but before he could ask one, Lieutenant Commander Wallace held up his hand and said, "I can't give you any more information than what I just said. She is alive and in Ravensbrück. Anything else would pose a danger to the source of my information. You have my card. If you decide you'd like to come to work for us, call me, and I'll get the application process going." With that, Lieutenant Commander Wallace turned and left.

Sidney just stood there in a daze. His prayers over the last three years had appeared to be answered. Rachel was alive. Not being able to tell anyone of the news was going to be difficult. He wished that he could at least tell her parents, but he recalled his security classes at the academy. There were enemy agents and those with sympathies toward Germany that could possibly hear that somehow word had come out of a Nazi camp. That information passed back to Germany could result in an OSS agent being caught, tortured, and executed. No, this information would have to remain with him alone.

Back at West Point, Sidney had to place more emphasis on his studies than he normally did. He was fighting an internal battle regarding his military career. Should he graduate in June and follow the prescribed path to the infantry school and then assignment to a line company in one of the infantry divisions or even the airborne division, or should he take Lieutenant Commander Wallace's offer and go to the OSS? The later decision would almost certainly see him in Europe much sooner than an infantry assignment. He wished that he had someone to discuss his decision with. There was a cadre mentor who was an infantry officer. But Sidney felt that his advice would be slanted toward selecting infantry, or at least serving as a line officer, not some "spook" working in civilian clothing. He could almost guarantee that his father would recommend Regular Army as well. Sidney didn't know an officer who was in the intelligence community. Then he remembered that there was that guy who worked for the Army Counterintelligence Corps; he processed the requests for the cadets' security clearances. Maybe he would be willing to listen and provide some advice. Sidney would look him up tomorrow and see if he were available to talk.

The next day after classes, Sidney went to the office of Special Agent Williams of the Army CIC (Counterintelligence Corps). He explained his situation and asked if he had some spare time to discuss his options. Special Agent Williams told Sidney that he was actually a captain in the Signal Corps detailed to the CIC. Working in civilian clothing with credentials identifying him as "special agent" made conducting investigations into the backgrounds of military members of all ranks much simpler. The soldiers he investigated couldn't try and intimidate him because of their rank as they didn't know his rank. Sidney asked what effect working for CIC had on his military career. Williams told him that the CIC was different than the OSS. The CIC leadership was all military, whereas the OSS had quite a few civilians and "acting officers"—civilians given military rank in order to blend in with the military establishment. The OSS hadn't really existed long enough to really establish a pattern for future military advancement or assignments. Sidney thanked Williams for his time and went back to his barracks, as undecided as he was before he spoke to him. Sidney figured that he would just have to ponder the problem some more and possibly hope for some sort of divine guidance. Sidney still had almost six months to make a final decision.

The start of the next and final class year at West Point for Sidney's class would begin in two weeks. Because the class of '44 was graduating in 1943, the school year would be starting earlier than normal. It also meant that their class was considered "firsties." This gave them the opportunity to conduct training of plebes and to receive more training with active-duty units. It also gave them the option of receiving training from the Navy if they so desired. Sidney thought that training with the Marine Corps could prove beneficial and interesting. Sidney applied for a four-week course at the marine base in Quantico, Virginia. The course taught the tactics and logistics of beach landings, something Sidney thought could be of use when the United States eventually invaded France in the liberation of Europe.

Sidney reported to Marine Corps Base Quantico on September 1, 1942. He was formally introduced to Gunnery Sergeant Murphy with the friendly greeting of "Drop and give me fifty, dogface!" This was nothing new to Sidney, who was already accustomed to such greetings.

Upon completion of the fifty push-ups, Sidney barked, "Permission to recover, Sergeant!"

The Marine looked down at Sidney and bellowed, "On your feet, doggie!"

Sidney snapped to attention.

Gunnery Sergeant Murphy pushed his Smokey Bear hat against Sidney's forehead and said to him, "I'm going to give you a break because you're a dogface and almost a second lieutenant. You see those stripes on my sleeve?"

Sidney had already figured out that addressing the Marine NCO as sergeant had somehow upset him, so he resorted to the only other form of address that he was familiar with, "Sir, yes, sir!"

Gunnery Sergeant Murphy looked as though he were about to have a stroke. His face was beet red, and his eyes practically bulged out of his head. "Do I look like a pussy to you, dogface? I'm not an officer. I work for a living! For your increased military knowledge, I am a gunnery sergeant in the United States Marine Corps! You will address me as Gunnery Sergeant or, if I'm in a pleasant frame of mind, Gunny. You copy that, dogface?"

Sidney replied, "Yes, Gunnery Sergeant!"

"That's just fine, dogface. Now drop and give me another fifty!"

"Yes, Gunnery Sergeant!"

Sidney assumed the position and counted out fifty more push-ups. "Permission to recover, Gunnery Sergeant!"

"On your feet, dogface!" said the Marine. "Welcome to Marine Corps Base Quantico, where I will strive to educate you in the intricacies of amphibious operations."

"Thank you, Gunnery Sergeant," replied Sidney.

Gunnery Sergeant Murphy proceeded to explain to Sidney where he would be billeted, where the mess hall was, and where he would report in the morning for training. Once he was satisfied that Sidney understood his instructions, he dismissed him with "Now get out of my space, doggie."

The next day, Sidney began training as a Marine infantry officer. The difference between Army and Marine tactics were quite apparent. The Marines were considered "shock troops." They hit the enemy positions with overwhelming firepower and maneuver to divide the enemy's defenses. Marine tactics were far different than those of the Army. After the four-week course in which Sidney learned beach assaults and Marine patrol and assault techniques, he completed the course.

On his way off Marine Corps Base Quantico, he happened upon Gunnery Sergeant Murphy. He walked up to the Marine gunnery sergeant and said, "It was a pleasure to be aboard, Gunny."

Gunny Murphy looked at Sidney and said, "You didn't embarrass the Army, which is easy to do. Wish you luck in your future, cadet."

Sidney replied, "Thank you, Gunny." And he departed.

Christmas of 1942 found Sidney visiting his parents at Fort Meyers, Virginia, where his parents were living while his father was assigned to the office of the deputy chief of staff for logistics. Unfortunately for his father, his genius in arranging for the correct supplies in the correct amounts, to be delivered to the correct unit, at the correct time had been realized by high-ranking generals as the proverbial "round peg in the round hole." This meant that Colonel Klein would most likely never receive a combat command or see stars in his career. Sidney felt sorry for his father as he knew that was the goal of his life. When his father asked him how things were going, Sidney was a bit apprehensive about telling his father that he had decided to basically give up his army career and join the OSS. But his decision had been made. He had already completed and forwarded the application forms to Lieutenant Commander Wallace and was only awaiting acceptance of the application and completion of the background investigation for the top secret security clearance. When he told his father, after two cognacs after dinner, he was greatly surprised with his father's response. His father told him that during these times, the path a man must take cannot be decided by tradition but by what a man felt must be done. Sidney's father understood why Sidney was making such a drastic career change; he just hoped that Sidney knew the consequences. Sidney appreciated his father's concern. He, of course, could not tell him that he had been made privilege to classified information regarding Rachel's status and whereabouts.

After New Year's, the tempo at the academy increased. The "firsties" were interviewed for branch assignments. Sidney was told by Lieutenant Commander Wallace to continue with such activities as if the OSS selection process had no bearing. By April, the cadets were fitted for their army uniforms in preparation for graduation. By mid-May, the cadets had received their orders for their active-duty initial training. Sidney, of course, would be returning to Fort Benning, Georgia.

On graduation day, Sidney graduated as brigade commander and first captain and received his father's gold second lieutenant's bars upon receiving his commission into the United States Army. His parents naturally came up for the graduation ceremony. Sidney's only desire was that Rachel could have attended. He had several class-mates who were going to be married over the next few days in the academy chapel, and it had been his dream that he and Rachel were one of them.

After graduation, Sidney told his parents that he would meet them later that evening at the Thayer House, and they would go to dinner together. Sidney went back to his barracks for the last time to change from cadet gray into army brown. Somewhere between then and when he reached the main gate, his path would cross that of an enlisted soldier, who would render his first salute, and Sidney would return that salute and continue a long tradition by presenting that enlisted man with a silver dollar. Sidney checked his uniform one last time in the mirror, ensuring that the parachute wings and expert marksman badges were centered before palming his silver dollar in his left hand and placing his officers cap under his left arm, took one last look at his room, and prepared to leave the United States Military Academy at West Point for what he assumed would be the last time.

As he left the building, a sharply dressed Marine in blue dress uniform stood before the doorway and presented a salute that would make any officer proud. Sidney placed his officer's cap upon his head, snapped a salute in return, and presented his silver dollar to Gunnery Sergeant Murphy.

"Congratulations, Lieutenant Klein!"

"Thank you, Gunnery Sergeant! What brings you all the way here from Virginia? Couldn't wait to see your favorite dogface become an official 'pussy'?"

Gunnery Sergeant Murphy smiled and said, "Partly, sir. I work for a mutual friend who would like to have a few words with you before you leave for dinner with your folks."

Sidney looked at the Marine and said, "Gunny, I can't imagine who we would have as a mutual friend."

Gunnery Sergeant Murphy motioned with his head in a "Follow me" movement and walked off. Sidney followed him to a secluded park area surrounding a statue of Robert E. Lee, former commandant of West Point. On a bench sat Lieutenant Commander Wallace.

Sidney saluted Lieutenant Commander Wallace and said, "Why does this unholy alliance not surprise me, sir?"

Lieutenant Commander Wallace smiled and offered his congratulations. "You won't be going to Fort Benning, and this weekend will be the last time you wear an army uniform for a while. After dinner with your parents, you will meet Gunnery Sergeant Murphy at Grand Central Station and take the train to Washington, DC. Once there, the gunny will arrange for onward transportation to the 'country club.' You are not to tell anyone of this change in your itinerary. All mail sent to you to Fort Benning will be rerouted to the 'country club,' and return mail will be postmarked from Fort Benning. Any questions, Lieutenant?"

Sidney saluted and said, "No questions, sir."

Lieutenant Commander Wallace looked at Gunnery Sergeant Murphy and said, "Gunny, you and Lieutenant Klein have your orders."

Gunny Murphy saluted and said "Aye, aye, sir."

Chapter 24

After the bloody battles in and around Moscow, the Second SS Panzer Division had suffered immense loses and was once again sent to France, this time for refit and resupply. The division had been badly mauled and was in dire need of replacements. Klaus's platoon of forty-four men was down to twenty men. Klaus considered himself fortunate in that his squad leaders and command element had all survived. Their vehicles had all been left behind in Russia as either spares or replacements for units that had remained around Moscow. The division was basically in the same condition. The only vehicles to come out with them had been their Opel Blitz transport trucks and their ambulances carrying their wounded.

Of Klaus's casualties, he had counted fourteen wounded and ten dead. They could reasonably expect ten to return within a few months, and four were too severely wounded to return to active duty. The battalion had sent down word that they would be on a modified training schedule, which would allow for soldiers to take some leave time. They were also informed that the replacements would only be requisitioned for those personnel who were killed in action or were not expected to return to duty. The rumor was that the division would remain in France for at least a year, if not longer. Soldiers were already inquiring if the rumor were true. Oberscharführer Winter asked them if they were asking because they were considering buying a house in France. Klaus and Oberscharführer Winter, being the seasoned veterans that they were, didn't believe a word of the rumors and advised their soldiers to be prepared to move out at any moment.

A month after setting up their bivouac area in France, Klaus, Oberscharführer Winter, Oberschutze Groenig, and Unterscharführer Gross were summoned to the battalion headquarters. Klaus and Oberscharführer Winter were presented with the Iron Cross First Class. Oberschutze Groenig was promoted to sturmmann and awarded the Iron Cross Second Class, and Unterscharführer Gross was awarded the Iron Cross Second Class and the Infantry Assault Badge. They also received a two-week leave. Klaus and Oberscharführer Winter flipped a coin to see who would go on leave first as they both couldn't be gone at the same time. But before anyone went anywhere, Sturmmann Groenig's stripes must be wetted down in time-honored First Platoon tradition. After so many months in close combat together, the party got to be a fairly drunken affair. First Sturmmann Groenig's promotion was toasted. Then there were toasts to all the comrades who had been lost in France, Yugoslavia, Greece, and Russia and then to all the soldiers who had been wounded and couldn't be there tonight but would be back. By the time they got to the last category, no one was feeling any pain. After several cases of French wine and bottles of cognac, the platoon members present had accomplished their mission—oblivion.

Two days after "the party," which would live in the annals of First Platoon parties, those selected for leave, except for Klaus, who had lost the coin toss, departed for home. Klaus had granted leave requests for at least half of his platoon, so there were just enough soldiers to perform required duties such as guard duty and other necessary tasks. Klaus was occasionally detailed to staff duty officer or officer of the day but otherwise had no pressing duties. He spent the majority of his time either writing in his war journal or writing letters to his mother. He already wrote her that he would be coming home in around two weeks on leave and was looking forward to seeing them.

Klaus spent a great deal of time with his war journal. His recollections of the engagements that his platoon had fought and the tactics they had employed, coupled with the end result of success or failure, gave him a great deal to consider. He clearly remembered every engagement that resulted in a loss of life or other casualty. He thought what could have been done differently to save that life or prevented that casualty. Klaus felt personally responsible for each man who had been lost in combat. Oberscharführer Winter had already warned Klaus that such lines of thought could lead to a loss in his ability to make combat decisions. If he overthought every decision, it could result in an inability to make any decision, which could cost lives. Klaus was very happy that he had Oberscharführer Winter as his platoon sergeant. He was not only an experienced noncommissioned officer but also an excellent mentor. Klaus could always count on Oberscharführer Winter for sound advice and his support of decisions he made. He could not ask for a better platoon sergeant.

Upon Oberscharführer Winter's return from leave, they sat together and talked about his time at home. Oberscharführer Winter, being from the Rhineland-Palatinate region of Germany, had brought back several bottles of a very fine Rhine wine, as well as a bottle of *birnen schnapps* (pear schnapps), a bottle of schnapps with a whole pear inside the bottle.

Just the sight of the pear inside the bottle intrigued Klaus. He looked at Oberscharführer Winter and asked, "Okay, how did they get the pear inside the bottle?"

Oberscharführer Winter suggested that they taste the schnapps, and then he would explain how it was made. Once the schnapps was tasted, along with a glass of beer, Oberscharführer Winter explained that the pear was actually grown inside the bottle. Once the pear was ripe, it was cut from the tree, and the bottle was filled with pear schnapps made from other pears. Klaus was impressed, and after he and Oberscharführer Winter consumed about half of the bottle along with another three bottles of beer each, the story of Oberscharführer Winter's leave was told. The time at home was very pleasant. His wife made every attempt to make everything like it was before the war. The only problem was the nightmares. There were nights when he would awaken, yelling orders to platoon members who were no longer alive, yet he could see them, plain as day. His wife tried to comfort him once, only to find that he had grabbed her around the throat and was stabbing her with a knife only visible to him, yelling, "Umri ty ublyudok!" (Die, you bastard!) When he finally snapped out of his nightmare, he could not believe what had happened. He said that he slept on the living room couch for the rest of the time he was home.

Klaus felt sorry for Oberscharführer Winter's problems at home but thought he might experience the same feelings when he went home. He had been having the same nightmares and problems sleeping. He was finding that the only thing that helped him sleep through the night was increasing levels of alcohol. The problem with that was in combat, that was totally unacceptable, and he would not tolerate such a condition from one of his soldiers and especially not from himself.

Klaus was surprised to find his father waiting for him at the train station. He hadn't been certain that all his connections would come together and so gave a general idea as to his arrival. As they were both in uniform, Klaus first saluted his father before embracing him. His father held him at arm's length and examined his son. "You've become quite the decorated hero, my son," said the elder Bergman.

"I'm just happy to be alive, Father," Klaus replied.

"Is the fighting on the Russian front as bad as they say?" he asked.

As they walked from the train station, Klaus told him that at times the German soldiers actually felt sorry for the Russian soldiers. Their equipment was in terrible condition, they were always short on ammunition, and their leadership was criminal. The Russians were sent in human wave attacks in which only every other soldier had ammunition. If the soldier with the ammunition were killed or wounded, the next soldier would pick up that man's rifle and continue to attack. If the attack were driven back, there were units of NKVD (Russian Secret Police) led by political commissars that would fire into the retreating Russian soldiers, killing them or forcing them to return to the assault.

"The poor bastards were caught in a cross fire between us and their own lines. They were slaughtered by the thousands and surrendered by the tens of thousands. Their advantages were in numbers of troops available. They swarmed the German positions like a kicked-over anthill."

Then there was the T-34 tank, which Klaus said was arguably the best tank in the world at this time. The German Mark IVs were absolutely no match for the T-34. Klaus's father said that Klaus shouldn't say too much about the Russian tanks. OKW was working very hard in getting German manufacturing to design and build a suitable response to the T-34. In the meantime, the T-34 was a sore point at headquarters.

Klaus's mother greeted him at the door, "Mein sohn, der held." (My son, the hero.) She kissed him on both cheeks, took him by the hands, and brought him into the living room. She poured three glasses of schnapps and handed them around. It was then that Klaus noticed that this was not the first schnapps that his mother had taken today. "Zum wohl!" (To your health!) And she tossed back the schnapps. Klaus looked to his father who silently shook his head as if to say, "Not now." After a few minutes of small took, Frau Bergman announced, "I'll go arrange some appetizers before dinner."

After his mother had left, Klaus turned to his father and asked what was going on. His father replied that there had been far too many death telegrams delivered in the last few months, and some of her friends had been recipients. The strain of comforting these women was starting to have the effect on his wife where she was taking to drinking a schnapps before going to visit her friends. Apparently, she had a couple with her friend and usually had one or two upon returning home. It was becoming quite common for Klaus's father to come home to find his wife sleeping after commiserating with a new widow or woman who had lost a son. Klaus was quite alarmed, as he had only seen his mother a little "tipsy" on New Year's Eve. Klaus asked his father what they should do.

Klaus's father just hung his head and said, "I don't know. Somehow end the war?"

Dinner that evening was rather tense. Klaus's mother drank two glasses of wine with dinner and knocked a third one over. Klaus could see the embarrassment in her face but didn't know what to do to help her. Klaus's father got up and took his wife by the arm and helped her upstairs. She stopped at the stairs and looked at Klaus, "I'm just a little tired, my boy. I'll be fine after a good night's sleep."

"Ja, Mama, you'll be fine in the morning. Gute nacht, Mama." (Good night, Mama.)

About a half hour later, his father came back downstairs. "She's sound asleep."

Klaus helped his father clear the table and wash the dishes. Afterward, they sat in the living room and sipped a cognac. Klaus's father asked him what the Army had planned for him. Klaus told his father of the horrendous casualties that his division had suffered. They had been ordered to leave all their tanks, armored vehicles, and heavy artillery in Russia for replacements. He had been told that the division would be rebuilt, but it would take a long time for that much equipment to come off the assembly lines and fill requests for replacement equipment for units in the field. Klaus said that he would not be surprised if the soldiers of the division were not simply fed into other units as replacements. Klaus's father finished his cognac and held up the bottle to Klaus, who nodded and held out his glass for a refill. After Klaus's father had topped his own glass off, he told Klaus he had it on good authority that the division would be rebuilt. He had all the requisition orders on his desk, and they had all been approved. The Second SS Panzer Division would be the first unit equipped with the new Panzer Mk. V tank, named the Panther. It was to be equipped with thicker armor and a new high-velocity seventy-five-millimeter (three-inch) gun to rival the T-34's seventy-six-millimeter main gun. Klaus said that almost anything would be an improvement over the Mk. IV. The only way they could destroy a T-34 with a single round was from behind into the engine compartment.

The remainder of Klaus's leave was like walking on eggshells. He could see that his mother was doing her best to stay away from the schnapps, but it was a struggle, and she was very edgy. It seemed it was almost a relief for her when Klaus reported back to his unit.

Klaus and Oberscharführer Winter got together to discuss what had transpired while he was gone. All the men who were due leave had either taken leave and returned or were on leave now and would return next week. There had been only one disciplinary problem to be dealt with. An oberschutze in the Third Squad had gotten drunk and had a run-in with the *Feldgendarmerie* (Military Police) who administered a bit of "field justice" before dropping him off at the Third Company Headquarters. Oberscharführer Winter picked him up from the company staff duty sergeant and confined him to his barracks, except for meals, latrine, and church services. He was to be in uniform and ready to perform any extra details that were required.

Klaus nodded his approval and asked, "How long is his restriction?"

Oberscharführer Winter thought for a moment and said, "Two weeks, so he has another four days."

Klaus once again nodded his approval. Klaus looked at his watch, noticed it was 1700, and asked, "Do we have any beer?"

Oberscharführer Winter reached into his footlocker and pulled out two bottles of Berliner Kindl beer. Klaus smiled in appreciation; it was his favorite hometown beer.

"Where did you manage to get hold of this?" Klaus asked.

"We senior noncommissioned officers have our sources, Obersturmführer."

As they enjoyed their beer, they discussed the training objectives for the coming months. They both agreed that supplies of winter clothing, which still had not been received, were desperately needed. Klaus said that his father told him that the high command was aware of the requisitions and were trying to fulfill them. The next item for discussion was readiness and training. If they got all their veterans back from the hospital, they would be in pretty good shape; they only had to integrate a few new replacement soldiers. They would have to work on new tactics that had been learned on the Russian front when dealing with the massive onslaught of Russian infantry and armor. The most pressing problem for the panzer grenadiers was the Russian tanks. According to Klaus's father, an influx of *panzerfaust* (bazookas) would be provided to them. Klaus said they would hopefully receive sufficient supplies to conduct training. They both agreed that training should commence in five days, starting with patrolling and road marches to get everyone back in physical condition.

By June of 1943, the division was back to combat strength and had been outfitted with the new Panzer Mk. V "Panther" tanks. They were a marked improvement over the Mk. IVs, which were still in use with many of the Wehrmacht panzer divisions. Extensive training with the new tanks revealed several problems that led to reliability issues, such as blown head gaskets, overheating, and engine fires. Still, the Panther was considered a much-improved tank equal to the T-34. New tactics were practiced for months, and the division was finally considered combat-ready. The division was ordered back to the Russian front in July 1943. The division was first deployed to the Kharkov area. Savage fighting in and around the Kharkov area resulted in a victory for the German forces and set up the Battle of Kursk. The division was committed to the southern perimeter of the Kursk salient and was tasked with driving that portion of the salient into the pincers of the German armored assault. Klaus, Oberscharführer Winter, and the squad leaders of the First Platoon went over the battle plan for the Third Company, First Battalion, Fortieth Panzer Grenadier Regiment in what was to be the largest engagement for the division. The battle plan was good. It appeared to be a sound plan and should succeed. What the Germans didn't know was that the Russians were aware of the German battle plan and had constructed defensive positions and placed armored units in position to counteract the German offensive.

The Fortieth Panzer Grenadier Regiment was assigned to support the First and Second Panzer Battalions in the initial assault. They were sent against Russian defensive emplacements to clear them of anti-tank guns. As The First Platoon advanced against its objective, they came under heavy machine gun and rifle fire. The many hours that Klaus had subjected them to assault training was proving to be very beneficial. The platoon managed to reach the Russian trenches with few casualties and began to lob hand grenades into the enemy positions. As Klaus was changing the magazine in his MP-40, a Russian grenade landed at his feet. Klaus pushed Oberscharführer Winter and Oberschutze Andreas out of the way and picked up the grenade. As he was tossing it back into the Russian position, there was a bright flash, and everything went black and silent. Klaus awoke to Oberscharführer Winter and Sturmmann Groenig leaning over him. He was having trouble focusing on their faces, and it sounded as if they were talking to him from several meters away. Eventually, their voices came to him.

Oberscharführer Winter was yelling, "Klaus! Klaus! Can you hear me?"

After a moment Klaus nodded and said, "What happened? How is the assault going?" Klaus attempted to get up, but both men held him down.

Sturmmann Groenig said, "Obersturmführer, please lie still. You've been wounded, and I need to treat your wounds."

Klaus looked up at his platoon medic and asked, "How bad?"

Oberscharführer Winter looked down at his platoon leader and said, "We need to get you to the rear right away."

Klaus reached for his face to rub his eye in order to clear his vision, but the medic stopped his arm. It was then that Klaus realized his left hand was missing at the wrist. He stared at the stump, which Sturmmann Groenig had already wrapped in a field dressing and said, "Scheisse, meine uhr is weg." (Shit, my watch is gone.) "Martin, what other injuries do I have?"

Oberscharführer Winter first looked at the medic, who nodded, then said to Klaus, "Klaus, you've also lost your left eye."

Sturmmann Groenig administered a syringe of morphine and marked Klaus's forehead with a *T* and an *M* in blood to indicate that a tourniquet and morphine had been applied. As Klaus was reacting to the sedative, he mumbled, "I just need a hook to become a proper pirate."

When Klaus awoke, he was lying on a table at the battalion aid station. A field dressing covered most of his head, and he could feel someone working on his left wrist. A doctor approached and inspected the work to his left wrist and told the person working on his wrist, "Wrap the stump with gauze and field dressings. I don't want to replace the tourniquet. It will only cause more tissue damage and make suturing more difficult after surgery." Next, the doctor removed the field dressing from Klaus's head and examined his eye. "Nothing to be done for the eye. Clean the wound and reapply a field dressing. Someone will suture the wounds once he reaches the field hospital." The doctor looked at Klaus and said, "You will survive, Obersturmführer."

Klaus replied, "Yes, but not to fight another day."

The doctor shook his head and said, "No, not to fight another day I'm afraid." The doctor patted Klaus's shoulder and moved on to the next patient.

The medic came around to where Klaus could see him and said, "Obersturmführer, I'm going to give you something for the pain, then I'll dress your head wounds."

Klaus felt the pin prick from the syringe and almost immediately started to fade away. He thought to himself, *Morphine is an amazing thing. I'll just have to be careful it doesn't become too amazing.*

Two days later, Klaus found himself in a very comfortable bed under crisp, clean white sheets. He vaguely remembered the trip from the battalion aid station. Along the way, the medics had kept him pretty doped up as the trip was very rough until they had reached the rail line and were placed aboard the medical evacuation train headed back to Berlin. At the Evacuation Hospital in Berlin, Klaus had undergone several surgeries. The first had been to cut back flesh and bones above his wrist in order to create a flap of skin that could be sewn together over the end of his wrist. The second set of surgical procedures had been to remove what remained of his left eye, reconstruct the eye socket, and suture the ten-centimeter-long (four-inch) wound that extended from above his eyebrow diagonally across his cheek to the side of his nose. The doctor came in to examine the surgeries performed and his general condition. The doctor consulted Klaus's chart and told the medic to continue the morphine for another two days.

Klaus stopped the doctor and told him, "No. No more morphine. There must be another medication for pain. I'm starting to look forward to the injections even when the pain is easily manageable."

The doctor looked at Klaus and told him that without the morphine, he would be in a great deal of pain. Why would he want to subject himself to that misery?

Klaus smiled at the doctor and said, "A little pain is good for the soul, Herr Doctor."

The doctor shook his head and told the medic, "Cease all morphine and give him the strongest aspirin we have. Let me know how well he tolerates the pain." As the doctor was leaving, the medic asked about visitors for the obersturmführer. The doctor looked at Klaus then at the medic and said, "That is up to the patient. I believe he is strong enough for visitors."

The medic looked at Klaus and said, "Well, Herr Obersturmführer, is there anyone I can contact for you?"

Klaus just shook his head and said, "No, nobody just yet. I'm not ready for the drama my wounds are bound to create."

The medic replied, "Well, sir, just let me know if or when you change your mind."

About four hours later, the last dose of morphine was wearing off, and Klaus was getting an indication of what the pain would be like when the drug was completely dissipated. He couldn't tell for sure which wound hurt more, the eye or the wrist. He just knew that he was going to do his damnedest to refuse the morphine or any other serious pain drugs. After another two hours, Klaus was bathed in sweat from fighting the pain. The medic came over to him and asked Klaus what he wanted him to do for the pain. Klaus answered, "The doctor said the strongest dose of aspirin available."

The medic went away and came back a few minutes later with the aspirin. "I can't give you too many of these because it will thin your blood to the point where future surgeries might have to be postponed."

Klaus nodded his understanding and said, "Just give me as many as you can. The doctor was right about the pain. It's pretty bad."

For the next three days, Klaus battled the waves of pain with a stoic resolve and a handful of aspirin. On the fourth day, he actually slept for six straight hours. When he awoke, he found that the pain was actually bearable without even aspirin.

The doctor came on his daily rounds and inspected his wounds. He told Klaus that they would do a little "cleanup" on his wrist to allow for a prosthetic hand and remove the sutures around his eye.

The doctor informed Klaus that damage to the eye socket was so severe that insertion of a glass eye was not possible; he would have to use an eye patch. Klaus nodded his understanding and thanked the doctor for all he had done.

September of 1943, Klaus was moved to the rehabilitation ward where he was allowed to wander the hospital and grounds. Klaus's parents had come to visit, and as he had feared, it was very traumatic for his mother. Apparently, no one had prepared either one for the severity of his wounds. His father turned ashen, and his mother had fainted. When she regained consciousness, she was practically delirious. Klaus's doctor came in and ordered a medic to give his mother a sedative to calm her down. Standartenführer Bergman sat with his son and inquired of his plans. Klaus told his father that he had heard nothing yet. He figured that if the military allowed *Oberst* (Colonel) Von Stauffenberg to remain on active duty, albeit as a staff officer, maybe the military would allow him to remain on active duty. Of course, Von Stauffenberg was a colonel, and a count, so that might count a little more than a lowly SS first lieutenant. Klaus's father knew a little more of the military's plan for him than he was letting on. He knew that Klaus would be retained on active duty. He even knew where his next assignment would be, but he could not tell Klaus any of this as there was an event that would precede his receiving orders.

A week after his parents' visit, Klaus was visited by a major from army headquarters. He asked Klaus if he had a serviceable dress uniform. Klaus replied that he did. The major told him to shave, put on his uniform, and wait. Klaus answered "Yes, sir!" and went to don his uniform. Lucky for Klaus, the medic was handy because this was the first time that Klaus had to deal with buttons, and to his frustration, he could not perform the task. Klaus waited in the hallway outside the ward until an *obergefreiter* (private first class) came looking for him. He asked Klaus to please follow him downstairs where he had a staff car waiting. Klaus asked the young soldier where they were going. He turned to Klaus and said, "Obersturmführer, no one has told you? You're to be decorated by the Führer today." The ceremony was to be held in the Führer's office at the *Reichs Chancellery* (Hitler's headquarter building).

Klaus was surprised to see his father there; his mother was feeling "unwell." The major from that morning and several other high-ranking officers of the general staff were there. Klaus was introduced around, and then Hitler's military aide-de-camp came out and announced, "Gentlemen, the Führer." Everyone came to attention. Adolf Hitler approached Klaus and shook his hand and greeted him warmly. The ceremony took place in two parts. Adolf Hitler waited while his aide read the citation for the award of the Knight's Cross of the Iron Cross. Then Klaus was presented with the Wound Badge in gold. The second part of the ceremony commenced with his father standing to one side of him and the Führer on the other side while the aide read the orders promoting Klaus to *hauptsturmführer* (captain).

Hitler looked to Klaus's father and said, "You must be very proud of your young man. A shame his mother couldn't be here. Mothers are very important to young men. I know."

After the ceremony, they were served coffee, tea, and various assorted cakes. Klaus overheard two of the generals saying that a good French cognac or a slivowitz was the only way to toast a promotion. Everyone knew that Hitler was very partial to sweets and was a teetotaler. Hitler soon retired to his office, which signified the end of the ceremony.

Before Klaus could leave, the major from this morning approached Klaus and presented him with his award citations and another envelope, which the major informed him were his transfer orders. Klaus opened the envelope and read his orders. He could feel the blood drain from his face. His father looked at Klaus and asked him if he was feeling all right. Klaus handed his father a copy of his orders, reassigning him as the commander of the security guard company at Dachau concentration camp. Klaus said, "I would rather return to the Russian front."

Chapter 25

After the evening meal on June 15, 1942, Aunt Sylvia decided she had no other choice but to tell Rachel that she would be leaving in the morning for Dachau. Aunt Sylvia had hardly slept in the last week after learning that everything was packed up and there was nothing left to do here at Ravensbrück. The news would be difficult for Rachel, but there was nothing more that Aunt Sylvia could do to postpone her departure.

Rachel took the news surprisingly well. She realized that it was not as if Aunt Sylvia had a choice in the matter. The hard part was losing the last bit of family that either one had. They sat up the entire night talking of the past and telling family stories. For the first time in ages, Rachel thought of Sidney and wondered what he was doing. She thought what might have been had she not followed a whim and gone on this disastrous journey. The only high point was realizing her dream of being a singer, even though she was singing for her jailers and possible executioners. Aunt Sylvia and Rachel embraced, and Rachel said, "Till we meet again."

In the morning, Aunt Sylvia and the remainder of the Siemens workers were loaded onto trucks with the last of their equipment and headed down the road to Dachau. Rachel returned to the officer's kitchen to finish preparing breakfast meals for the SS officers. Life without Aunt Sylvia settled into the same routine as before. The only differences that Rachel noticed were that on those nights that she sang in the officers' club, there were more officers than were stationed at the camp. They must be coming from other nearby units. The second thing she noticed was that there were hardly any Jews left in the camp. One other oddity was the construction of a strange-looking building at the far end of the camp. The building was segregated from the rest of the camp. Later, they learned that Ravensbrück would have its own gas chamber soon.

October 10, 1942, after morning count, a list of names was called out. Rachel's name was one of them. They were told to get their belongings and form up to be marched to the railroad siding. Rachel was thinking this must be some kind of mistake. She desperately looked around for Scharführer Kolbitz but couldn't see him anywhere. She had no choice but to wait at the siding. As their names were called, they were loaded onto the railcars. Just as Rachel was stepping onto the railcar, Scharführer Kolbitz arrived with a written order from the commandant, pulling her from this shipment. Rachel's life was spared, for now.

After the rail yard incident of last week, Rachel realized how precarious her hold on life really was. She continued to live merely on the whim of the camp commandant. If he were to wish it, she could be placed on the next shipment to Auschwitz or simply wait until Ravensbrück's gas chamber was completed. Rachel had absolutely no control over her own destiny. It was a feeling of utter helplessness and dread. More and more, the thought of suicide occupied her mind.

Unknown to Rachel, Scharführer Kolbitz was working behind the scenes to keep Rachel alive. At great personal risk, he had approached the camp commandant and made inquiries concerning Rachel. He knew that if the camp commandant misinterpreted his suggestions, the camp commandant might think that Scharführer Kolbitz was romantically involved with her, which would result in the harshest of punishments for both of them. Scharführer Kolbitz must convince the commandant that his wish to keep her alive was for the music and nothing else. Her singing worked wonders for the morale of the officers who were occupied with the elimination of enemies of the state, a most unappreciated endeavor. He pleaded his case to the camp commandant, and much to his surprise, the camp commandant made a pledge to him that as long as Rachel was not the last Jew left in Ravensbrück, she would be spared. When she became the last Jew, he could make no more promises as to her longevity on this earth as he had sworn an oath to the Führer to rid Germany of all Jews. Scharführer Kolbitz received the commandant's assurances that Rachel's name would not appear on any transport orders for the foreseeable future.

The news that Rachel would not have to live under the cloud of uncertainty lifted her spirits, but still she knew that her time might still come. Still, watching other Jews waiting for their names to be called was hard on her because she knew she was safe from selection. Her life and routine continued on. Her only bright spot was on Friday nights when she changed from prison rags to evening gown and jewels and immersed herself in her fantasy world as nightclub entertainer. The audiences grew larger every Friday to the point where the officers' club was standing room only. High-ranking officers were traveling from as far away as Munich and Augsburg to come to her show. Scharführer Kolbitz hinted that they might add a show on Saturday night because of the crowd size. After the show, Rachel was allowed to circulate among the officers and was treated as though she were not a Jew but a real person. Rachel found out that Scharführer Kolbitz simply neglected to inform the officers of her religion or that she was a prisoner in the camp. The officers just assumed she was possibly a local brought in to entertain the troops.

Over time, with tutoring from Obersturmmann Mueller, Rachel spoke very good German. This added to the belief that she was German. It was only after the show when Rachel returned to her "alter ego" that the German officers would have not welcomed her so graciously.

By May of 1943, the Ravensbrück camp was predominantly occupied by Russian prisoners. The gas chamber was operating at full capacity, and the bodies were being sent down the road to the crematorium as fast as they could be loaded onto trucks. It was interesting that Jews were still being sent to Auschwitz to be gassed, but the Russian non-Jews were gassed here. Nazi segregation at its finest.

Scharführer Kolbitz greeted Rachel at her dressing room door the following Friday with some disturbing news. It was rumored that the camp commandant was being transferred to another camp. He didn't know which camp, but the transfer was to take place next month. Rachel asked how that was going to affect her and the show. Scharführer Kolbitz told her he didn't know yet but would keep her informed. That night, Rachel displayed true showmanship by putting on a stellar performance, although it might be her last. A week later, Scharführer Kolbitz again met Rachel at her dressing room door. Stacked outside were several boxes and suitcases. He told her that after the show tonight, she was to pack all the evening gowns and other paraphernalia and leave it in the dressing room. She was then to go to her barracks room and do the same.

Rachel took a deep breath and, with tears in her eyes, said, "So this is the end."

Scharführer Kolbitz said, "This is the beginning—the beginning of a new phase of your career. The camp commandant is being transferred and has arranged for us to accompany him. We will go to Dachau with him."

Rachel could not believe her ears. She would get to see Aunt Sylvia again and would continue to sing. This was simply a miracle! The news made Rachel forget herself, and she threw her arms around Scharführer Kolbitz's neck. Almost immediately she remembered who he was and stepped back and lowered her eyes and said, "Entschuldigung, Scharführer." (Excuse me, Scharführer.)

Scharführer Kolbitz looked around and saw no one had seen what had just happened and smiled at Rachel. "I understand your joy, but in the future, please be more careful." Rachel nodded and began moving boxes and suitcases into her dressing room.

The day came when everything was loaded into a transport truck for the trip to Dachau. Rachel figured that she would ride in the back of the truck as she was, after all, a prisoner. Prior to leaving, Scharführer Kolbitz gave Rachel a set of civilian coveralls to replace her camp striped uniform. "With these, you'll draw less attention on the trip." After Rachel changed, she was escorted to the car with Scharführer Kolbitz, the camp commandant's personal cook, and the nanny for the camp commandant's children. The camp commandant, his wife, and two children rode in another car. The cook and the nanny had also been prisoners at Ravensbrück camp. The cook had packed a very large hamper into the trunk of the car, which contained a variety of cold cuts, cheeses, fruit, bread, and a few bottles of beer and wine for a picnic lunch along the way. It was going to be at least a twelve-hour drive to Dachau.

Scharführer Kolbitz dozed most of the trip, while the three women took in every sight along the way. After years of imprisonment, anything outside the perimeter fence of Ravensbrück camp was like witnessing the wonders of the world—hills, valleys, and streams; cows and sheep in the fields; farmers tilling the soil and people shopping in the stores in the towns and villages they passed through. It just amazed Rachel that life actually continued on as normal, while they lived in a hell on earth. Did these people know what was going on in the camps? The torture, deprivation, and death? The murder of thousands of innocent men, women, and children put to death for the crime of being of the wrong religion? For that matter, did they even care? The people all seemed so content with their lives as if they had not a care in the world. It was definitely two totally different worlds.

About one hundred kilometers (sixty miles) south of Leipzig, the three vehicles pulled off the road for their picnic. Rachel helped the cook lay out the food in the hamper while the nanny tended to the camp commandant's children. The cook told Rachel that there was a second smaller basket in the trunk that contained sandwiches and fruit, plus she had smuggled three bottles of beer for them. They would, of course, not be eating with the Germans. After the food for the commandant's family and entourage was laid out, Rachel and the other two women sat by themselves behind the vehicles and ate their lunch. The cook opened the three beers and held up her bottle to the two other women and toasted, "Zum uberleben." (To survival.) They touched their bottles together and took a healthy swig.

After lunch, the cook and Rachel packed up the remnants of the meal while the nanny accompanied the camp commandant on a walk before getting back on the road. Scharführer Kolbitz walked up to Rachel and asked how she was enjoying the drive. Rachel just said, "It's another world out here. If I'm not careful, I could forget that this isn't real life and my life hangs on the whim of the camp commandant or some other person who knows nothing about me or even cares. I'm just another filthy Jew!" Scharführer Kolbitz was taken aback by Rachel's outburst. She had always been so mild-mannered, and this was totally unlike her. Rachel immediately regretted lashing out at the scharführer and blamed it on the beer at lunch but didn't mention the beer to him. "Excuse me, Scharführer, I must help the cook pack up the car." She turned and went to help the cook.

The camp commandant and family returned from their walk, and everyone got into the vehicles and returned to the road.

It was starting to get dark by the time they reached the town of Dachau, which was about three kilometers (two miles) from the concentration camp. The camp commandant, his family, and the nanny would stay in the hotel in town, which had been requisitioned for use by the SS. Scharführer Kolbitz would take Rachel and the cook, along with the vehicle drivers, to the camp and arrange billeting for everyone. The camp commandant called Scharführer Kolbitz aside and told him to "discreetly" ensure that Rachel and his cook were not placed into the camp. They were to be provided with similar quarters as they had at Ravensbrück. Scharführer Kolbitz came to attention and said, "I understand completely, sir."

Before he could leave, the camp commandant said to him, "Also, please present my compliments to the present camp commandant and inform him that I look forward to seeing him in the morning. Make sure that the car and driver are at the hotel by 0730."

"Yes, sir!" replied Scharführer Kolbitz. He saluted and left.

At Dachau camp, they were met by the duty officer who told Scharführer Kolbitz that Rachel and the cook would be billeted in the Siemens AG facility with the essential workers there. Scharführer Kolbitz could barely suppress his happiness at hearing the billeting arrangements for Rachel; she would have no trouble seeing her aunt again. Their vehicles would be secured in the camp motor park, and the drivers would be billeted in the transient enlisted barracks. Scharführer Kolbitz would be billeted in the senior noncommissioned officers quarters. Scharführer Kolbitz told the duty officer he was to present his commanding officer's compliments to the Dachau camp commandant and inform him that he would join the Dachau camp commandant for breakfast in the morning. The duty officer got the camp commandant on the telephone, and Scharführer Kolbitz passed on his commander's message. Scharführer Kolbitz then carried out his billeting instructions, escorting Rachel and the cook to the Siemens AG billets. He went inside and spoke to the billeting NCO and asked if there was room for another person in the quarters of a Sylvia Silbermann. He was told there was, and he asked that Rachel be assigned that bunk, which she was. Scharführer Kolbitz came outside and gave each woman her billeting assignment and left.

Rachel went to her assigned barracks, and when she entered, there sat Aunt Sylvia on her bed. At first, they just stared at each other in disbelief. Aunt Sylvia jumped from her bed and ran to Rachel, and they embraced. Tears of joy flowed freely as Aunt Sylvia asked, "Is it really you? How did you get here?" They sat and talked into the wee hours, relating what had transpired over the last months and how Rachel had managed to get here. Aunt Sylvia confessed that on the day she left Ravensbrück, she fully expected to never see Rachel again.

The months went by. June 1942 turned to September 1943. As time went by, more and more laborers were moved into Dachau to work on "special projects"—extremely delicate and intricate timing devices that required fine motor skills and sharp eyesight. Aunt Sylvia, because of her vast experience and longevity, was made a supervisor of an assembly team. Aunt Sylvia had determined long ago that the timing devices were for detonators. She learned later on, from overheard conversations by engineers, that the other delicate devices were for a guidance system for something called a V-2 rocket. She didn't know what that was but apparently was some sort of weapon that was fired from North Germany and traveled all the way to London. Aunt Sylvia didn't know much about weaponry, but this thing didn't sound good for the Allies. She asked that Rachel keep her ears open when she sang at the officers' club for any conversations concerning rockets.

Aunt Sylvia actually got to see Rachel before she went on stage one Friday night. The transformation was absolutely astounding.

She was wearing a shimmering red evening gown with a slit that went from floor to hip, black silk stockings, and matching red stiletto heels. At her throat, she wore a single red ruby about the size of a quarter in a silver mount. Her jet-black hair cascaded across her shoulders to frame her face. In a word, she was exquisite.

Aunt Sylvia said, "I can't believe it's you."

Rachel smiled and said, "In a few hours, Cinderella will be back. But there will be no prince coming to find her and take her away from all this."

Aunt Sylvia said, "You never know. Don't give up hope."

Rachel replied, "Hope is all I have left."

"Well, off to the ball."

With that, Rachel left for the officers' club and her secret life.

If the Nazi officers only knew that the young woman who sang for them and they lusted after was an "untermensch" (subhuman), they would all be appalled.

Just as the evening show was about to begin, there was the wail of air raid sirens followed by blackness as the power to the camp was cut for blackout purposes. Everyone stayed where they were because there were no air raid shelters. It had long been determined that Allied intelligence knew that this was a prison of some sort and held no strategic value to the war effort. Therefore, they had no fear that the camp would be bombed and were far enough from valuable targets such as Augsburg or Munich to worry about near misses. The lights were off so that they didn't provide a navigational waypoint for Allied bombers on their way somewhere else. They listened as the bombers flew overhead. As it was night, they had to be RAF (Royal Air Force) planes because they only bombed at night. A few minutes later, they could hear the explosions as the bombs were dropped on Munich, only sixteen kilometers (ten miles) away. It sounded very much like a summer thunderstorm. After a period of time, they could hear the bombers returning on their trip back to England.

After they had passed, the sirens sounded the "All clear" and the lights came back on. Life went on, or at least this charade of life. After Rachel had finished her first set of the night, she walked to the bar to get a glass of club soda. She noticed a young severely wounded officer sitting alone at the bar. She didn't know how, but he appeared vaguely familiar. She walked over to him and introduced herself, "Good evening, Hauptsturmführer. For some reason, you remind me of someone. My name is Rachel."

The officer looked at her and stood up. "My name is Klaus, Klaus Bergman."

Rachel took a step back and put her hand to her mouth.

The young officer said, "I realize my appearance can be off-putting to some people, but I have yet to make someone ill at the sight of me."

Rachel stuttered, "N-n-no, it's not that. Do you happen to know a Sidney Klein?"

It was Klaus's turn to be taken aback. "Yes, I do. We were schoolmates in Berlin. He was my best friend. How do you know Sid?"

Rachel replied in English, "I'm Sidney's girlfriend."

C hapter 26

June 20, 1943, found Lieutenant Klein standing before the entrance to a building with a sign that read, "Blackthorn Country Club and Golf Course." Beneath that sign, there was another one that read, "Private Club—Members Only." As Sidney approached the door, there was yet another sign, "NOTICE: Because of the war, the club is closed until further notice. Thank you for your understanding. BUY BONDS." It had been explained to Sidney that this was the cover for the OSS being given free reign over the club and its grounds. Sidney was told that when he reported, he was to ring the bell, and someone would be there to start his in-processing. Sidney followed his instructions, and shortly, a young man about Sidney's age unlocked the door and granted him access to the clubhouse.

The young man held out his hand and said, "Hello, my name is Albert. And you are?"

"I'm Sidney Klein. Glad to meet you."

"So, Sidney Klein, I believe you have some paperwork for me, along with identification proving who you are?"

Sidney produced all the required documentation and signed what looked like a visitor's log before being led down a hallway to a room that contained what appeared to be a photo studio and a fingerprint station. Sidney was photographed and fingerprinted. He was asked if he had any tattoos or identifying scars. He said no tattoos, but he had a scar on his abdomen where his appendix had been removed. He was instructed to remove his shirt, go back to the photo station, and show the scar to the technician, who duly photographed the scar and annotated a form that Sidney was carrying with him.

After the photos and fingerprints, there was a form that he had to read and sign that stated that all information that he would be presented with was classified *Secret*, and failure to protect that information and unlawful dissemination of that information was a violation of the War Department Classified Information Act of 1941 and was punishable by twenty years of imprisonment, a 50,000-dollar fine, or both. After Sidney read and signed the form, he was escorted down the hallway to another room with another young man who introduced himself as Stephen. He had Sidney sit down at a desk that held a set of headphones, a telegraph key, a pad of paper, and several number 2 pencils. He was told that he would be undergoing several evaluation tests to determine his language skills and proficiency in receiving and sending Morse code. Sidney placed the headphones on and began to transcribe coded messages in German. At various times, the message required him to send back a reply or repeat a segment of a message. After an hour, the messages stopped, and Sidney was told to hand over his pad so that Stephan could read what Sidney had "received."

Stephan looked at Sidney and said, "Very impressive. A 100 percent score is seldom achieved."

Sidney was told to exit the building at the end of the hallway and wait for his next evaluator. The man outside was not a young man but a man in his early forties. He introduced himself as Franklin, and he led Sidney to a nearby golf cart. They puttered along in silence for a good fifteen minutes until they reached a building with no windows and a heavy steel door. Once inside, Franklin turned on the lights, and Sidney could see that they were at an indoor shooting range. On the counter before him were an M-1911A1 Colt .45-caliber pistol, a Smith and Wesson M&P .38-caliber revolver, and an M-1923 Thompson .45-caliber submachine gun. Further down the counter were some weapons he had only seen in pictures or newsreels. There appeared to be an MP-40 Schmeisser nine-millimeter machine pistol, a Luger P-08 nine-millimeter pistol, a Walther P-38 nine-millimeter pistol, a Mauser 98K eight-millimeter rifle, a Sten nine-millimeter submachine gun, and lastly, a Webley Mk. VI .455-caliber revolver.

Franklin turned to Sidney and said, "Now, Mr. Klein, are you at all familiar or qualified with any of these firearms?" Sidney informed Franklin that he had qualified *expert* with all the American weapons but had never fired any of the German or British weapons. "Well," Franklin said, "let's start with the devils we know. Please begin with the 1911, Mr. Klein."

Sidney picked up the Colt pistol, inserted a magazine loaded with five rounds, and engaged the target at seven meters (twenty-one feet). When the last round was fired, the slide locked to the rear, and Sidney ejected the empty magazine. He placed the pistol and magazine on the counter and was about to go down range to retrieve his target when Franklin said, "Stand fast, Mr. Klein. We have all of the most modern conveniences here." Franklin pressed a button on a console behind Sidney, and the target was hauled in on a steel cable. "We wouldn't want you to exhaust yourself running back and forth for targets and possibly affecting your accuracy." Franklin examined Sidney's target. Out of a possible score of fifty points, Sidney had scored forty-eight. Franklin looked at Sidney and said, "Very impressive, Mr. Klein. I can only imagine how you'll improve after we've taught you how to shoot our way." And so it went with the remainder of the American-issue weapons, with Sidney firing "high expert" with them all.

They then moved on to the European weapons. Sidney's personal favorite was the P-08 Luger. He admired its design and engineering but realized that it could be unreliable in combat because it would be a high-maintenance weapon. The Walther P-38 was much better suited for combat. The Mauser 98K was an excellent infantry rifle, but it was a bolt-action rifle, whereas the M-1 Garand and M-1 carbine were semiautomatic rifles with much larger ammunition capacity. Of the two submachine guns, the MP-40 was better built and designed, but the Sten was much easier to maintain. Once Sidney had the opportunity to familiarize himself with the weapons, he again fired "high expert" with these weapons.

At the end of firing, Franklin walked up to Sidney and told him, "Sidney, I believe you have a natural talent for shooting. But as I said, once you learn our way of shooting, you will be absolutely lethal." Franklin looked at his watch and said, "And now it's time for lunch."

Over the next two months, Sidney participated in classes that taught him how to create explosives from common household chemicals. He was taught how to employ explosive devices for demolition and as mines and booby traps. He spent an entire week on the firing range learning the OSS way of shooting. This involved moving targets, firing while on the move, and using silenced weapons. This was followed by two weeks in intensive hand-to-hand combat training and the use of the Fairbairn dagger. This was followed by training in the use of ciphers and code books. There was more language and signals training. They were taught the use of disguises and the creation of counterfeit identification and other documents. They received training in the use of microdot photography methods and the concealment of the microdots within seemingly innocent correspondence. Their training in land navigation was relentless. They were blindfolded and dropped miles from where they were to rendezvous. They were equipped with a map, compass, canteen, their Fairbairn dagger, and a silenced .22-caliber pistol. They had three days in which to reach the rendezvous point. They were to live off the land while evading an enemy force that was searching for them. All in all, a very interesting exercise.

Afterward, the candidates were notified that the land navigation course was the final exam, and the next day, those who had made the cut would be announced. Sidney found this to be more nerve-racking than West Point. You didn't have to wait until the very end to find out if the last three months were for nothing. The class had started out with one hundred candidates. By the time they had reached the hand-to-hand training, they were down to seventy-five. After hand-to-hand, they lost another ten, those who could not employ the dagger. The remaining sixty-five candidates awaited the final results.

September 30, 1943, found the remaining sixty-five candidates gathered outside the "clubhouse," which was the headquarters building for the OSS training facility. Franklin and another older gentleman whom they only knew as the General came out of the building. A hush fell over the assembled candidates as Franklin unfolded a sheet of paper.

"When I call out the fifteen names on this list, will those gentlemen please move over to the dining facility."

Franklin began calling out names. The names were in alphabetical order, and Sidney's was the eighth on the list. Sidney felt his heart sink into his stomach as his name was called, and he moved to the dining facility with the others who had not made the cut. He was both puzzled and angry. How could he have not been selected? As the fifteen entered the dining facility, they were told to take a seat and remain silent. About ten minutes after the last candidate was seated, Franklin and the General entered. They proceeded to the front of the dining room and said, "Gentlemen, congratulations. You have successfully completed the OSS training course and will be certified as OSS agents."

There was stunned silence. They had all thought they had been gathered to be dismissed and sent back from where they came.

The General looked them over and said, "Is that all you've got to say? I think I'd let out a big cheer!"

It finally sank in that they were not going home, and they all let out a cheer. At that moment, the chef and wait staff emerged from the kitchen with a large cake and at least two cases of chilled champagne. Champagne corks popped, glasses were filled, and toasts were made. They had made it!

Franklin tapped a champagne glass and announced, "Gentlemen! Although your training is finished here, there is still work to be done. In the morning, you will assemble at the clubhouse to receive your OSS credentials, your issued service weapon, and your follow-on orders. Wherever your orders take you, we here wish you Godspeed!"

The voyage to England was interesting. The speed of the convoy was determined by the best speed of the slowest ship. In the case of this convoy, it was an oil tanker making about fifteen knots (about seventeen miles per hour). Doing some rough calculations, Sidney estimated that their crossing would take about eight days.

There were frequent U-Boat alarms and abandon ship drills, which called for all passengers to don their life jackets and proceed to their assigned lifeboat stations. Depending on the weather, they actually practiced launching the lifeboats by untethering them from their moorings and lifting the boats with their davits. This gave everyone the opportunity to experience the amount of work required to launch the boats. Everyone seemed very pleased with their ability to confidently launch their lifeboats. Sidney thought them all overconfident. During the drills, the seas were calm, the weather was fair, and the ship was on an even keel. He knew that if they were required to launch the boats, it would most likely be at night with mass confusion and with a listing ship that would most likely be on fire. This was quite unlike what they were experiencing during these exercises.

Sidney once asked one of the ship's officers why they didn't hold the drills at night. The officer looked at Sidney and said, "Mister, half of these idiots would fall overboard or injure themselves if we tried this in the dark. I see your point as far as realistic training, but we couldn't risk the casualties such training would produce."

As it was not unduly cold at night, Sidney had taken to sleeping on deck, which he thought would give him a better chance for survival in case of a U-Boat attack. There were two attacks during their trip across the Atlantic but were in different areas of the convoy. These were accompanied by the sounding of alarm bells and the sight of the destroyer escorts racing around the convoy like sheepdogs guarding their flock. The escorts apparently did their job well, as no ships were hit during this convoy.

October 10, 1943, found them safely in Liverpool, England. The passengers disembarked the ship with the military personnel proceeding to a processing center and the "civilians" directed to a customs and immigration kiosk at the other end of the pier. Sidney approached the kiosk and presented his passport along with his OSS credentials to the customs agent. He stamped Sidney's passport and cocked his head toward a door to Sidney's right and, in an unmistakable Cockney accent, said, "Your lot are to proceed through that door, Guv'na."

Sidney retrieved his passport and thanked him. Sidney knocked on the door and entered. A middle-aged woman sat at a desk behind a typewriter, pounding furiously on the keys. She looked up at Sidney and said, "A copy of your orders and your credentials, please." Sidney produced the requested documents and waited further instructions. The woman checked Sidney's orders against his credentials and then pulled a well-worn journal from a shelf behind her desk. She selected the tab she was looking for and made some annotations in the journal. She then picked up the telephone from her desk and, consulting the journal, dialed a two-digit number.

"Hello, Jaime. Edna at receiving here. Number 441 has just checked in. Do you want to send someone round to fetch him, or will I have to lock up and escort him down there?" She listened for a moment then said, "You're a love. I've got paperwork up to me eyeballs at the moment, and leaving here just to go to the loo sets me back. Yes, he's all set to go. Ta-ta, Jaime, and thanks." She hung up the phone and looked at Sidney. "Right then, just have a seat, and your escort will be here shortly. I'd offer you a cup of tea, but as you probably heard, I'm literally swamped with reports."

Sidney smiled and told the woman he understood perfectly and thanked her for the offer. A few minutes later, a young man came in and introduced himself as Jaime. Sidney stood and shook the young man's hand and said, "I guess I'm Number 441, but you can call me Sidney."

Jaime smiled and grabbed Sidney's suitcase and motioned for him to follow. They entered a warehouse-looking building, and Sidney was told to grab a seat while Jaime called Sidney's future supervisor. Jaime sat at a desk and said to Sidney, "There's tea if you'd like, although I guess you yanks prefer coffee instead." Sidney thanked Jaime for the offer and made himself a cup of tea. After a few minutes on the phone, Jaime said to Sidney, "Right, after you've finished your tea, I'll run you down to the train station and get you on the overnight to Southampton. You're to be assigned to Detachment 441 in Southampton. Your 'supervisor' is Major Thomas Fielding, USMC [United States Marine Corps]. I'm not at liberty to divulge any other information regarding Detachment 441. That will have to come from Major Fielding."

The train departed Liverpool Station at 1700 and was scheduled to arrive in Southampton at 0700. Sidney hadn't eaten since breakfast that morning aboard ship, so he set out in search of a dining car. He happened upon a porter who told him that the dining car was two cars down and would commence dinner service at 1800. Sidney thanked him and turned to leave when the porter asked him, "You do have pound sterling, don't you, sir?" Sidney shook his head and said he did not. The porter told Sidney to speak to the bartender in the dining car and tell him that Finnegan had sent him. He would exchange US dollars for sterling. Of course, it would be at an atrocious exchange rate, but what was one to do? Sidney once again thanked the porter and proceeded to the dining car. He was quite sure that the porter would get a percentage of the "atrocious" exchange rate. True to his word, the bartender would exchange five US dollar for one pound sterling. It was an atrocious rate as the current "legal" exchange rate was three to one.

The next morning, as Sidney stepped off the train in Southampton, he got his first look at the devastation that had resulted from the Blitz. German bombers had leveled a good portion of the city and its industrial center. As he wondered how the citizens had managed to survive the bombings, a US Army corporal approached and asked, "Lieutenant Klein?" Sidney turned and said that he was. "If you would come with me, sir. Is that your only bag, sir?" The corporal reached down and took Sidney's suitcase and headed for the exit. The soldier placed Sidney's suitcase in the back of a jeep and, once Sidney got in, pulled into traffic. Sidney almost screamed until he remembered the English drove on the left—wrong—side of the road.

After a trip of forty-five minutes, they arrived at a walled compound with an armed gate guard. The corporal and Sidney had to produce their identification in order to gain access. Once verified against a roster, the guard opened the gate and allowed them to pass. They entered what appeared to be the main house where Sidney was ushered into the office of Major Fielding, Commanding Unit 441.

Sidney came to attention, saluted, and reported to Major Fielding. Major Fielding did not return Sidney's salute, and Sidney remembered that the naval service, which included the Marines, did not salute indoors. Major Fielding pointed to a chair and told Sidney to have a seat. There followed a forty-five-minute briefing on the mission of Detachment 441 and its area of operations. Detachment 441 was tasked with training, supplying, and aiding the local "Maquis," French resistance fighters. Detachment 441 agents would parachute into Southwestern France and participate in intelligence gathering, sabotage, and other activities as required.

Sidney was assigned to Team Baker and, over the next six months, participated in eight infiltrations into France. Dealing with the Maquis was hazardous at times. They tended to select their targets more on the headlines they would create rather than their strategic importance. Sidney had to try and keep a tight rein on the resistance without causing too much friction. One of their more spectacular raids was the sabotaging of a railroad bridge that was detonated just as a freight train carrying tanks and other armored vehicles was crossing. The explosion resulted in the destruction or severe damage to thirty-two Panzer Mk. V "Panther" tanks and forty other armored vehicles, along with over one hundred casualties among the troops on board the train. The tanks, vehicles, and troops were all headed to the Second SS Panzer Division, which was being rebuilt after suffering horrendous loses at the Battle of Kursk. The loss of such a large amount of equipment would delay the return of the division to combat status for many months.

Upon Sidney's return to England, he spent two weeks preparing his after-action report, along with intelligence assessments and target recommendations. A few days after Sidney submitted his reports, he was called to Major Fielding's office. Major Fielding went over Sidney's intelligence reports, highlighting on his target recommendations. Major Fielding mentioned that Sidney had recommended the destruction of several road and railroad bridges leading to the French coast. Sidney provided his rationale for selecting those particular targets, and Major Fielding agreed that they were sound strategic targets. Their destruction would greatly hinder the Nazis' ability to move reinforcements to the coast. For reasons that Major Fielding could not reveal, Sidney was to instruct the Maquis in the Normandy area that all bridges were off-limits as targets. Major Fielding asked if Sidney understood his instructions, which Sidney answered in the affirmative. Sidney would be going back to France next week to brief his Maquis counterparts.

Sidney left Major Fielding's office somewhat perplexed until he glanced at a large wall map of France in the outer office. Suddenly, Sidney put the pieces together, and he thought he realized why the bridges were suddenly off-limits for sabotage. If the Allies landed in Normandy, they would need those bridges as badly as the Germans would. Sidney also realized that if he mentioned his theory to anyone, he would be removed from his assignment as a possible security risk.

Throughout March and April of 1944, Sidney spent most of his time in France with the Maquis units. One of his tasks was to gather as much intelligence as possible on the Second SS Panzer Division, which was being held in reserve in the event of an allied invasion. The German High Command, OKW, had determined that when an invasion came, it would be in the Pas-de-Calais area further to the north. The Second SS was still rebuilding after Russia and was still largely understrength because of the Maquis sabotage actions late last year. Sidney and one Maquis member, Jean-Claude, conducted over a dozen surveillance missions in the Second SS bivouac area. They discovered the severe shortage of tanks along with the startling revelation that almost 60 percent of the soldiers were boys between the ages of fifteen and seventeen. With absolutely no combat experience, the Second SS would not be very combat effective. Sidney forwarded his reports back to England and awaited further orders.

The last two weeks of May brought a flurry of coded radio traffic with instructions to monitor a specific BBC (British Broadcasting Corporation) radio frequency. Every evening, they listened to what sounded like nonsensical public information announcements. Each Maquis unit had received a specific "announcement" to listen for and instructions to follow. Sidney's unit was tasked with the destruction of a railroad bridge. On the night of June 5, 1944, the message

"Madame Dubois a achete un nouveau chapeau" (Madame Dubois has purchased a new hat) was broadcast. That was their alert order. The team assembled their explosives and proceeded to the railroad bridge. As they were preparing to detonate the explosives, the sound of hundreds of aircraft were heard. The ground shook from the sound of the planes, and then the flash and explosions from German antiaircraft fire lit the sky. Between the flashes, they could pick out the canopies of parachutes in the distance. The liberation of Europe had begun.

Over the next three months, Sidney's Maquis unit participated in many more raids and sabotage assignments. The destruction of telephone and telegraph lines, cutting of electrical power to German installations, and the assassination of German couriers, sentries, and officers were their main tasks. By the end of August 1944, the campaign in Normandy was declared over. Sidney was ordered back to England for reassignment. Major Fielding informed Sidney that the OSS detachments in France were being disbanded as the missions of the Maquis were being phased out. Detachment 441 would be reorganized, and its assets (personnel) would be attached to line units as intelligence analysts at division headquarters. Major Fielding asked Sidney if he had a preference as to which division he would like to be attached to. Sidney had already done some research into the order of battle and assignments of units and knew that General Patch's Seventh Army was being assigned the southern portion of Germany, which would include Bavaria and the Dachau concentration camp.

Major Fielding had already figured that was where Sidney would request to go and already had orders prepared to attach him to the Seventh Army Intelligence Section. He told Sidney that he would be leaving to catch up with the command element in two days north of Toulon, France. "But before you leave us, we have a little going-away present." Major Fielding led Sidney to what had been the dining room and had been converted to a briefing room. The majority of the detachment was present, and Major Fielding called out, "Attention to orders!" The detachment senior sergeant read from a set of orders announcing the promotion of First Lieutenant Sidney Klein to the rank of captain. In addition to the promotion, Sidney was awarded the Silver Star and the French Croix de Guerre for his missions with the Maquis in France. Captain Klein was also presented with a star for his parachute wings, which indicated a combat jump. Major Fielding wasn't sure how the Army would classify the parachute jumps that Sidney had made into France, but he figured that he should get credit for at least one combat jump.

On August 15, 1944, Sidney reported to headquarters of the Seventh Army near Toulon, France. He was back in the Regular Army.

Chapter 27

Klaus was dumbfounded. He couldn't believe what this young woman had just told him. That she was Sidney Klein's girlfriend was simply preposterous. How could she be here, in this place, of all places? He looked into the woman's eyes and said, "I'm sorry. Could you please repeat what you just told me."

She said, "I am Sid Klein's girlfriend."

Klaus shook his head and said, "You must understand how unbelievable I find that statement to be. The last letter I received from Sidney was just before the war began in September 1939. He had written that he had met and fallen in love with a beautiful girl, and they intended to marry once he completed West Point. As far as I knew, you were still in the American Midwest somewhere waiting for Sidney. To have you show up here is just too difficult to comprehend."

Rachel gave Klaus a sad smile and told him how she and her Aunt Sylvia managed to end up in Dachau. After Rachel finished her story, Klaus shook his head again and said, "Mein Gott, das ist unglaublich!" (My god, that is unbelievable!)

At that moment, another officer walked up and asked in German, "What is unbelievable, Hauptsturmführer Bergman?"

The look that Klaus gave the other officer was unmistaken distaste. Where Klaus's black SS uniform was adorned with medals, badges, and campaign ribbons, the other officer only displayed his Nazi Party membership pin—a clear indication that he had not seen combat his entire career. Rachel could see the jealousy in the other officer's eyes when he looked at Klaus's tunic.

Klaus turned to Rachel and said, "Fraulein Silbermann, may I introduce Hauptsturmführer Stefan Freitag, the camp deputy commander."

Rachel offered her hand to Hauptsturmführer Freitag, who looked down at Rachel with unmistaken disgust in his eyes and turned to Klaus and said, "She doesn't actually think that I would touch a Jew, does she? And tell me, Bergman, why do you address her as fraulein or even speak to her at all? You realize she's a Jew and not a real person? The only reason she is here at all is that the camp commandant has brought her along from Ravensbrück as his pet Jew to entertain him with her singing and possibly other ways. I can assure you that if I become commandant, she will be one of the first to be liquidated. As a matter of fact, I might spare the Reich the cost of the poison gas and simply shoot or strangle her myself." With that, Hauptsturmführer Freitag knocked back his glass of schnapps and walked off.

In all the years that Rachel had spent in concentration camps, she had not experienced such a feeling of dread and foreboding as she did at this moment. Rachel lived each day with the expectation that she survived on the whim of a Nazi guard, but there was a set of rules that if you followed them as best you could, you had an expectation that you might survive the day. Hauptsturmführer Freitag's statement was a death sentence just waiting to be carried out. Rachel was glad that she had finished her last set for the night because she didn't think she could stand on stage, let alone sing.

Scharführer Kolbitz approached and introduced himself to Klaus and asked Rachel if she wanted him to escort her back to her barracks. Klaus looked at Scharführer Kolbitz and said, "Es ist nicht notig, Scharführer. Ich will Fraulein Silbermann begleiten." (It's not necessary, Scharführer. I will escort Fraulein Silbermann.)

Scharführer Kolbitz looked to Rachel, who smiled and nodded. Scharführer Kolbitz nodded to Rachel and said, "Wie Sie wunchen, Fraulein." (As you wish, miss.) He turned to Klaus, clicked his heels, and said, "Herr Hauptsturmführer." Then he left.

Klaus escorted Rachel back to her barracks after she had changed back into her prison garb. Aunt Sylvia was still awake, as she always was when Rachel sang. Rachel was torn about telling Aunt Sylvia about her encounter with Hauptsturmführer Freitag. There was no reason to cause her concern that she could do nothing about. Instead, she told her about meeting Klaus, who she had often heard Sidney talk about as a close friend. She was about to ask about Aunt Sylvia's day when she noticed that Aunt Sylvia had fallen asleep. Rachel had noticed that the workers assigned to the Siemens plant were working longer and longer hours. She still had no idea what Aunt Sylvia was involved in, but it must be vital to the Nazis. She figured that Aunt Sylvia must be very necessary to the Nazis because about a month before, Aunt Sylvia had become very ill, and instead of just leaving her in the barracks to either recover on her own or die, she had been moved to the camp infirmary. Rachel had been allowed to visit once and observed that she was well taken care of.

Over the following months, Rachel noticed that Hauptsturmführer Freitag seemed to be everywhere she went, stalking her, but not drawing the attention of the camp commandant. When she performed at the officers' club, he was always somewhere in the audience, always watching her. Where he sat depended on whether the camp commandant and/or Klaus were in the audience.

There were almost daily air raids now. One evening during her show, there was an unusually long raid and, per usual, a prolonged black out. It was during this blackout that Hauptsturmführer Freitag sidled up to her in the darkness. He pressed the point of his SS dagger against her heart and whispered into her ear, "On a night such as this, I may come to you and fulfill my promise. Don't think that the commandant would avenge your death. After all, you are a Jew, and I am an SS officer. Sweet dreams." He melted back into the darkness before the raid ended and the lights came back on. When they did, Scharführer Kolbitz noticed immediately that there was something wrong. He asked Rachel if she was all right. To which she replied that she was suddenly feeling unwell.

"Could we cancel the remainder of my show tonight?"

He looked around and noticed that many of the officers were already leaving and told her that it would be no problem and he would escort her back to her barracks.

That night, Rachel had the most terrifying nightmares, all featuring Hauptsturmführer Freitag coming out of the darkness and murdering her in one way or the other with unbelievable clarity and brutality. During one of these nightmares, Rachel must have cried out in her sleep loud enough to wake Aunt Sylvia, who normally could sleep through the air raid sirens. Aunt Sylvia was sitting on the edge of Rachel's bed and trying to calm her down.

"What scared you so badly, Rachel?" she whispered to Rachel.

Not wanting to alarm Aunt Sylvia, Rachel said, "I can't remember exactly. I think someone was chasing me. Just a silly nightmare. Go back to sleep, Sylvie."

Aunt Sylvia stroked Rachel's cheek and went back to her cot. Rachel thought for sure that she would not fall asleep again, but the next she knew, the morning reveille was sounding. Rachel hurriedly dressed and went off to her duties in the officer's kitchen before Aunt Sylvia could ask any questions about last night. Aunt Sylvia came from the washroom to discover that Rachel had already left for her duties. Aunt Sylvia went to her workstation at the Siemens plant.

After morning roll call, the workers were assembled and notified that the workforce would be reduced by half. A list of names was called out, and Aunt Sylvia joined the others whose names were called. They were told that they would work at another plant on the other side of the camp and were ordered to get aboard two trucks waiting outside. The workers were driven to a patch of forest outside the camp where they were lined up next to a trench and machine-gunned to death. Two SS Scharführer then went into the trench and fired a single bullet into the head of each worker, ensuring they were dead. A third truck had carried a work detail that was charged with burying the dead.

As the two Scharführer smoked a cigarette, one said to the other, "I thought these were such essential workers. Why did we get rid of them?"

The other replied, "I heard one of the scientists say that the plant that produces the rockets had been destroyed by RAF bombers and they had more of the guidance systems that these people were assembling than they had rockets, so they were no longer essential. They had to make sure that in case things go wrong, the information they had could not fall into enemy hands."

When the burial detail was finished, they returned to the camp.

Later that evening, when Rachel returned to the barracks, she noticed that Aunt Sylvia's meager belongings were gone, and another prisoner had taken over her cot. Rachel asked the new prisoner where Aunt Sylvia was and received a shrug of her shoulders and a grunt. Rachel went to one of the women who worked with Aunt Sylvia to discover that she, too, was missing. Finally, Rachel found a woman who worked at the Siemens plant and was told what had transpired that morning. Rachel asked if the woman knew when the other workers would be back. The woman looked around to see if anyone was listening. She said, "I don't think they are coming back, ever. About twenty minutes after the trucks left, I happened to be outside when I heard a burst of gunfire. Later, there were single shots. Two hours later, the trucks came back empty. I think the workers were executed."

Rachel could not believe what she had just heard. Her vision blurred, and all she could hear was the beating of her own heart. This just could not be true. Aunt Sylvia couldn't be dead. After all they had been through together, the thought of continuing on without her just seemed to be beyond belief. Rachel turned and walked back to her cot in a zombie-like trance. She sat on her cot and wondered why she didn't cry. All emotion had been drained from her soul so long ago that there was none left. She had come to the point where she felt that she was dead inside. There was no love, no joy, no sadness, no pain. Nothing was left inside. At the moment, she thought that she would welcome the visit from Hauptsturmführer Freitag. She realized that she no longer cared if she saw another sunrise. There was nothing the Nazis could do to her that made a difference anymore.

The next day, Rachel went about her duties like a robot. The other women noticed but said nothing. Word of Aunt Sylvia and the other women's "disappearance" had already spread throughout the camp. If the Nazi's plan had been to make the workers disappearance a secret, it had failed miserably.

June 1944 brought an electrified atmosphere to the camp. Something big was going on, and the attitude of the SS guards was definitely affected. It took until the tenth of June before the prisoners started hearing the rumors that the Allies had landed in France. Many of the guards were concerned that now that Germany was fighting on two fronts that they would get pulled off this safe assignment and sent to the front. Hauptsturmführer Freitag assured his men that their duties at Dachau were required for national security. They would not be sent to the front until every last Jew was eradicated.

Klaus would prefer to be sent to the front than stay at this death factory. He lacked the sadistic, inhumane personality that being an SS guard at a concentration camp required. Klaus was glad that his duties were securing the outer perimeter of Dachau, and therefore, he had very little interaction with the poor wretches inside the camp, except for Rachel. He didn't actually talk to her that much; he simply kept an eye out for her and kept track of Freitag as much as he could. Klaus had no doubt in his mind that given the opportunity, Freitag would follow through on his promise to liquidate Rachel. Klaus just couldn't understand how a man could be so twisted in his beliefs that one of his goals in life was to kill a young woman because of her religion.

One day in July 1944, Hauptscharführer Kreuzman, the security company first sergeant, entered Klaus's office and announced the arrival of a new platoon sergeant for First Platoon, a Oberscharführer Gross, transferring in from the Second SS Panzer Division's Fortieth Panzer Grenadier Regiment. Klaus was very curious about this new man coming from his old unit.

"Have him report in Hauptscharführer."

When the "new" man entered the office and reported to Klaus, both men had a huge grin on their faces. Oberscharführer Gross had been Unterscharführer Gross of Klaus's First Squad. Klaus had Oberscharführer Gross take a seat then pulled a bottle of Jägermeister and two glasses from his desk drawer. "This calls for a drink!" Klaus poured two shots and touched glasses with Oberscharführer Gross. "To the Fortieth Grenadiers and all the comrades we left on the field." They knocked back their drinks, and Klaus poured another.

"So, Gross, tell me everything after I was hit and evacuated from Kursk."

The battle was a massacre. Somehow, the Russians had captured a copy of the battle plans and anticipated every move the Germans made. The Führer would, at first, not allow German forces to withdraw and straighten their lines, which almost resulted in another Stalingrad. Finally, the German line was consolidated, and the Russian onslaught stopped. Casualties were horrendous. The Fortieth Panzer Grenadier Regiment went into the battle with three thousand men and eight hundred armored vehicles. They came out with less than one thousand troops and one hundred armored vehicles, twenty of which were tanks. The rest were destroyed or captured. Klaus was shocked at the number of casualties.

"What about First Platoon? How did we fare?"

Oberscharführer Gross sadly shook his head and said, "The only survivors from the command element were yourself and Oberscharführer Winter, but he was wounded even worse than you. He lost both legs when a retreating Russian T-34 ran over him while he was pulling the radio operator, Sturmmann Andreas, back to cover. Then our medic, Sturmmann Groenig, was gunned down by the Russian tank when he went to render aid to Winter and Andreas. I visited Oberscharführer Winter at the military hospital at Bad Kreuznach. He doesn't regret requesting to go to a combat posting from the Fahnenjunker Schule and was very concerned as to your well-being. If you get the opportunity, you should try to visit him. I think it would greatly improve his morale."

Klaus nodded and said that he would try to visit Oberscharführer Winter.

Gross went on, "Of the thirty-six remaining members of the platoon, sixteen were killed and eighteen were wounded, twelve seriously. I was slightly wounded by shell fragments and spent a month in the hospital before being returned to full duty. For some reason, I was not returned to the regiment but sent here. Tell me, Hauptsturmführer, what kind of a place is this?"

Klaus took a long look at Oberscharführer Gross and said, "In a word, hell. This is the idea that we have been fighting for all these years. This is the goal of National Socialism, the ideal that our Führer Adolf Hitler has been preaching since he came to power. This place is designed to carry out the goal of the Nazis and eradicate all Jews from Europe and eventually the world. This place, my dear Oberscharführer Gross, is a death camp, an extermination factory designed and built to facilitate the removal of Jews and any other group of people determined to be subhuman by the Nazi party."

Oberscharführer Gross was silent for a few moments then said, "And why are combat soldiers being sent here with these murderers?"

Klaus poured another round of Jägermeister and said to Oberscharführer Gross, "We combat soldiers are here to protect the murderers from being disturbed by outside forces from accomplishing their task of saving Germany and the world from the Jews, Gypsies, communists, homosexuals, and all other 'untermenschen.'" Klaus raised his glass to Oberscharführer Gross and said, "Prost."

Klaus told Oberscharführer Gross that he would be the platoon sergeant for Third Platoon, then he summoned Hauptscharführer Kreuzman into his office and informed him of Gross's assignment and asked that he take the new platoon sergeant and introduce him to his platoon leader. Klaus stood and shook Oberscharführer Gross's hand and welcomed him to Dachau's External Security Company.

After Oberscharführer Gross left, Klaus called his company clerk into his office and asked him to find the address for a Oberscharführer Winter attached to the Military Hospital in Bad Kreuznach as a patient. Klaus thought that if he couldn't get away to visit Oberscharführer Winter, he might at least be able to write or call him. Klaus was worried about leaving Dachau because of Hauptsturmführer Freitag's threats against Rachel. He couldn't go to the camp commandant because he had no solid proof against Freitag, and besides, he didn't know how the commandant would receive such information. He might even consider it part of Freitag's duty.

The next morning, the company clerk provided Klaus with the address for the Military Hospital plus the telephone number of Oberscharführer Winter's doctor and the phone number for the ward in which he was assigned. Klaus thanked him and was about to dismiss him when the clerk said, "Herr Hauptsturmführer, the *krankenschwester* [nurse] that I spoke to suggested that you speak to his doctor before you try to contact Oberscharführer Winter." Klaus thought for a moment then nodded and dismissed his clerk. He could well imagine why the doctor wanted Klaus to speak to him first. He, too, had to deal with survivor's guilt for a long time after he first heard of the casualties that his platoon had sustained. Even after being horrifically wounded, one still felt that he should not have survived after so many of his comrades hadn't. Why them and not me?

On the twentieth of July, the news of the attempt on Der Führer's life by members of the military reached Klaus with mixed emotions. Had the conspirators succeeded, would that have hastened the end of the war? For although Klaus spoke to no one of his opinion, he sincerely hoped that this madness would come to an end sooner rather than later. Of course, to voice such thoughts was treason, and one could end up like the assassination collaborators, hung up by piano wire and left to slowly die of decapitation. As a result of the attempted assassination, the only branch of the military that Hitler would trust was the SS. Several SS units were reassigned as additional security wherever the Führer was located. As the Führer took greater control of the war effort, the military seemed to do worse in the field. After the battle of Kursk, the Russians seemed to be unstoppable. A German Army would become encircled, and the commander would want to fall back to straighten his lines, only to be ordered by Hitler to hold at all costs. It would take days of pleading and explaining that if the forces were not allowed to fall back, the entire formation, sometimes fifty to sixty thousand troops, would be lost. Hitler would wait until the last possible moment before allowing a withdrawal, which resulted in unnecessary casualties and loss of vehicles, especially tanks. These were tanks that could not be replaced.

On the Western Front, the Allies had finally broken out of the hedgerows around Normandy and, with General George Patton leading the Third Army, were charging toward Germany. As the Allied juggernaut rolled toward Germany, it became increasingly evident that the loggerheads at Cherbourg and Antwerp were slowing the advance because of the extended supply lines. In September 1944, Field Marshall Montgomery came up with a plan to cut across Holland into the Ruhr Valley, thereby cutting off Germany's industrial centers. The plan Operation Market Garden was a massive airborne assault that would seize and hold the Rhine River bridges and allow a British armored corps to follow and cross the bridges into Germany. Unfortunately for the Allies, the plan failed with great loss of life to the British First Airborne Division.

By December 1944, General Eisenhower had to call a halt to the Allied advance in order for supplies to catch up with the leading elements of his armies. New replacement units were brought up to relieve frontline units that had been at the front the longest. These replacement units had little or no combat experience and were placed on the line where it was thought there would be no enemy activity, which would allow the "green" troops time to acclimate themselves to the combat zone. It was during this time that Adolf Hitler came up with his plan for the Ardennes Offensive. His plan was to attack out of the Ardennes Forest, which was considered tactically impossible because of heavy forest and narrow paths, which would not support an assault by heavy armor. The initial attack caught the American troops completely by surprise, and they retreated in panic. The German success depended on their forces reaching American fuel dumps as the Germans had no fuel to spare. The Germans also depended on current weather conditions, which prevented Allied air superiority from being employed.

The German assault proceeded according to plan until it reached the city of Bastogne. There were seven roads into and out of Bastogne, and it was not a city that could be bypassed. The Germans had to take the city, but it was where the American forces made their stand. A heroic defense of the city led by the 101st Airborne Division held out until finally reinforced by Patton's Fourth Armored Division. Fighting continued until Hitler gave permission for all German forces to be withdrawn from the Ardennes around January

25, 1945. The Germans had suffered approximately sixty thousand to eighty thousand casualties and had to abandon large amounts of their armor and artillery. This would be the last major offensive on the Western Front. The beginning of the end came in March 1945 with the capture of the Ludendorff Bridge at Remagen. With its capture, the Allies gained a crossing into Germany.

Chapter 28

On September 30, 1944, Captain Sidney Klein was assigned to the G-2 (intelligence) section of the Forty-Fifth Infantry Division. He was given a twenty-man detachment of soldiers who had a wide variety of language, engineering, and geographical skills with which to assemble and analyze field intelligence from observation and prisoner interrogation. As the Forty-Fifth Division joined in the push through France toward Germany, it was Sidney's job to gather intelligence and determine what the enemy's plans and capabilities were. These duties placed Sidney and his detachment very close to and sometimes ahead of the front lines.

On November 25, the division crossed the Moselle River and passed through the Maginot Line into the Alsace region very close to the German border. Several prisoners, including officers, captured at this time complained among themselves that if they had been able to get reinforcements, they could have turned back the American advances. Sidney found this information extremely interesting and probed further. It turned out that the entire German reserve units were being withheld for another operation, and the German High Command would not release any of these units for any reason. The question was where these units were going. Sidney prepared an intelligence analysis and forwarded it to the division intelligence officer.

In his analysis, Sidney predicted that the Germans were planning an offensive somewhere around the Ardennes. He further predicted that this offensive would occur within the next thirty days.

The division intelligence officer didn't agree with Sidney's assessment but forwarded the report along with his own assessment on to the division commander. Two weeks later, the Germans launched their Ardennes Offensive known to the Americans as the Battle of the Bulge. Unknown to Sidney, his analysis had been forwarded all the way to the Third Army Headquarters where it had been read by General Patton, who agreed with Sidney's report and had his operations staff prepare three plans to move three divisions north within forty-eight hours of the order to execute.

After the Battle of the Bulge, German resistance grew increasingly weaker. German prisoners uniformly complained of the lack of food and ammunition. Medical supplies were almost nonexistent. The Germans were surrendering in greater numbers. Officers were very reluctant to sacrifice their men in one-sided engagements. The feeling that the war was lost was growing daily. Only the most fanatical Nazis still believed that the war could be won or at least fought to a draw where Germany could retain some sense of honor. These soldiers had no idea what had played out in the concentration camps across Poland, Germany, and other occupied countries.

From January 2, 1945, the division took up a defensive line along the German border. On the seventeenth of February, the division was pulled off the line for rest and training. After this rest period, the advance continued. The division smashed through the Siegfried Line on the seventeenth of March and crossed the Rhine River on the twenty-first. Nuremburg was captured on the twentieth of April. Sidney thought it rather ironic that Nuremburg, one of the great symbols of National Socialism, should fall on Adolf Hitler's birthday. The division's next objective was Munich. Sidney was starting to pick up rumors of some sort of prison complex twelve miles northwest of Munich. Sidney's detachment captured a group of SS soldiers who said that they had been assigned there and that it was a concentration camp with mostly Jewish prisoners, but there wouldn't be many left as they were being shipped out to Poland as fast as they could load them on the trains. These SS soldiers could not know that the Americans had already cut the rail lines in this area, and there was no place for the trains to go. Sidney asked them what would happen to the prisoners if they could not be shipped out. They answered quite simply, "They would be either gassed or shot. They would not be released." Sidney inquired about security forces, and they reported that the exterior guard was Waffen-SS who did not seem to be at all pleased about their mission and, at this point in time, would most likely not fire upon any inmates who managed to escape the compound. They would also offer the least resistance to the Americans.

The interior guards were the more fanatical "Death's Head" SS. Their mission was to dispose of any Jews left in the camp using any means possible. These troops would more than likely resist to the end. Next, Sidney asked how many prisoners were inside the camp and if there were any women. The prisoners answered that there were women prisoners but could only guess at the number of total prisoners at around thirty to forty thousand. As they said, the camp guards were loading them up as fast as possible.

Sidney brought this information to the division security officer and requested permission to lead a rescue mission to free the prisoners immediately. The intelligence officer took Sidney in to see the division commander, Major General Frederick, and had him explain what he had discovered. The general went to the situation map and told Sidney, "Our 180th Regimental Combat Team is currently passing out of Augsburg, which is about thirty-seven miles from Dachau. Get your detachment over to the 180th and pick up two platoons of mechanized infantry and whatever medical personnel and supplies they can spare and head for this camp at Dachau. I'll call over to the 180th and let the commander know you're coming and to give you everything he can spare. We've heard a lot of reports concerning these camps, and if only 10 percent is true, I'd hate to see the inside of these places." As Sidney saluted and made to leave, the general said, "When you get over to the 180th, see if you can find a couple of chaplains that aren't busy, especially a rabbi."

Sidney saluted and left the general's office to gather up his detachment.

April 26, 1945. In the 180th Regimental Combat Team Headquarters just outside the city of Augsburg, Sidney's detachment of twenty-five men, including him and two medics, with six jeeps were formed up outside the headquarters tent. Each jeep was equipped with a pedestal-mounted .30-caliber machine gun along with as many cases of C-rations, cans of ammunition, and jugs of water that the jeeps would hold. With four men per jeep, two for the medics, there was not much extra room. The medic jeeps were crammed with medical supplies, blankets, litters, and water jugs. The 180th commander greeted Sidney and detailed the support that he could provide.

"You understand, Captain, that this formation is still actively engaged in the attack, and I'm giving you vital resources that I hope I'm not going to regret giving up."

Sidney replied, "Yes, sir. I greatly appreciate the support that you can provide to this mission."

The colonel looked at Sidney and nodded. "What I can provide are two platoons of infantry, plus an antiarmor detachment armed with 3.5-inch bazookas. I'm also going to provide a full medical team to include a surgeon, four ambulances, and enough supplies to equip a battalion aid station. Please take good care of the medical people. They're irreplaceable, as you know."

"Yes, sir," Sidney replied. "What about rations, sir?"

The colonel replied that he had spoken to the division medical staff, and they said that these prisoners were probably near starvation, and solid food would probably kill them. "There are two problems. First, we have to liberate them, count them, and then feed them. The division surgeon said that they should be fed nothing more solid than oatmeal for several days. The next problem is how to come up with enough oatmeal for, what did you say, thirty thousand to forty thousand starving people? Phase 1 is to liberate them and provide basic medical care. Once that is done, we'll get the logistics moving to feed them. Any other questions, Captain?"

Sidney replied, "No, sir. Let's get this show on the road."

Sidney was introduced to the two infantry platoon leaders and the doctor. The doctor went over a few items with Sidney and the platoon leaders regarding the treatment of the prisoners and the possibility of infectious diseases. He also stressed not giving them any food, as hard as that would be to resist. Details concerning the formation of the column, tactics in the event of attack, and alternate routes if necessary were decided. With the details hashed out, the troops were loaded up and the convoy moved out. Sidney and one other jeep from his detachment ranged out ahead. They had anticipated that with no resistance, they could cover the thirty-eight-mile trip in approximately four hours. Sidney's two jeeps proceeded down the road toward Dachau. They had gone a little more than five miles when they came upon the first column of refugees. Many were old men, women, and children carrying what appeared to be all their worldly possessions on their backs or in small carts. They appeared to have evacuated from Augsburg just ahead of the American forces.

Further down the road, Sidney began to notice younger men wearing parts of Wehrmacht uniforms but carrying no weapons. Sidney stopped several of these men, and for a cigarette, they would tell him everything they knew. They told Sidney what unit they had belonged to, where they were going to, and where their unit was located when they left. Sidney always asked if they had heard of the concentration camp at Dachau. The answer was always the same— they had neither heard of nor knew anything about such a place.

About twenty-five miles from the town of Dachau, they encountered a roadblock. Through his binoculars, Sidney could make out that the roadblock was manned by a small detachment of Feldgendarmerie (Military Police) stopping all military-age males and checking their identity papers. One individual, obviously a deserter, broke and ran from the roadblock. A military policeman raised his MP-40 and, with a short burst, cut the man down. Sidney could see several other men further away from the roadblock slowly fade into the woods alongside the road, not wanting to take the chance that their papers would pass scrutiny. Sidney got on the radio and called for reinforcements and started toward the roadblock. When they were within machine gun range and no civilians were in the line of fire, Sidney had his machine gunner fire a short burst at the roadblock. Two of the military policemen went down; the other four dropped their weapons and raised their hands. Sidney and his men approached in their two jeeps, taking the four Germans prisoner.

Sidney questioned them about the location of further roadblocks. He was told that the next roadblock would be at Odelzhausen, about ten miles down the road and ten miles before the turnoff to Dachau. Once the reinforcements from the main column arrived, Sidney placed the prisoners in their custody to be handed over to American Military Police for transport to the rear. Sidney's two jeeps proceeded down the road toward Dachau. After the first roadblock, the stream of refugees thinned out, allowing them to make better time.

Ten miles and forty-five minutes later, they came upon the second roadblock, which appeared to be abandoned. Sidney observed the roadblock for a good twenty minutes to ensure there were no enemy soldiers in the area. Satisfied that the area was clear, they moved on. When they reached the roadblock site, they found weapons and uniforms scattered around. A three-quarter-ton truck left at the area was out of gas. Sidney had his men remove the bolts from the rifles and machine pistols to render them harmless. He radioed back to the column that the roadblock was clear, and they were proceeding on to the camp another ten miles distant.

Near the little town of Rothswaige, there was a sign pointing to Dachau. Sidney spotted an old farmer coming out of a wheat field and asked if that was the way to Dachau. The old man looked at Sidney and said, "I don't believe you want to visit the town. I imagine that you're looking for the other place, where people go in but never come out."

Sidney said, "Yes, that's the place I'm looking for. Do you know about it?"

The old man nodded and pointed down another road that had a barely visible sign, "KZ [*Konzentrationslager*] concentration camp—Dachau." Sidney asked the old man about guards. The old man said that the guards outside the wire were pretty decent lads, considering their job. They would talk to you if you walked by them. The ones inside the wire with the skull and crossbones on their collars only talked to each other. They were very unfriendly, and the old man thought they were all a bit crazy. Sidney asked about the location of the guards outside the wire, and the old man drew them a map. Then Sidney asked the old man why he had provided so much information. The old man looked at Sidney and said, "I was a soldier during the Great War. I served with honor and was proud to be a soldier. Those people inside the wire are not soldiers. They have no honor. They disgrace Germany and the German people." Sidney watched as the old man shuffled down the road toward a farm in the distance.

Sidney radioed the column that they were less than five miles from camp and would conduct a reconnaissance of the area to determine threats. The lieutenant leading the column said that they were about four miles from Rothswaige and would be at Sidney's location in about ten minutes. By the time the column arrived, Sidney and his men had reconnoitered the area and found that the map the old man had drawn was very accurate. Fire teams were assembled from the First Platoon and crept into place opposite the German positions outside the wire. Sidney and the Second Platoon approached the main gate and announced that they were Americans and they should drop their weapons and come out with hands raised. As hoped, the guards outside the wire complied with Sidney's order. As expected, some of the guards opened fire. The fire teams had targeted the watch towers around the fence and quickly dispatched the guards in the towers with accurate rifle and machine gun fire.

Sidney, along with his detachment and the Second Platoon, breached the main gate and commenced mopping up guards inside the compound. They assembled those guards who surrendered in the main parade field. Sidney and his detachment proceeded to the main headquarters building.

* * *

Klaus entered the headquarters building searching for Rachel. He had left his guard company to a trusted lieutenant and told him not to resist the Americans when they came. He didn't want anyone dying unnecessarily this close to the end of the war. Klaus knew that Hauptsturmführer Freitag's last act would be to kill Rachel. Klaus had already ensured that she was no longer in her barracks, and the women there had reported that Freitag had taken her away at gunpoint. The only thing that Klaus could imagine was a threat he had once made that he would enjoy a last glass of cognac as he strangled Rachel to death. When Klaus asked him why he would do that, Freitag smiled and said, "Because it would please me."

As Klaus crept through the headquarters building, he figured that Freitag would be in the commandant's office. As Klaus entered the office, he noticed that Freitag's adjutant was also in the office and holding a pistol in his hand. Freitag was just pouring cognac into a crystal snifter while Rachel sat in a chair to Freitag's left near the office door. Freitag turned to see Klaus standing there and said, "Ah, Hauptsturmführer Bergman, I'm glad to see that you arrived in time to witness my promise come true."

* * *

Sidney carefully entered the headquarters building, followed by his four-man security team and two medics. Outside, he could hear intermittent gunfire interspersed with screams. Sidney thought that there must still be resistance by some fanatical Nazis. What he couldn't see was the result of what the American soldiers were finding inside the compound. There were naked bodies in piles, looking more like stick figures than the bodies of human beings. Two railcars were full of bodies locked in the cars until they starved to death. Once the Nazis had loaded Jews into the railcars for transport to Auschwitz, Treblinka, and Sobibor and the Allied air raids had cut the rail lines, the Nazis had no further use for the railcars and simply left the Jews to starve. A few of the loaded cars were doused with gasoline and set afire, but that practice was soon halted due the shortage of fuel. All these atrocities were witnessed by the American soldiers, and some just could not handle the horror. They shot SS guards or let the prisoners beat their former guards to death and did nothing.

Sidney was unaware of these events as he continued to search the headquarters building. Sidney held up his hand to stop his team as he heard voices down the hallway. Suddenly, there was a burst of MP-40 fire followed by a single pistol shot and then a woman's scream followed by another pistol shot. From the second door on the right, a female prisoner's body fell out of the doorway, followed shortly by an SS officer with a pistol pointed at the woman's head. Sidney called for the German officer to drop his pistol and surrender. The man tossed a P-08 Luger pistol at Sidney's feet. Apparently, the German officer thought the sight of the much-prized Luger would distract the American officer and he would be able to use the second pistol he had to shoot the American. As Freitag raised Klaus's Walther P-38 to shoot the American officer, Sidney fired a burst from his .45-caliber Thompson submachine gun, stitching Freitag from belt buckle to throat, killing him instantly.

Sidney warily approached the dead German to ensure that he was dead. For some reason, he picked up the Walther pistol before checking the female prisoner who had a bullet wound to the back of the head. Sidney looked down at the pistol in his hand and noticed the engraving. The pistol belonged to Klaus Bergman. It was then he heard a groan from the office. There was another German officer lying on the floor. Sidney entered the office and recognized Klaus on the floor. Sidney called, "Medics, on me!"

One medic began checking the woman out in the hallway while the second started treating Klaus. Klaus explained how he came to stop Freitag, and his adjutant pulled his pistol on Klaus. Klaus fired a burst from his MP-40, killing the adjutant, but Freitag shot Klaus before he could shoot Freitag. Klaus looked up at Sidney and said, "My friend, please take my decorations and get them to my father, and I want you to keep my pistol."

Sidney tried to tell Klaus that he could give his decorations to his father himself.

Klaus looked at Sidney and said, "Why are you here with me? You should be with Rachel."

It suddenly dawned on Sidney that the woman in the hallway with the bullet wound to the head was his Rachel. He looked over at the medic who just shook his head.

Klaus took Sidney's hand and whispered, "Till we meet again."

Sidney looked at Klaus, and as tears ran down his face, he repeated, "Till we meet again."

From out in the hallway, the second medic called out, "Hey, Captain! This woman is still alive!"

Chapter 29

April 27, 1955. Dachau Concentration Camp Memorial. Lieutenant Colonel Sidney Klein; his wife, Rachel; and their seven-year-old daughter, Sylvia, entered the memorial compound. Rachel could not suppress a shiver as they entered. Sidney leaned over to her and asked, "Are you sure you want to go on?" Rachel nodded, and taking Sidney's hand, they walked down the parade field where the prisoners assembled for head count. They walked down the memorial wall until they found the name SYLVIA SILBERMANN engraved on the wall. Rachel gave a silent prayer and placed a bouquet of flowers at the base of the wall.

On the far side of the compound segregated from the memorial was a small German cemetery. Buried here were the remains of German soldiers who could not be returned to their families. There were no "Death's Head SS" soldiers interred here. Sidney found the grave of KLAUS BERGMAN, 1923–1945. Sidney deposited a bouquet of flowers and said to Klaus, "I got your decorations to your father. He was very proud of you and glad that you died as a true soldier."

Sidney took Rachel's hand in one hand and Sylvia's hand in the other, and they left Dachau for the last time.

End

$\mathcal{A}$cknowledgments

Till We Meet Again was inspired partly by my eighteen years of living in Germany. The remaining inspiration was my brother, Tim, who infected me with the idea of writing a book. Tim and his wife, Deb, encouraged me to write the book and provided much appreciated and necessary guidance along the way. This advice was easy to follow as they were both published authors, so they kind of know what they were talking about.

I would also like to thank my wife, Ruta, who was a driving force in accomplishing my mission. Ruta also assisted as my Polish and Russian translator. When she would come home from work each day, she would ask how the book was coming. She is an endless source of encouragement, and I don't know what I would do without her.

$\mathcal{A}$bout the Author

Allen Sweetsir is a retired US Army sergeant first class living with his family in Arizona. After serving twenty-two years in the Army, he worked for defense contractors in the communications, electronic warfare, and electronics maintenance fields in Germany and Arizona. He then worked as a field maintenance engineer for a mobile television production company and finally as a regional purchasing manager for a global metal recycling corporation until his retirement.

During his eighteen years in Germany, he traveled extensively throughout Europe, visiting many of the battlefields of both the First and Second World Wars. He has visited the Dachau Concentration Camp Memorial on several occasions.

Allen is an avid student of military history and gun collector. He enjoys traveling with his wife, Ruta, visiting the wineries of Arizona and enjoying the Red Rocks of Sedona and other wonders of the desert Southwest.

This is his first published work; he already has a second novel in the works.